Guiteau's desperate voice rose above the crackling of flames and thunder

"Any moment a hundred armed sec men'll be on top of you, Cawdor. Give up and the boy lives. Best offer you'll get all day."

He stepped into the open, crouched and almost totally hidden behind Dean, the muzzle of the Armalite digging into the boy, his finger on the trigger.

"Let him go, or I'll put you down." The voice, surprisingly calm, was Mildred's.

From the corner of his eye, Ryan saw the doctor standing like a statue, her right arm extended, the ZKR 551 target pistol pointed at the sec sergeant.

"The boy dies before I take a hit," Guiteau called, crouching even lower, so that she could see very little of his head of body.

But that didn't matter. The Czech revolver snapped once, and at forty paces and in poor light, Mildred put the .38-caliber round precisely where she aimed it.

Both Harry Guiteau's index finger and the trigger of his automatic rifle were blown off. The Armalite clattered to the ground, and Dean scampered toward his ~~~~

"Best damn shot I ever s~~~~
through his pain.

Mildred's second sh~~~~
nose, ensuring the c~~~~

They turned and head~~~~

D1059335

Also available in the Deathlands saga:

JAMES AXLER

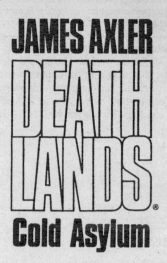

DEATH LANDS®

Cold Asylum

A GOLD EAGLE BOOK FROM

WORLDWIDE®

TORONTO • NEW YORK • LONDON
AMSTERDAM • PARIS • SYDNEY • HAMBURG
STOCKHOLM • ATHENS • TOKYO • MILAN
MADRID • WARSAW • BUDAPEST • AUCKLAND

This dedication, belatedly, is to the countless legions of
fans of the Deathlands series. The people who love
Ryan, Krysty, Doc, J.B. and the company as much as I
do. Thanks for riding the dangerous highways of this
alternative future at my side. Onward into new
tomorrows, together. This is for you.   —James Axler

First edition April 1994

ISBN 0-373-62520-0

COLD ASYLUM

"Kansas... John Stewart has sung movingly of it, and Dorothy so wanted to return there. But during the War Between the States it earned its name of 'Kansas, bloody Kansas.' So it was and so it will be again."

—*The Great Plains, Yesterday, Today and Tomorrow,* by Tecumseh Shelby, 1987

Prologue

Ryan Cawdor paused, his hand on the heavy door, ready to pull it shut and trigger the mat-trans system that would propel them into elsewhere. "Here we go, friends."

He sat on the floor beside Krysty Wroth, with his son, Dean, on his left. Doc Tanner was opposite, lying on his side, his knees drawn up to his chin. The rest of the companions had assumed the positions that they knew from previous experience would be the most comfortable for making the jump.

Ryan took Krysty's hand in his.

The lamps outside the chamber dimmed, and he heard the crackling of a major electrical circuit malfunctioning. The metal disks in floor and ceiling began to glow, and the pale yellow armaglass walls started to pulse with the familiar misty light.

The inside of Ryan's brain was already beginning to float in the nauseous way that he hated so much. He closed his good eye.

"Something's wrong."

The voice was his father's, but it couldn't be. The man was long dead at Front Royal in the Shens.

"Something."

It was an old man's voice. Doc Tanner. Something felt wrong.

Ryan gripped Krysty's hand more tightly, seeking some portion of her mystical power, the Earth Mother's power, trying to hold her.

But they were suddenly wrenched apart with a dreadful force and violence.

Now he could hear the roaring of a mighty water, and his breathing was being choked.

Tidal wave off the Keys.

"Wrong."

The word sounded flat and unemotional.

Now a profound darkness engulfed Ryan, and he realized with a chilling terror that he was completely alone, alone in a different time and place.

"What's happening?" His lips formed the words, and his brain could hear them.

Wrong.

"Happening?"

Alone. One.

Chapter One

Ryan opened his eye.

He swallowed, tasting the yellow bitterness of bile at the back of his throat, the inside of his skull still swimming in its own secret sea. His muscles ached as if he'd been on the wrong end of a beating in an alley behind a frontier gaudy.

"Fireblast!" His voice was so quiet it hardly carried as far as his ears.

The mist in the chamber of the gateway was clearing slowly, the metal plates losing their silvery glow. He noticed that the armaglass walls were a rich, deep purple. Coming out of a jump, the brain never functioned all that well, but Ryan couldn't remember seeing walls of that color before.

He felt more deeply sick and confused than he could remember, and he looked around the six-sided room to check on how the others were feeling.

The others.

There was nobody else there.

He was on his own.

That wasn't possible. He'd closed the door himself and triggered the jump mechanism in the buried redoubt in Florida, and everyone had been there then.

Ryan took a sudden harsh breath, biting back the desire to vomit. He closed his eye again, battling for self-control and checking in his memory where everyone had been sitting.

Krysty had sat next to him, her brilliantly red hair dark and wet, pasted to her head, her long legs stretched out in front of her, back against the wall, fingers clasped in his. Some incredible force had torn them apart. Ryan remembered that.

She'd been on his right, with his eleven-year-old son, Dean, on the left. The boy had been toying with his beloved turquoise-hilted knife as he sat and waited patiently for the jump to begin. His big 9 mm Browning automatic pistol had been jammed into a holster at his belt.

Who'd been next in the circle?

"Mildred Wyeth."

Ryan could see the black doctor in his mind's eye. A relative latecomer to the group of companions, the thirty-six-year-old woman had been wearing a cotton shirt and quilt-lined denim jacket over reinforced military fatigue pants, tucked into calf-length boots. In December of the year 2000, Mildred, an expert on cryosurgery, had been taken into hospital for minor abdominal surgery. Things had gone wrong, and she'd been placed in cryogenic suspension—frozen—a state from which Ryan and the others had eventually freed her nearly a century after her "death."

Recently she had deepened her relationship with the Armorer of the group, John Barrymore Dix, who'd sat next to her. About the same age as Ryan, J.B. was his oldest friend. The two of them had traveled for years with the legendary Trader, rising in the ranks to become his two most trusted lieutenants, as they ranged all across Deathlands.

Thinking about the Trader brought a flicker of memory to Ryan. Abe, another comrade from the savage days riding the war wags, had gone off to search for the man. How long ago? Weeks? Months? Years? Ryan couldn't remember. He knew that his old leader had vanished during one long-ago night. Everyone thought that the rad cancer had overwhelmed him and he'd gone off to die like an animal in some cramped, dark place. Then the rumors started that Trader might not be dead after all.

"Abe?" Ryan said, trying to remember whether the little gunner had been with them in the gateway in Florida. He was sure that he hadn't. But there had been others.

Krysty Wroth.

J. B. Dix.

Dean.

Mildred Wyeth.

"Doc."

Of course. Doc Tanner, lying doubled up on the far side of the chamber, knees cracking as he composed himself, his mane of bedraggled white hair framing his lined face. Doc's age was a bizarre enigma that Ryan had never been able to understand.

He knew that Theophilus Algernon Tanner had been born on the fourteenth day of February in the year of Our Lord, 1868. He'd been married to Emily, née Chandler, on the seventeenth day of June, twenty-three years later. He'd obtained his doctorate in science at Harvard and a Ph.D. from Oxford University in England.

Tall and skinny, Doc had been a happy man, with a three-year-old daughter, Rachel, and a little son, Jolyon. Then white-coated, faceless scientists a hundred years in the future had destroyed his life.

He'd been plucked into 1998 from 1896 as one of the few successful guinea pigs from Operation Chronos, a time-trawling government project that generally brought only mangled piles of unidentifiable meat, blood and raw bones from the past.

Doc had proved so difficult a guest of that particular present that they had eventually pushed him forward another ninety years or so into Deathlands.

"And Michael," Ryan announced triumphantly.

Michael Brother had been brought into their world as another faulty experiment of Chronos. Since his birth he had been an oblate, a trainee monk, in a closed community called Nil-Vanity, above Visalia in the Sierras. Nineteen years of age, he had been disciplined into the martial art of Tao-Tain-do and had the fastest fighting reflexes that Ryan had ever known.

That was all of them.

The name of Jak Lauren came unbidden into Ryan's mind. Had Jak been with them in Florida?

"No."

The albino youth had traveled with Ryan and the others through many lethally desperate adventures.

Now he was married to Christina, and they and their child, Jenny, lived on a spread in New Mexico.

Ryan managed to get himself upright, conquering the sickness, trying to get his brain working. They'd all been together as the jump began, but there had been some kind of electronic malfunction. He recalled that. Could that have been responsible for the jump going so wrong?

Were the others together, or had each of them been sent tumbling through time and space to different locations?

He breathed deeply, trying to deduce some clue from the taste of the air.

Most gateways were buried deep within old top-secret military installations called redoubts. They were generally powered by long-lived nuke generators that kept the heat and lights in the complexes functioning at survival levels.

The air didn't smell like it normally did. Most jumps took the companions to gateways where the air was stale, dusty and dull. It often hadn't been breathed by anyone for close to a century, since the nuke cataclysm of 2001 that had wiped away civilization.

This air was fresh and clean, warm, with a strange, foreign scent to it that Ryan couldn't quite identify.

Automatically he checked through his personal armory of weapons, then adjusted the long white silk scarf around his neck, fingering the weighted ends that turned it into such a lethally effective garrote.

A fresh wave of dizziness made Ryan stagger, and he leaned his hand on the cold glass wall. What was happening didn't hang together for him. How could they all have been in the Florida gateway and then end up in different destinations? Assuming that the others had materialized somewhere else in Deathlands. The idea that they hadn't was too appalling to entertain.

To try to steady himself, Ryan drew his blaster from its holster. The familiar shape made sense to him, and he lifted it closer to his face to peer at it.

"Schweizerische Industrie-Gesellschaft Sauer." The trusty SIG-Sauer, Model P-226, that he'd carried for so many years had never let him down.

Ryan took several more slow, deep breaths, reciting the vital statistics of the gun. "Nine millimeter. Fifteen rounds with push-button mag release. Weight twenty-five and a half ounces. Barrel length 4.4 inches. Total length 7.7 inches. Built-in baffle silencer."

He holstered the blaster and stopped to pick up the rifle that lay on the floor by his feet. His free hand had been gripping the sling on the Steyr SSG-70 during the jump, which explained why it had come along with him. The bolt action, 10-round blaster fired the uncommon 7.62 mm bullets, and Ryan had intended to try to find some way of changing it for a long gun that used a more standard caliber. Ammunition was a whole lot better than gold in Deathlands. If you didn't have any, it was almost impossible to obtain. If you had plenty, then you could generally find a way of getting hold of even more.

It had been something that Trader had constantly drummed into every man and woman who rode and fought with him on the lumbering war wags. "No bullets gets you dead" was one of his more succinct and memorable sayings.

Ryan was feeling better.

There were two simple options.

One was to open the door and then close it again. About the only thing that they managed to learn about the lost science of gateways was that this would normally speed you straight back to where you'd been.

But Ryan's prime guess was that the Florida mattrans chamber might well now be destroyed, flooded full ten fathoms deep in saltwater.

The other option was to go out and try to find where in Deathlands he'd landed and begin the monstrously difficult quest of trying to track down Krysty, Dean and the others.

Ryan drew the SIG-Sauer in his right hand and reached out with his left toward the control on the door.

Chapter Two

Mildred Wyeth recovered consciousness, doubled-up, a pool of vomit inches from her eyes.

"Don't remember eating that," she said, aware that her throat was dry and painful and that her voice hadn't risen above a hoarse whisper.

Suddenly, like a rush of cold wind across a midnight desert, came the realization that she was alone.

"Bastards. Might've waited." She struggled to sit up, the only sound the tiny clicking of the beads in her plaited hair. The floor and the walls were cool. No, they were cold. Bitingly, icy cold. Mildred jerked her hand away.

The walls of the previous gateway had been a sort of pallid yellow. These were a light greeny-blue. So, the jump had been made successfully, but where were the others?

"John?" she said, coughing as she stood, blinking at the rush of pain behind her eyes. She cleared her throat and tried again. "John?"

The chamber was quiet, and she couldn't catch any noise from outside the armaglass surround.

In the last-ever Olympic Games, held in Miami in the summer of 1996, Dr. Mildred Wyeth had won the silver medal in the free-shooting pistol. Back in her home town of Lincoln, Nebraska, she had been chairperson of the local shooting club, the first black, and the first woman, to hold the position.

She felt for the butt of the 6-shot target revolver on her hip, the ZKR 551, originating in the Zbrojovka Works in Brno, and designed by the Koucky brothers. The weapon was chambered to take a Smith & Wesson .38 caliber bullet.

"John? Ryan? Anyone there?"

Mildred had made enough jumps to be utterly bewildered. She knew that everyone suffered to varying degrees, but there'd never been a situation where someone would be left totally on his or her own by the others.

She stretched the stiffness out of her spine, finally making the positive decision to draw the revolver. Its familiar weight and beautiful balance gave her the momentary illusion that she felt better.

It was so cold in the heart of the mat-trans unit that Mildred's breath frosted the air in front of her.

Her fingers touched the handle of the door and she paused a moment, reaching the conscious decision that this was about the most frightened that she'd ever been in her adult life.

"Ready or not, here I come," she said, and opened the door.

KRYSTY CAME TO, finding herself holding Dean's hand. At some point, as consciousness faded into the dark, the young boy must have climbed into her lap and now lay with one arm around her shoulders, his dripping, tousled hair pressed against her breast.

"Like father, like son," she whispered to Ryan, wincing at how much it hurt her to speak.

There was no answer, so she blinked her emerald eyes and looked at Ryan.

Who wasn't there.

"Ryan!" She was more bewildered than concerned, and light-years away from real fear.

Even when she realized that nobody else was in the scarlet-walled mat-trans chamber.

Just her and the boy.

Krysty had "seeing" powers. Not like those of a genuine doomie, but with enough precognition to sometimes be aware of the threat of some imminent danger.

Now she felt her fiery hair shrinking around her skull, gripping the damp skin across her nape, clamping so tight that it almost made her cry out. With it came an utterly overwhelming feeling of total disaster. Not along the line or even around the next corner, but right now and right here.

"Now, Krysty," she said sternly, "no time for giving in. Gaia, help me."

She stood, lifting Dean gently in her arms. He stirred and woke, smiling sleepily up at her. "Hi, Krysty."

"On your feet," she said. "We're in deep shit."

"What?" He recovered awareness almost as quickly as his father would have, sliding from her grip and drawing his heavy blaster. Then realization dawned. "Where's everyone?"

"Don't know. Something terribly wrong here. Taste it flat on my tongue like the skin of a week-old corpse."

She had drawn her own Smith & Wesson double-action 640, a 5-shot, snub-nosed .38.

"Walls are different color," he noticed. "Could the others have come around quicker and then... No, that's stupe thinking, isn't it?"

"I heard some kind of electric explosion as we were beginning the jump. Reckon it affected the transmission. We came here, wherever 'here' is. Rest might be someplace else. Might have split up in different redoubts." She suppressed a charnel image of the others being dismembered in the jump.

"Why just you and me?"

The woman was touched by the courage of the eleven-year-old. It was all too obvious to both of them that they were in the gravest peril, isolated and lost. But he had braced his shoulders and almost, *almost*, managed to hide the tremble in his voice.

"You were on my lap when I came to. Real close contact. Gaia!"

"What?"

"Just remembered. The last thing was Ryan's hand being torn from mine, like some giant had ripped us apart."

"You think they all gone together?"

"Could be."

He sniffed and rubbed the back of his hand across his forehead. "But they'll all be safe, won't they?"

"Of course." The woman hoped that her own doubts hadn't shown up in her voice.

"We could open the door and close it again."

Krysty shook her head. "I don't know. Might try it. We've always reckoned that these gateways are programmed not to send you to mat-trans units that no longer exist. If that tidal wave hit, then Florida's probably done for."

"Then we might finish up where the others have gone. Mightn't we?"

She nodded. "First things first." The air had the familiar scent of one of the long-abandoned, buried redoubts, air that had been refiltered and recirculated countless times for the past century.

Krysty moved quietly to the door and readied herself to open it.

MICHAEL BROTHER'S realization that he was alone affected him, oddly, less than the others, with their combined vast experience of making jumps.

Almost all of his nineteen years had been spent in a closed community among the tall, snow-tipped mountains, a world away from the world.

He had been a complete innocent about life around the turn of the millennium and had found the brutality of Deathlands difficult to handle. Only recently had Ryan been able to persuade him to carry a gun, a Texas Longhorn Border Special that held six rounds of centerfire .38s.

But the bizarre jumps remained a blank mystery to him. The way that one could go into a small glass-walled room and just close the door, fall unconscious, wake up feeling like a rabid wolf had shit in your mouth, then discover that you'd arrived somewhere completely different. It had bewildered Michael Brother from the very start.

Now that it had obviously gone totally awry, he wasn't in the least surprised.

"Knew it," he croaked.

He stood and leaned for a few moments against the olive-green walls. Ryan had also told him that he couldn't go around Deathlands in bare feet and a knotted robe, insisting he dress more sensibly. He'd acquired a black denim shirt and quilted vest, and an ancient pair of black jeans with silver thread along the seams and small copper rivets. A pair of good quality knee-high lace-up hiking boots completed his ensemble.

During his time with the small group of friends, Michael had seen enough to know that they wouldn't have walked off and abandoned him. That wasn't their way.

They must have jumped to somewhere else.

Back at Nil-Vanity, there hadn't been many opportunities to master technical devices. Life was deliberately very simple and basic.

Though Michael hadn't taken too much interest in the few jumps that he'd already made, he had a vague memory that you could trigger a matter transfer by simply closing the door. He also knew that you didn't have any control over how the system worked or where you might end up.

All that had been lost during the endless nuke winters and the time of dark nights.

"Nobody moves by standing still," he said, unaware that he was echoing one of the Trader's sayings, which he'd picked up from J. B. Dix.

Michael forgot to draw his blaster, simply reaching out to open the door.

J.B. PICKED UP his worn fedora and jammed it on his head. He took his spectacles from a secure pocket and held them up to the overhead lights, then polished a smear from one of the lenses before placing them on his nose.

He'd been aware at the beginning of the fateful jump that something seemed to be going wrong. The feeling of spinning and disorientation had been worse than usual, and he'd detected the brief smell of overheating circuitry.

It had been absolutely no surprise to find that he was alone in a chamber with walls of orange armaglass, one of which was cracked from top to bottom.

Nor did he waste any time on speculating where the others might be. Mildred's face swam into his mind, but he resolutely pushed it away.

He quickly itemized the possessions in his jacket, then glanced over his weapons. The powerful Smith & Wesson M-4000 12-gauge with pistol grip and folding butt. He slung it over one of his narrow shoulders. J.B. also carried an Uzi machine pistol, with several mags that held twenty rounds of 9 mm full-metal-jacket ammunition. A priority would be to fieldstrip and check and oil his blasters, after their immersion in saltwater.

He sniffed at the air, catching the flavor of pine trees and fresh-turned earth. That meant that some part of the redoubt was probably open to the outside. That, in turn, probably meant there could be people around.

J.B. decided that the first and safest option was to open the door of the mat-trans chamber, then close it again immediately. His calculation was that this wouldn't return him to Florida, which he guessed probably no longer existed. But it might possibly link him up with some, or all, of the others.

Life was all possibilities that weren't very safe. Or probabilities that weren't that good, either.

"Don't believe much in certainties," Trader used to say. "Not unless you count death."

The sec lock clicked as J.B. turned the dull steel handle of the door. He hesitated for a moment as he considered the value of the Uzi and the scattergun, going in the end for the machine pistol, sliding the catch onto full-auto.

"For what we are about to receive," he muttered blasphemously, as he pushed the door open and stepped through.

"BY THE THREE KENNEDYS!"

Doc Tanner knew from bitter previous experience of jumps that the single worst moment was when you peeled back your eyelids to the harsh light of the new chamber.

The longer that could be postponed, the less vile it was likely to be.

His skin itched but he tried to ignore it, assuming that it was simply a new and unpleasant manifestation of the consequences of going from place to place via a mat-trans Unit.

"Damn and blast Project Chronos and Project Cerberus to Hades and back," he whispered. During his brief and difficult stay in 2000, Doc, a brilliant scientist, had been used on both of these highly secret operations, involving sec clearances of at least B19 or above. Cerberus had been matter transfer, and Chronos had been time trawling. The former had been amazingly successful and the latter had been almost completely disastrous.

They had both been a part of what was known as Overproject Whisper, which, in its turn, had been a sector of the wide-ranging Totality Concept.

Doc had inched his left eye open, finding that the back of his right hand was close to his face. The skin was mottled with pale brown patches and covered in fine white hair.

"Silver threads among the gold, darling, I am growing old," he sang, in his fine, melodious voice.

The words echoed around the chamber as though it were a vaulted marble tomb.

"A doleful thought," he muttered. "This grave's a fine and private place, but none I think…" He opened both eyes, and looking around, the rest of his words faltered and faded away into a deep stillness.

He had been lying down, knees drawn up to his chin. Very slowly the old man straightened, his ancient boots creaking, joints cracking. As he sat up, Doc noticed that the walls of the unit were a smooth gray, speckled with tiny spots of green. It was an unusual combination, and he reached up and rubbed his hand over the armaglass, peering at the emerald stain on his fingers.

"Moss. Some sort of subterranean sphagnum, probably of the genus of—" He stopped. "Come now, Theo, my dear fellow. Not the time for scientific theorizing. I think that it is time to set your pathetic and appallingly aged brain to work on the fascinating proposition that you have completed this jump alone and that Master Cawdor and the other good, good companions have ended up...finished up...where?"

He was aware of more bothersome itching, around his midriff. For the first time since recovering, Doc looked down at his feet.

Without any conscious effort from any of his muscles, he suddenly found himself standing upright, hands held level with his shoulders, as though he were about to surrender to some unseen enemy. He was also attempting the shamanistic trick of removing both feet from the ground at the same moment.

The consequence was that he staggered around, banging into the smooth walls, getting smudges of green lichen on the shoulders of his black frock coat.

At the same time he was shouting out in shock and disgust, an incoherent stream of revulsion.

"Coleoptera in excelsis . . . Oh, the horror, the horror . . . Ortheopterous vileness . . ."

Beneath his dancing, clattering boots, the floor seemed to be composed of innumerable tiny pieces of a shimmering mosaic, opalescent and glittering, with a dark coppery turquoise the dominant color.

A mosaic that was moving.

It was rustling with a ceaseless susurration, as though invisible hands were turning the countless pages of arcane grimoires with their invocations for devils and the spirits of the dead.

"Cockroaches!" Doc yelled, crushing dozens of the scuttling insects under his feet.

His unstable mind was tipped into underdrive by the horror that flooded the gateway, seeping through a narrow gap beneath the entrance. Without pausing for a moment to consider the possible repercussions of his action, Doc grabbed the handle and threw himself out through the door.

Chapter Three

As Ryan opened the door of the gateway chamber, he was struck by the strange taste of the air. It wasn't the flat dull taste that he was so used to in other redoubts. This had an exotic scent of lustrous flowers that had become sickly and overblown, a warm and damp smell that also carried with it another taint.

Human sweat.

Finger tight on the trigger of the SIG-Sauer, Ryan stepped silently out into the anteroom that was always a part of the mat-trans complex.

But something barred his way. A scarlet rope with yellow tassels had been strung across the entrance.

A large rectangular piece of car was fixed to the thick cord. Ryan carefully stepped over the rope, making sure he didn't touch it, then looked back.

Keep out.

The room was bare, with two short shelves fixed to the wall near the distant door, which Ryan knew would open into the control room for the gateway.

He paused to listen, wondering whether he'd actually heard voices beyond the door. He decided that he'd imagined it, but didn't put the blaster back in its holster.

The handle of the second door was clean and polished. Ryan turned it very slowly, pressing his eye to the narrow gap and seeing what he'd expected—rows and rows of chattering comp consoles.

The smell of human perspiration was stronger, overlaid with something sweet, like popped corn with honey.

"Don't touch anything!"

The voice was so loud that it made Ryan jump and nearly squeeze a round from the SIG-Sauer.

"When this building was uncovered during the digging of foundations for a new housing development, great care was taken not to tamper with it. There have been many lookings to find how it worked, but so far no successes with that."

It was English, but with an odd accent and with peculiar phrasings. Ryan's first guess was that it was someone speaking who came from below the Grandee, but it wasn't quite like the usual sort of Mexspeak.

"We think it was closed up in the month of January, which is the first of the year, in 2001, which was when skydark came and long nights lived for many times. Please keep the children away from that next room, lady. It's double-real out of bounds."

Ryan flattened himself back in the little room, knowing that any attempt to close the control-section door would draw attention to him. There were others out there, apart from the speaker, who almost sounded as if he were taking them on a conducted tour.

"Story is that a big bomb exploded in Washington and that set off the war." A harsh laugh. "Not that war is correct word. More like nukes in noon and night and morning, and after the noon also. About twenty lived from every ten thousand. In the big villes, more like one living."

Another voice asked a question that Ryan couldn't quite catch.

But he heard the answer. "We know it was called 'mat-trans,' and we think somehow sent food or stuff through space. We reckon it was a nuke trick. But... Won't tell you again to watch that child, lady. But we don't know nothing how it worked. Could be locked in some way so doesn't function."

Ryan bit his lip, not knowing what was happening. Why was there a working gateway that they hadn't been able to use to carry out jumps? Could it be that it was only able to receive? If so, he was in serious trouble. Or mebbe it needed some kind of priming, like a hand pump. Otherwise, the first of these strangers to go in and close the door behind him would have had one of the great all-time shocks.

"Want to go in and see, Grandy?" The voice of a whining child sounded less than a yard away from Ryan.

"Shut up, Langdon." The admonition was followed by a muffled slap and a cry of pain.

"Thank you, lady. These things we look at are old and rare and can't be touched or ruins come fast. The Museum of Our Past got more things to show. Let's move on now. Hey!"

Ryan had been backing away toward the gateway, ready to chance another quick jump to get away from wherever he was. Then the door to the control area burst open and a skinny boy, looking around twelve, pushed in. He was dressed in scruffy cotton pants and a torn vest, with a red peaked cap struck on his foxy skull. In his right hand he held a bright plastic windmill.

"Who the fuck're—"

The room was only a couple of strides from one wall to the other and Ryan wasted no time. He swung the blaster with all his strength, catching the wincing boy across the side of the head with the barrel. There was a loud crack and the boy went down like a felled calf.

Then a woman stood in the doorway, hand to her mouth in shock at the sight of the armed figure and her child slumped at his feet. "What are you—"

Ryan shot her through the center of her narrow forehead, the bullet exiting from the back of her shattered skull and striking a uniformed guard of some kind who was pressing immediately behind her. His face was covered with her blood and brains, and pocked by splinters of bone. The partly spent 9 mm round, distorted and tumbling, ripped a gouge beneath his left eye, driving a crimson furrow through the stubbled flesh of the cheek, removing most of his left ear before angling upward and burying itself in the plaster of the white ceiling.

The entrance to the mat-trans unit became a screeching, flailing chaos.

Half of those outside didn't know what was going on and were trying to push forward, while the other half had seen the woman and attendant shot and were shoving back in panic. Everyone was shouting and screaming, the wounded man loudest of all.

"Chill the bastard spy!" someone yelled, and a knife flashed through the air, missing Ryan by a hand's span.

He snapped off a couple more shots, aiming into the press of bodies that jammed the doorway, dodging backward, intending to get straight into the chamber. Once the lock had engaged, the armaglass walls would protect him from anything short of a concerted gren attack.

But he'd forgotten the red rope that blocked off the gateway, and it caught Ryan behind the knees, sending him toppling over on his back.

"Cut the balls off the murdering bastard!"

A stout man had drawn what looked like an old cavalry saber and was running boldly toward Ryan, flourishing the weapon above his head. But the dying woman was thrashing around and he caught his foot on her arm, fighting for balance, feet slipping in the spreading lake of blood.

An alarm bell had started to ring, and Ryan could see a flashing light above the heads of the throng in the doorway.

He scuttled back, still on his ass, until he was finally inside the chamber, firing half a dozen more bullets from the SIG-Sauer, more or less at random, seeing and hearing most of them strike home in the angry mob.

"We got him now!"

"Yeah, the shithead can't escape from there."

Ryan stood quickly, pulling the purple door closed, whistling between his teeth with relief as the massive sec lock clicked shut.

"Right. Time to move on," he said, squatting with his back to the wall, facing the door.

Despite its thickness, the glass still showed the distorted faces of the strangers, pressed against it, and he could hear their vicious yelps for his life. Fists and metal banged and crashed all around the gateway.

Ryan held the SIG-Sauer in his hand, waiting calmly for the jump to start. He felt confident that nobody would break in, but he'd been counting bullets. As the mist began to gather and thicken around the silvery disks in the floor and ceiling, he calmly reloaded the blaster.

"What the fuck's happening in there?" someone bellowed. "Break the door down!"

"No chance," Ryan whispered, hearing his own voice swirl and echo around his brain, shifting into some unguessable and infinite distance. The darkness closed his eye and then began to squeeze his brain in a shroud of raven's velvet.

Ryan slipped once more into unconsciousness.

Chapter Four

Outside the actual chamber of the gateway, the air was even more perishingly cold. Mildred rubbed her hands together, the Czech revolver stuck clumsily in her belt. Though the greeny-blue door was wide open, she hadn't taken a single step into the small adjoining room. She was aware that her pulse and respiration were both racing.

Through the half-open door beyond she could see into the control room. The air itself felt as though it were shimmering with suspended frost crystals. Already Mildred was aware of tiny lumps of ice forming inside her nose, and her facial skin felt like a badly made mask.

"No," she said. "Thanks, but no thanks."

The woman reached out to close the door again, triggering the mat-trans mechanism that would send her on another jump.

WHEN KRYSTY OPENED the gateway door, Dean pressing at her back, she found that the usual small room outside was filled with cardboard boxes.

"What're they?" the boy whispered. "Might be ammo or blasters or knives or some real old jolt we could use."

She shook her head. "Doesn't look like bullets, guns or drugs, Dean."

"What's it say?"

Letters were stenciled on the sides and top of each of the boxes, but the ink had faded over the past hundred years.

"Says 'This Way Up' on the top of the boxes. Though some of them are upside down."

"How about the other words?"

Krysty laughed. "Contents are a disappointment for you, though I might take some for myself."

Dean crouched, the tip of his tongue between his lips as he spelled out the words. One of the overhead lights was broken, making it even more difficult to read. "Oh," he said.

Tampons—Female Officers & O.R.—Internal Use Only, it read.

Beyond the piled boxes, Krysty could see through into the control area of the redoubt. Farther beyond were the massive closed sec doors that would lead them out into the rest of the complex.

"I think we might as well try for a return jump, Dean. What do you reckon?"

"Can't we explore?"

"Think logical. We want to try and link up with Ryan and the others. Now, where is the one place in Deathlands that we know none of them are?"

"Here."

"Right. The mat-trans screwed up, but I figure there could be a chance…only a small chance…that if we rejump straight away we could find the others."

"Worth a try." He turned and sat down again on the floor of the chamber, the scarlet armaglass walls giving his pale face a ruddy glow. "Come on, Krysty."

She was standing in the doorway, looking at the heaped boxes, head to one side. "I was just thinking that me and Mildred might both be grateful for this little trove. I'll help myself to a few. Won't take a minute."

Dean waited until she came back. "I hate these jumps," he complained. "Makes my head feel double-grunge."

"Me, too. Still, you ready?"

"Yeah."

"Then here we go." She pulled the door firmly shut, sat down and put her arm around the boy's shoulders.

MICHAEL WALKED around the control room, humming a setting of the ode to Saint Cecilia. He ran his finger along the dust-free tops of desks, eyes entranced by the amazing array of colored lights that flickered ceaselessly across the dozens of comp consoles.

He'd noticed the dark green double doors that dominated the area, the steel lever alongside them that was in the down, "closed," position.

From his previous jumps, the teenager knew that the lever would open the sec-steel shutters and enable him, if he wanted, to go out and explore the rest of the...what was it called again? The word had slipped from his memory.

"Redoubt," he said aloud, nodding at the recognition.

Perhaps it would be much safer to go back into the gateway chamber and simply make another jump. But Michael hated the unpleasant sensation of jumping, with the sickness and the whirlpool sucking at your brain.

He put his hand on the cold metal of the lever and gently eased it upward. His Texas Longhorn Border Special remained holstered.

There was the slightest humming sound, deep within the gray walls of reinforced concrete. Gears engaged for the first time in a century.

Michael recalled that J.B. and Ryan had been careful at times like this. He returned the lever to a central position, stopping the sec doors rising. There was a gap of around ten inches between the floor and the bottom of the doors.

Michael knelt, laying his face sideways to peer through the opening.

"Nothing."

But there was something.

A soft sound, like padded feet running quickly, or like scales moving over stone, or feathers being brushed across a sheet of rusting iron.

The gap was just wide enough for Michael to push his head a little farther, though the thought of the colossal weight of the sec doors poised above him gave him a moment's hesitation. But the strange noise was definitely coming closer, making him feel oddly uneasy.

He wriggled down, giving himself a view of a lot more of the winding passage beyond. To the left there seemed to be a blank wall, but to the right he was able to see for fifty or sixty yards. The strip lights in the curved ceiling gave a bright, flat illumination, and the two vid cameras that Michael could spot had both pivoted to point away from him, as though they were reacting to the oncoming noise.

It was definitely some living creature, and it was moving fast in his direction, as though it had somehow heard, or sensed, the opening of the double door. Michael didn't have anything like the fighting reflexes of the others, or their highly developed awareness of impending danger. But he began to think that whatever he'd disturbed might not be friendly.

Just as he was about to get up, he glimpsed it.

For a near-fatal moment the young man was paralyzed by the sight, unable at first to see quite what it was, and then unable to believe the evidence of his own eyes.

It was a kind of lizard, sort of a snake, with a ruff of spiky fur around its throat and long claws on each of its six legs. The body was about eight feet in length, colored a dirty white. A long tail whipped back and forth at incredible speed, seeming to help propel it toward Michael. The eyes were like scarlet golf balls on protruding tubes, and there were at least eight of them. The head was as pointed as a prairie rattler's and seemed, in that first ghastly glimpse, to be almost entirely mouth. Michael had just enough time to see that the triple-mutie creature had several rows of thin, needled teeth, hanging over its bleached lips.

"Mother of God!" He scrambled to his knees, heaving himself up by the green lever, inadvertently pulling it downward, setting off the release mechanism that would lock the doors.

The gap immediately began to shrink, but with an agonizing slowness that made the youth start to scream.

One inch less.

Two.

The noise was now on top of him, overlaid with a mindlessly ferocious hissing that nearly made Michael pass out in a panic.

Three.

He realized that he should have run for the gateway chamber and slammed the door shut on the horror, and he would have been safe and on his way out of this place.

Now it was too late.

The thing was partly under the door, its front legs scrabbling at the floor as it sought to thrust itself all the way through. One of the eyes was knocked off in the struggle, the severed stalk spouting a thick green ichor that stank like the bowels of death itself.

If the mutie was able to wriggle itself more than halfway through, its body tapered down to the forked tail and it would be unstoppably into the control room.

In that moment of truly terminal fear, Michael Brother's training in Tao-Tain-Do came to his salvation. His right hand flowed to the butt of the gun, drew it, aimed it and fired it, all in less than a second.

And missed.

The small revolver, at point-blank range, kicked upward and surprised him, the .38-caliber round hitting the descending vanadium-steel doors a hand's span above the thing's head, doing it no harm whatsoever.

But the thunderous noise, in the confined space, made it pause in its determined attempt to get at its prey, pause for only a splintered segment of time, barely even measurable.

But long enough.

As Michael watched, holding the warm blaster, he saw the thing pinned to the concrete floor by the doors, flattened by it, gripped just behind the elongated skull, so that it could move neither backward nor forward.

The hissing stopped and it began to howl with a sickeningly human cry, like a hungry baby. All of its eyes waved like the tentacles of a sea anemone in its death agonies and then burst, one by one, soaking the ruff of pale fur around its crushed throat.

"Die, you forsaken mess of blasphemous shit!" Michael was trembling so much that he could hardly slide the gun back into its holster.

Now the hundreds of tons of steel were inexorably closer to the floor, pulping the thing.

The noise had stopped, and there was just a faint bubbling sound as the sec doors ceased moving.

While Michael stared at the dead creature, something slithered out of its mouth and began to crawl toward him, leaving a trail of gleaming slime. He realized to his disgust that it was like an embryonic version of its parent, deformed, unfinished, sent before its time.

As he crushed it under his heel, the thing made a tiny cheeping sound, like a baby chick.

Michael spun and walked straight to the mat-trans unit and pulled the door smartly shut behind him. He sat down with his arms folded around his knees and tried very hard to stop himself shaking.

But the mechanics of the jump were already in operation, and the blackness came first.

J.B. TOOK A SINGLE GLANCE outside the chamber of the unit, seeing that it looked just like a run-of-the-mill mat-trans unit. It smelled like there was fresh air close by.

There was no logical reason to wait around at all, so he stepped back one pace and closed the door again. He took off his spectacles and carefully folded them into a pocket, removed the fedora and laid it on the floor beside him. Then he sat and composed himself for what he knew wasn't going to be a particularly enjoyable experience.

THE GRAY, MOSS-SPECKLED chamber was empty of human life, though the countless army of cockroaches scuttled across the floor as though it was celebrating its triumphant eviction of Doc Tanner.

The old man was standing in the outer room. Though his face was turned toward the broken-down sec doors, his eyes weren't seeing them.

"Call in the pest-control firm, Emily," he said, smiling and nodding. "It's the only thing to do with an infestation like that. I fear that it must be that slovenly maid you insisted on taking on without a single reference to her name." He paused as though he were listening to the other half of a conversation. "Oh, I know all about her widowed mother and her eight little babies. You and your soft heart, Emily, my dearest dove. I fear that it will be the death of you, one of these days."

The air was damp, and every single surface was spotted with the intrusive lichen. It was a tribute to American workmanship from a hundred years earlier that most of the computer consoles were still functioning.

Doc sniffed and nodded. "Of course. It was my responsibility to see to that leak of rainwater that we had in the larder above the meat safe. Perhaps that *is* a part of the problem. But to see such horrible creatures in such numbers. I thank goodness that little Rachel and dear Jolyon have not become aware of them. By the Three Kennedys but—" He stopped and wrinkled his forehead. "Who *were* the Three Kennedys, Emily? That is a puzzle and no mistake. I am reminded of the Schleswig-Holstein issue of yesteryear. So complex that only three men in history ever properly understood it." He laughed, ignoring the torrents of insects that bustled around his feet. "One of them is dead, one went insane and the third of them has forgotten."

In the corridor outside the shattered sec doors, a small stream of dank water was threading its sullen way past the entrance. The lights outside were faint, barely shining through the layer of clinging moss.

"One dead and one... One was Jack and he was the shining knight who ruled over Camelot. Second was Bobby and he was the panther in the hurricane, the oldest living son who paid the blood price. Third was... No, Emily, I disremember his name."

Behind him a warning light had begun to flash, and there was an insistent beeping.

Doc started, the glazed expression disappearing from his eyes. "Malfunction, Ryan. Triple-red alert." He hesitated. "Ryan? Where have you... where have all the flowers... to graveyards? Krysty and the laconic John Barrymore, the argumentative Dr. Wyeth and all, and all... I fear that I have lost them, every one, and they have lost me."

At his elbow one of the blue screens began to flash a message—Instant Mat-Trans Return To Previous Location Destablized. Error De-processing In Ninety Seconds From Now.

In the corner a clock was already counting down.

"Seventy-five seconds. Ah, but my poor old brain is more addled than usual. It says the return facility isn't working. Now, that means I lose any hope of rejoining my loyal and trusty companions. Sixty-two seconds and—''

The beeping had stopped suddenly as its control circuit burned out.

Simultaneously the screen went blank.

Doc started to run, his huge Le Mat blaster flapping clumsily at his hip, ignoring the dozens of roaches that perished under his ancient boots.

''Thirty seconds,'' he panted, pausing. ''Perhaps it could be more like forty seconds. Then again, I suppose that a timing as low as twenty seconds is not impossible. Time is, after all, subjective, is it not?''

A digital repeater clock set above the door of the gateway showed nine seconds remaining. Doc noticed it through the bug-infested anteroom, and broke again into a frantic gallop for his very life.

But the combination of pulped insects and the damp lichen had made the floor treacherous and he stumbled and slipped, banging his shoulder against the frame of the door. Falling over, he saw the clock tick inexorably to zero.

''No.'' He sighed.

''Reset after twelve-second malfunction,'' said a disembodied comp voice. And the clock started to run down once again, starting from twelve.

Eleven.

Ten.

Doc was on his knees, roaches chittering up his sleeve, but he ignored them, looking across the small room to the gray walls of the unit.

''Seven, six,'' he said.

Powering himself forward in a racing dive, he skidded on his stomach into the gateway, turning with an alien skill and speed born of utter desperation and snatching at the door. He managed to claw it shut just as the digital repeater clock reached the single, ultimate figure "one."

Doc was about to assume his usual doubled-over position on the floor, when he realized that he was still lying in the middle of a seething mass of coppery roaches.

"By the Three . . ."

He pulled himself upright, wiping sweat from his forehead. He knew that it was extremely risky to start a jump while vertical, but he was unable to face the prospect of lying unconscious in the midst of that carpet of churning horror.

The mist gathered around his head, and the disks in the ceiling began to glow, those on the floor mainly obscured by the cockroaches. Doc Tanner felt his head beginning to swim, nausea gripping his intestines, and knew that, for better or worse, he was on his way again.

Chapter Five

It was closing on midnight, and the frontier gaudy was beginning to quiet down. Most of the raddled whores had gone off to finally get themselves some well-earned sleep after a busy night.

The thaw, carried on a warm westerly from the nearby Cific Ocean, had brought in the local trappers and a few miners and hunters. Many, like Abe, had been stuck in isolated camps or cabins during the recent severe blizzards, and had headed for the dubious delights of the nearest ville of Andromeda, a community of forty or fifty ramshackle houses, three stables, nine gaudies and a burned-down church. All were under the benevolent rule of the local baron, Big Rodge Peyton.

The bar of the largest gaudy, called the Hammer of War, was almost deserted. A scar-faced half-breed solemnly wiped up the puddles of spilled beer and gut-rot brew. In most establishments like the Hammer of War you'd expect to find a number of dealers, sharp-eyed and twitching, doing a good trade in jolt, the lethal cocktail of heroin, cocaine and mescaline that was the fatal bane of its users.

The Trader used to say that jolt made you feel like a new man and the new man always wanted more jolt.

But Abe had heard that Rodge was opposed to the drug, proud of running a clean ville, and had a short way of dealing with the dealers. A row of half a dozen severed hands, nailed above the bar in varying stages of mummification, proclaimed his policy better than any written sign could.

Abe looked around the room, with its rickety furniture and floor covered in damp sawdust. Two trappers sat at a table near the door, heads close together, sharing a bottle of whiskey. A single man, looking like a traveling merchant, was stubbornly resisting the blandishments of one of the gaudy sluts. Her name was Kim, and she sported a better mustache than most men. She was drunker than her prospective client, and the barkeep had to keep walking around to pick her off the floor and set her back on the chair. Neither Kim nor the merchant seemed to notice anything wrong.

Abe had also noted the only other occupants of the gaudy—three men who'd been drinking quietly and sending away any women who approached them. They sat under a guttering oil lamp that one of them had risen to turn off, so that it was difficult to see their faces.

Abe kept his hand on the stainless-steel Colt Python Magnum that he kept tucked into the front of his belt.

He'd booked a room on the second floor and was feeling about ready to go up to it. But he decided to read the mysterious letter from the Trader one more time. He pulled out the stained, crumpled piece of paper and angled it to catch the best of the light that remained.

Trader himself was virtually illiterate, but he'd apparently dictated it.

"Abe, glad the mutie bobcat didn't chill you. Always sleep with one eye and two ears open." It was touches like that that had convinced Abe that the missive was genuine. The reference to "one eye" was obviously intended to make Abe think of Ryan Cawdor, and it had.

"Known for some weeks you had been on my trail. Should've known I couldn't just walk out like I hoped. Still rather been lost and stayed lost. No point weeping on account of a spent round." Another clue there. It had been one of the Trader's notorious sayings about the meaning of life in Deathlands.

"Time you read this I'll be moved on some. But not far. Reckon we might meet soonish, Abe, and jaw over old times like old men does. Watch your back. Trader."

"That wouldn't be some sorta fucking map, would it, shit for brains?"

The triple shadow across the letter and his table told Abe that he was in trouble.

"No. Letter from a friend."

"Sure," said a different voice. "But the word is that you're some little prick of an outlander. Come around the Northwest here, after fucking predarkies. Might know about some lost blaster store. What do you say, outlander?''

"Never been here before. That's true, mister.'' They were ranged behind him so that he couldn't actually see their faces without straining his head around. "But I'm not into predarkies. Trying to track down an old friend. Could be you might be able to give me some help.''

Though Abe knew there was a whole subculture in Deathlands who scavenged through the nuked ruins of predark buildings for all sorts of salable souvenirs, blasters were the best treasure. And he also knew that gaudies were hot spots for the sale of "genuine maps, guaranteed from before the long winters, showing plenty of undug places.''

"Help you, asshole?''

"Why not?''

The third man mumbled, like someone had knocked out all of his teeth. "Why not? Help's a one-way highway, you runty cunty bastard.''

"I don't know a thing that could help you boys,'' Abe said, laying the letter on the table, allowing his hands to drop naturally into his lap.

Three armed sons of bitches standing close behind tended to push up the chances of catching the last train west. But there might be a hope of taking one with him, if he could draw, cock and fire his .357 blaster before they gunned him down in the spit, beer and dirt.

"You got a gun in your belt, fuckface?''

Something cold pressed against the back of Abe's neck that he knew wasn't the handle of a spoon.

One of the trio giggled. "Little cocksucker gone whiter than the main-street slush."

There was a muffled sound as the whore fell off her chair again. This time, though, the barkeep didn't go to help her up.

"Wasting time, G.W.," the third speaker said. "Let's take him out the back and fill his mouth from the privy till he tells us about the predarkies."

Abe felt a slight draft as though someone had opened a door to the cold night outside.

"You got a room here, barkeep?" one of the trio asked.

"Yeah."

"Best take him there. Be quieter and more kind of private to ask him what we want."

The new voice was harsh, and sounded weary. "Best step away slow and careful."

"Butt out, you white-head sheep fucker, or you get what this runt gets."

Abe knew precisely what was happening, knew whose voice it was, knew what he would do now. He prayed passionately that the man with the blaster pushed against his skull didn't pull the trigger as he died.

The Armalite was set on single shot, but the three shots came so close together that it sounded like full-auto.

The triple shadows vanished from the table and Abe stood, drawing his one Colt, seeing immediately that it wasn't needed.

"Don't you ever learn, Abe? I said in that letter to watch your back."

Trader smiled.

Chapter Six

Ryan blinked his eye open and promptly closed it again, unable to bear the instant lancing pain that drove through the optic nerve into the heartland of his brain.

The one-eyed man slowly took stock of his body, not risking any sort of sudden movement. He lay on his right side, knees drawn up to his chest in a fetal position, hands clasping each other for comfort. Apart from the ferocious headache, there was also a gut-roiling sickness and a faint tremor running through all his limbs.

"Better never to have jumped at all," Ryan muttered through clenched teeth.

Though he knew that wasn't true.

He risked another glance, wanting to check on the color of the armaglass walls. Pale yellow would mean a return to Florida, which wasn't something that he contemplated with any pleasure. Purple would mean he was back in that strangely alien gateway that had seemed like some sort of museum.

The walls were a cheery cherry red.

It was so positive and bright that Ryan groaned, taking in plenty of shallow breaths to hold away the nausea that threatened to erupt.

While lying very still, he tried to taste the air. It had the familiar flat, recirculated flavor, though maybe a tad less arid and dull than usual.

Moving in extreme slow motion, Ryan sat up, shuffling sideways until he could rest his back against the nearest wall. Like someone squinting into the brightness of the rising sun, he eased open his eye again.

He took stock of his possessions, beginning with the blasters and the two knives. He'd always had the irrational fear that making a jump would, one day, land him in a foreign place, completely naked.

But this one was all right. Apart from feeling that a day-old lamb would take him over five rounds.

Ryan stretched, forcing the variety of cramping kinks from his muscles. The threat of vomiting was fast receding and he risked standing up, swaying a little, steadying himself with one hand on the cool glass of the wall. Using some of the basic remedial skills that Krysty had taught him, he powered himself along the road to recovery.

In less than three minutes he began to feel that he could at least give that day-old lamb a run for its money.

THE DOOR HISSED OPEN with a hydraulic perfection, revealing the small room that led through to the usual main control area of the mat-trans unit.

Ryan stepped out of the chamber, SIG-Sauer preceding him, the barrel of the blaster moving from side to side. Other than the usual faint sounds of the comp controls clicking and whirring, the place was as silent as the grave.

He noticed some boxes on nearby shelves, padded brown cardboard, dried and brittle. Their contents were announced in watery-blue stenciled letters that ran diagonally across each box: Surgical Gloves—Twelve Dozen Pairs—Green; Sterile Face Masks—Surgical/Pathology—Twenty-four Gross; Op Room/Morgue/Laboratory   Boots—Midcalf—Plastic—White—M/F—Sizes L & XL.

For several long seconds Ryan stood and stared at the boxes, puzzled. He'd never come across anything remotely like this in any of the other hidden redoubts that he'd visited.

His guess was that this particular military complex had been used mainly for medical purposes, perhaps as some sort of secret hospital.

It crossed his mind to wonder whether there might still be some stores of predark pharmaceutical drugs. Vacuum-sealed and often still usable, they were one of the most sought-after commodities in all Deathlands. When he'd ridden with the Trader they'd almost always had stocks of drugs on board the war wags.

The rectangular digital clock on the opposite wall of the control room was showing 0805. Ryan checked his wrist chron and corrected it. The only person who would be able to find out where they were with any accuracy would be J. B. Dix, who always carried a miniature sextant in one of the capacious pockets of his coat.

From the apparent time change, Ryan could only guess that he was probably somewhere in what had once been called the Central Time Zone. But that could mean anywhere from the Canadian Arctic clear down to the Gulf of Mexico.

Thinking of J.B. made Ryan realize once more the isolation of his position.

There might well be clues if he moved out from the mat-trans unit into the remainder of the complex, clues that would tell him precisely where he was.

But there was no possible way of finding out where Krysty and Dean and the others had gone.

Alive or dead?

Now that he'd made the fresh jump, Ryan hadn't really done that much to improve his position. He could either try a third jump or he could cut his losses and go out to explore the redoubt.

On balance, that seemed the only viable option.

So he took it.

THERE WAS NO TRACE of any human activity within the whole of the mat-trans section, no sign that anyone had been there since the first fatal weeks of 2001.

Ryan reached the control lever for the sec doors. Finding it in the down, "closed" mode. He had the Steyr slung over his shoulder, the SIG-Sauer in his hand. Cautiously he eased the green lever upward, stopping the doors when they'd moved only a couple of inches toward the ceiling.

He flattened himself and peered through the gap, sniffing the faint draft that seeped in from the corridor beyond. There was no sign of freshness that might indicate the redoubt had been broken into. At least the immediate area seemed to be secure, though Ryan could detect an odd, vaguely chemical scent, which he figured could have something to do with the building having once been used as a hospital.

He pushed the lever again, lifting the doors another eight or nine inches, alert to drop them if he caught any hint of danger. But the passage beyond was silent and seemed to be completely deserted.

Finally the gap was wide enough for him to slide through, checking both ways. As was often the case, the mat-trans unit was placed at the farthest extremity of the redoubt, with a blank wall beyond it. To the right he looked along a fairly narrow passage, slightly curving, with the usual overhead strip lighting and the occasional ruby gleam of sec cameras.

Confident he was in no immediate danger, Ryan stood and closed the locking lever on the outside, watching as the dark green vanadium-steel doors slid smoothly down. The last thing he saw was the clock on the wall, showing 0819.

THE DIGITAL CHRON clicked over to 0820. The armaglass door of the jump chamber trembled as though an invisible hand had been laid on it, then began to close slowly and silently.

Outside, high in one of the corners above the rows of unmanned comp consoles, a crimson warning light flashed while a voice crackled through the speakers, inaudible beyond the double sec doors.

"Matter transfer in progress. Any personnel with a sec rating below B19 must leave immediately, repeat immediately. Matter transfer in progress."

The metal disks in the top and bottom of the chamber were beginning to glow, and a faint mist was beginning to appear like ectoplasm emanating from a successful medium. The cherry-red color of the walls seemed to be fading.

"Matter transfer completing. Matter transfer completing. Do not open chamber door."

Inside the armaglass, someone was appearing. Someone or something.

RYAN WALKED along the center of the passage, oblivious to what was happening behind him.

It was a familiar experience, following the broad curve, all his nerves on double-red alert. But there was a massive difference to other times.

Now he was a man alone, on the edge.

The scent of chemicals, both tart and sweet, was definitely stronger. It seemed that the place was in excellent condition, with all of the lights functioning and every camera swiveling to follow his progress. The walls were flawless, the smooth concrete showing no sign of any cracking or deterioration. The floor was virtually dust-free, and Ryan could just detect the faint vibration of the hidden, distant nuke generator still faithfully keeping the redoubt serviced.

He passed only three or four side doors, all locked and comp coded. The likelihood was that they were service quarters for the personnel who maintained the mat-trans section. In some of the redoubts that they'd discovered, the gateways had been completely self-contained.

Ryan glanced down at his chron, seeing that it was a few seconds shy of 0825, less than half an hour since he'd completed the jump.

J.B. SIGHED, rolling back his sleeve to check the time on his wrist chron. Twenty-five minutes past the hour. And the hour didn't much matter as that would only be resolved by finding where he was.

By and large he'd found that Deathlands still conformed to the old tradition of time zones, though many of the frontier villes either operated their own eccentric time scale or, sometimes, had no real time at all.

The Armorer stood, clutching his fedora, and placed it carefully on his head, wincing with the effort. The walls of the gateway were an unrelenting cherry red, a color that appeared to pulse and throb in time with the beats of the heart.

He opened the door and sniffed, peering through his spectacles at the boxes on the shelves.

"Hospital," he said quietly.

J.B. dropped to his knees, staring closely at the floor. There was something that almost looked like the print of a boot in the fragile layer of fine dust, but it was impossible to be sure. In an unchanging environment the mark could easily have been made the best part of a hundred years ago, when the redoubt was finally being evacuated.

He moved into the main control area, glancing around him and checking the time on the wall, which now showed 0831. J.B. altered his chron accordingly.

There was no sign of any human life around, so he immediately and unhesitatingly made his way toward the main sec doors into the mat-trans section of the redoubt.

He paused by the green lever, sniffing the air. "Some sort of chemicals. Yeah, definitely like a hospital." For a moment J.B. considered leaving a note in case anyone else came after him, but decided that it would be pointless.

There wasn't much doubt that he was now on his own, cut off from Ryan and Mildred and the rest of the group by some fault in the jump mechanism back in Florida.

All he could do was to emerge from this vault and work out where in all Deathlands he was, then begin the near-impossible task of tracking down the others.

He pushed the control up, kneeling with the Uzi on full-auto, ready to spray a burst of lead at any threat from outside. But the rising door revealed only an empty expanse of corridor, slightly less wide than the usual, closed off to the left, curving away to the right.

Once outside, J.B. threw the lever down to close the doors again, sealing the complex, and set off at a brisk walk to his right, heels clicking on the barren stone.

His wrist chron showed him a time of precisely 0837.

Behind him the control area was still and quiet, with only the dancing lights on the comp screens moving, and the wall clock inexorably ticking around to 0840.

The gateway began to run through its mat-trans cycle all over again.

Chapter Seven

Ryan saw the elevator at the end of the passage and his heart sank into his boots. The last time he'd traveled in one, the result had been close to terminal. Also, as he walked carefully toward the dull gleam of the sliding sec door, he could see that there was a complicated comp-code control panel at the side, one containing a mixture of letters, numbers and colors. It was probably a four-symbol code, but it would take, literally, millions of random attempts before you hit on the correct combination.

"Fireblast!" He stopped a few yards away from it and shook his head. The thought of having to go back and make a third jump was physically sickening.

Then he saw that there was something printed on the pale cream wall by the elevator door. Fortunately the overhead lights were all full bright; otherwise he could easily have missed the time-faded writing.

Ryan moved in, glancing automatically behind to make sure that nobody was threatening him.

"Green C M, one, nine, blue five, E E red."

A ten-symbol code showed how triple-secret Cerberus had been in Overproject Whisper. What was amazing was that it had actually been written on the wall. Ryan knew enough about the way the military had run its redoubts to be certain that it would probably have been a capital offense to betray a code like that. His guess was that it had been done in the very last days.

The Washington bomb had gone off and the skies had darkened all across the planet with the preemptive and retaliatory strikes. Nukes rained in from their space launching platforms, as well as from buried silos and from ships and planes.

Evidence from other stripped redoubts showed how panic had overridden expert training in those last crazed hours. Here it was a fair bet that someone had lost control over B-ratings of personnel and access to codes, taking the easiest option and scribbling it on the wall so that no time would be wasted during what could have been the wild panic of evacuation.

Ryan turned and looked back along the corridor, whose steady curve prevented him from seeing more than sixty or seventy yards. He frowned and concentrated, closing his eye to try to listen better. There was a faint and regular sound, like boot heels clicking on bare stone.

But he'd passed a tiny leak in the roof a minute or so ago, which was steadily dripping water from an eroded crack in the concrete. He waited, deciding that it was the tumbling spots of liquid that he'd heard.

"Green . . . C . . . M . . . one . . . nine . . . blue . . . five . . . E . . . E . . . red."

As he pressed each recessed button, the code was entered on a green liquid display above the panel, ready for confirmation. Ryan waited.

There was a slit beneath the controls that might have been used for personnel-coded ID cards. If that was also needed, then he was out of luck.

But after a couple of seconds the word "Accepted" flashed, and he heard the distant rumble of machinery. There was another small panel at the top of the door of the elevator, with two letters. *U* and *D*.

Up and Down.

The cage was coming steadily down toward him.

Ryan checked his chron again and saw that it had taken him nearly twenty minutes to walk from the mat-trans unit to the elevator, a sign the size of the redoubt above him.

The elevator took two minutes to descend, arriving with a pneumatic hissing of brakes and the flicker of light behind the transparent letter *D*.

And nothing happened.

"Come on, you bastard," Ryan urged, unable to believe his ill luck. To have gotten this far and have the astounding luck to find the code for the elevator, and now the door wouldn't open. He kicked at it, hearing only the dull ringing thud of his boot on the inert metal.

The glowing golden light on the control panel shone cheerily, drawing Ryan's angry stare, which changed to a slightly sheepish grin as he realized what a double-stupe he'd been.

For on the bottom was "Open Door."

He pressed it and the door slid back.

The elevator was much larger than he'd expected. It was twelve feet square and capable of holding at least forty people.

Ryan hesitated before stepping in, listening again for the regular sound from along the corridor. But it had ceased. All was silent.

The cage rocked very slightly under his weight, and he immediately faced outward, the SIG-Sauer still in his right hand. But there was no sign of life. On the wall was another control panel, but this had only five buttons: Up, Down, Open Door, Close Door and Alarm.

Ryan pressed the fourth, then the first, flexing his knees as the door shut. There was a distant whining sound from the driving engine, and the elevator began its ascent.

J.B. HAD HEARD the muffled ringing noise and immediately stopped. He had been walking at good speed, confident from the dull taste of the air that nobody had been in that section of the complex for many, many years.

"Dark night!" he breathed. He had no doubt at all that someone else was inside the redoubt with him.

MILRED RECOVERED consciousness, feeling as though she were suffering from the worst migraine in the history of the universe.

There were a whole mess of things that she couldn't stand about living in Deathlands, but the sickening horror of making a mat-trans jump was among the worst. She sat up very slowly, holding her head in both hands, not yet willing to open her eyes.

When Mildred eventually did, the flaming brightness of the cherry-red armaglass walls of the chamber almost made her pass out again.

THE CHEMICAL SMELL GREW stronger as the elevator climbed the endless shaft. Ryan waited patiently, trying to work out the speed he was traveling at and, hence, the depth of the mat-trans section of the redoubt. But it was impossible to judge. All he could tell for sure was that it was seriously deep.

There was a tiny, bell-like pinging sound, and the upward movement slowed and then ceased. Ryan's finger hesitated over the button that would open the sliding steel door.

He ran his mind over the code in case he needed to get back quickly to the gateway. In case he needed to get back to the gateway *at all*. The overwhelming probability was that he would never be able to return if he forgot the comp sequence.

"Green, C, M, nineteen, blue, five, E, E, red," he recited, making sure he had it right.

Numbers had never been his strong point. Trader, even though he was nearly illiterate, was able to reel off strings of map coordinates or quote endless details of muzzle velocities or the populations and sec strength of dozens of villes throughout Deathlands.

Here, at the top of the shaft, the air seemed a little fresher, though it also carried a stronger taint of the medical smells. Ryan couldn't believe that the place was still working as a hospital. During his travels with War Wags One and Two, he would surely have heard something about such a place.

But he gripped his blaster more tightly, eased the shoulder strap on the Steyr rifle and pressed the button.

J.B. SAW THE ELEVATOR, with the light showing that it was at the top. He also spotted the code written out on the wall alongside the control panel.

He moved in closer and waited.

"FIREBLAST."

The impenetrable sec door slid open and the elevator cage was flooded with the hospital smell, so strong and sickly that it made Ryan gag. It was overlaid with more familiar scents—the sweetness of decay and the unforgettable gut-churning odor of much dying.

He wished profoundly that he had J.B. on his right hand to face whatever it was that lay out there. Perhaps whatever it was might walk alone.

There was an open area immediately in front of him, with a number of other passages leading off it. Ryan saw there was a large wall plan of the redoubt opposite, but it had been daubed with what could have been paint, tar or old, dried blood. Whatever it was had completely obscured the map.

The floor outside the elevator was in stark contrast to that around the gateway. It was muddy and scuffed, showing the blurred marks of dozens of feet. As Ryan stepped out of the cage, with infinite caution, he saw that the walls on either side of it had been hacked and scarred, the reinforced concrete gouged and the vanadium steel of the door itself and its surround showing innumerable bright scratches.

But there were no marks of gunfire. No evidence that anyone had tried to use a gren to break into the elevator and get down to the mat-trans section. The damage looked like it had been done with nothing more lethal than knives or chisels.

The control panel had also been attacked, but the cover was sheet armaglass and had hardly been touched. Ryan pressed his finger to the contact pad marked "Door Close" and stood back, mentally rehearsing the control code to himself.

The steel slid silently across, the light above it showing that the elevator was at the top.

Since there was no visible sign of life, Ryan obeyed one of the Trader's cardinal rules and stood still for several seconds, listening.

He could feel a draft on his stubbled cheek and half turned to face it. Apart from the vile stench it carried, he could actually detect what might be fresh air. It wasn't by any means certain, but Ryan was beginning to think that the redoubt had probably been penetrated.

There didn't seem to be any distinguishable noise coming from any of the corridors.

The two simple choices were to either explore as much as possible of the military complex and see if there was anything worth the taking, or to simply head for the nearest exit and get into the open.

Out and away.

Partly because of the smell, Ryan's heart inclined toward the latter option. But his head guided him toward a recce of the redoubt first.

Since the wide passageway immediately ahead of him brought the wind, and also seemed to have been most used, he decided to try it first.

As he walked away from the elevator, Ryan's boots scraped on the pebbles and mud, drowning the tiny pinging sound from inside the cage. If he'd turned around at that moment, he would have seen that the light had vanished from the letter *T* and would, in a couple of minutes, glow once more behind the letter *B*.

J.B. STOOD PATIENTLY at the bottom of the shaft, awaiting the arrival of the elevator. He could hear the gears turning. Years of painfully learned caution made him turn to check the corridor behind him, but there was no sight or sound of any living thing anywhere near.

MILDRED HAD MANAGED to get out of the chamber without throwing up and was now sitting in front of a comp console at one of the desks in the large room.

While she sat there, Mildred started to doodle on the keys, using a one-finger hunt-and-peck technique, watching as the white letters appeared dutifully across the bright blue screen.

"My name is Mildred Winonia Wyeth, and I was born on the seventeenth day of Decembre— Shit." She backspaced and made a correction. "December, 1964. That's more than one hundred years ago. I'm a qualified doctor of medicine, specializing in freezing techniques for human tissue. Ironic, considering that's what happened to me eleven days after my thirty-sixth birthday. I got frozen. My father was a Baptist minister murdered by the white-sheet cowardly bastards of the invisible empire of the Klan only a year after I was born. My father's brother, Josh, helped—"

She stopped, feeling the short hairs prickling at her nape and turned in the revolving chair.

Through the anteroom, Mildred watched as the main armaglass door of the gateway chamber began silently to close.

"Holy...!" She jumped to her feet and raced toward the exit doors, reaching out for the green lever, not bothering in her panic to check for safety. She plunged under the rising mass of steel as soon as it was high enough and immediately reversed the direction. She knelt the other side, panting as if she'd run a half mile across a plowed field, the revolver in her hand.

She could hear the recorded voice inside, shut off by the sec doors. "Matter transfer in progress. Any personnel with a sec rating below B-19 must leave...."

The clock on the wall showed precisely 0859.

Krysty Wroth and Dean Cawdor were just completing their second jump.

Chapter Eight

Out in the corridor, Mildred was more aware of the odd smell in the redoubt.

"Formaldehyde? Can't be. Surgical disinfectant and some kind of gangrene."

The mix of medical scents was puzzling.

To her left the corridor ended in a totally blank wall, blocking off any thought of progress in that direction. The other way was a winding, well-lit passage, like ones that she'd seen in other redoubts. Mildred noticed that the ceiling was dotted with miniature surveillance cameras, reminding her of visits to the shopping mall in Lincoln, Nebraska.

"Here goes nothing," she said, keeping the ZKR 551 in her right hand.

J.B. WOULD NEVER HAVE admitted to anyone, not even Ryan or Mildred, that he suffered from claustrophobia, but the truth was that he found any confined spaces extremely difficult to handle.

It dated back many years, before he met the Trader and Ryan Cawdor.

He'd been born in Cripple Creek in Colorado, a beautiful town that had boomed during the nineties with the legalization of gambling in the old mining township. A boom that was predictably followed by bust, not long before skydark, when that same legislation was repealed.

The hills around the township were littered with hundreds of old mine shafts. Since the long winters, many had been used by the ragtag collection of radsick survivors, countless numbers of them dying in those cold, barren caverns.

The young John Dix had been a great explorer, preferring his own company to that of the teenaged gangs around Cripple Creek. He knew that some of the mummified corpses in the tunnels had died with blasters in their possession. Even at the age of ten, J.B. had been fascinated by weaponry.

He'd taken to roaming for days on end, living off the land, exploring the more isolated diggings.

It had been called the Lucky Chance Mine. Boards across its entrance had been pulled down for burning, and the entire site had almost vanished under a rock slide. But there was a gap just big enough for a skinny little boy to wriggle through, his pocket oil lamp primed and ready.

At first it had looked like it was a deuce on the line. No signs of human habitation. J.B. had persevered and gone deeper into the winding passage.

At first he thought he was imagining it, holding the light higher, so that its flickering golden glow reached into the deeper shadows.

A cabin was built within the mine. Using the old props and timbers, the rickety roof actually held up the roof of the mine. As the boy had walked closer, the echo of his feet brought down a fine dust from the curved ceiling, a sure sign of serious danger of collapse.

There was a glider on the porch, its swing long rusted through. A dried corpse lay among the tattered rags of a blanket. J.B. had looked at it from a few yards off, seeing to his disappointment that there was no blaster around.

Moving as if he were treading on eggshells, he'd picked his way past the body, the lantern ahead of him, into the ramshackle hut, aware that even his light weight was making beams shift a little, creaking in protest, like a sleeper being pulled back to the light of morning.

There was a table with a couple of plates on it, both covered in a sheen of gray dust; a collapsed armchair and a fireplace, soot-blackened and empty; half a dozen empty bottles and a few cans, still silver-bright in the dry atmosphere.

And a double bunk bed in the far corner.

As the lad had stepped across toward it, he'd felt the floorboards shift, and somewhere there was a brittle, snapping sound.

But he'd seen the gun, glittering like a jewel in a pirate's den. He'd recognized it immediately as a chromed Colt Cobra 1973, a 6-round double-action revolver that fired a solid .38 round. It had a snub-nose two-inch barrel, and J.B. reckoned he could get a handful of jack for it at the general trading store.

There was a bundle shape on the top bunk that he figured might well be the partner of the corpse out on the porch. Likely they'd both starved to death or succumbed to the long-term effects of rad sickness. He'd seen enough of that himself in the previous few years, hair loss and bleeding gums, and sores that spread to cover most of a person's emaciated body.

He had moved like a frail ghost, setting one foot slowly down in front of the other, trying to ignore the ominous sounds of straining timbers and the fine dust that floated around the sheltered flame of the oil lamp.

As the boy knelt to pick up the gun, his hand brushing the checkered grips, the cabin collapsed. The ceiling gave way, bringing down part of the roof of the old mine shaft. The bunk bed folded over on top of J.B., knocking him to the floor, trapping him faceup, boulders and splintered wood confining him in a tiny cave.

For a few moments the shock robbed him of his senses. But when he opened his eyes he realized that the lamp was, amazingly, still lighted at his side. And that the body from the bunk now lay above him, pinning him to the floor in its dry embrace.

The skull face was inches from his.

The mane of long brittle golden hair that caressed J.B.'s cheeks told him the corpse had been female. The eyes had long vanished into the smeared sockets, and the skin of the cheeks had shrunk and tightened across the planes of bone. The lipless mouth was wide open, the irregular yellowed teeth actually nipping at his own skin, below his left eye.

J.B. had started to scream then, screamed for so long that his throat became raw and the sound of his voice faded away to a croaking whisper in the echoing stillness.

His arms and legs were pinned by the tumbled hut and the heaped rocks, the skeletal figure in the torn shreds of a plaid shirt hugging him in a ghastly parody of a lover's embrace.

It took perhaps the greatest effort of will for J.B. to ever reassert self-control. Faced with this ultimate horror, the lamp beginning to gutter and die, virtually anyone—man, woman or child—would have given in to insanity and despair.

Not John Barrymore Dix.

He closed his eyes and breathed slow and thought about the rolling mountains and the sunlight, and fresh snow and crystal streams and live oaks in the spring, and shivering aspens in the fall. He also mentally rehearsed some of the encyclopedia of arcane blaster knowledge that he already possessed, gleaned from some old gun books he'd found.

"At two hundred yards a five-seventy-seven rifled musket ball with standard charge will penetrate seasoned white pine to a depth of eleven inches. A .69-caliber smoothbore to half an inch less. A .58 rifle to just over nine inches. And a .58 pistol-carbine to below six inches."

Gradually the boy's heart stopped pounding like a miniature trip-hammer in his scrawny chest. He was able to consider his position with a careful objectivity, trying to move first each foot and then each hand, working out what was holding him down and precisely where his best option for escape lay.

The light was close to being done, and he knew that he had to get free before that happened. The idea of being held forever under the leering skull in total darkness was so appalling that J.B. consciously thrust it away from him.

His left leg moved most, and the boy concentrated all of his attention on that, wriggling and pulling, trying to ignore the suspicion that the whole mountain was poised above him, ready to tumble and blur him into infinity.

Something slid away and the leg was free. J.B. brought it up and used it to push at the part of the bed frame that was trapping his left arm. He was caught near the wrist and he tugged, feeling skin tear and warm blood flowing over his fingers.

But it was moving. By turning half on his side he could lever his right arm out, finally flailing away at the brittle corpse, a moment of panic returning as the jagged teeth clamped on a fold of skin at the front of his throat.

He could never quite remember how he got his other leg free, or how he made his way in the utter velvet blackness, after the tiny flame died, to fresh air and safety.

And ever after J. B. Dix had been unhappy in confined spaces. Spaces like the cage of the waiting elevator.

But he did eventually manage to get a good handful of jack from the sour-faced storekeeper in Cripple Creek for the chromed Colt Cobra.

DEAN CAWDOR WAS PARCHMENT pale, and threads of vomit dappled the front of his black denim jacket. He looked at the gateway, where Krysty Wroth stood staring at the labeling on the piled boxes.

"Yeah. I think that means we could be somewhere farther west than we were in the Keys."

Krysty's hair was almost dry, but it still clung to her skull like a small fiery animal. She was recovering from the second jump, feeling surprisingly well, though there was a nagging worry at the back of her mind. Something wasn't right about this gateway, but she couldn't put her finger on what that was. The air smelled strange.

"Where's Dad?"

"I don't know, Dean."

"He here?"

She really hadn't thought about that possibility. After the last jump and the horrific experience of finding that she and the boy were all alone, it hadn't occurred to her that Ryan—or any of the others— could be here.

"No way of knowing."

"He might come, though? Or he might have gotten here before we did?"

Krysty shook her head doubtfully. "We don't know how many redoubts like this were built, Dean."

"Before skydark?"

"Yeah. I've lost count of the ones I've visited. Couple of dozen, easily. And loads more must have been destroyed by the nuking."

"But they're mostly well hid. They reckoned they was a hot pipe to survive."

"Were."

"What?"

Krysty managed a smile. "Like father, like son, Dean. You should say 'they were' and not 'they was.' That's all. But, yeah, it's true. They picked mainly isolated places for the redoubts and buried them deep. I suppose it's a remote statistical chance that Ryan or one of the others might have ended up in the same one as we have."

"Let's go look."

The clock showed 0914.

"Hey, wait up. Don't touch that control lever. Not yet."

Dean started to run up and down the aisles of desks, punching his fist in the air, brimming with excitement at the chance of being reunited with his father.

"Cool it down," Krysty called. "Odds are dozens to one. No, they could be hundreds to one." She noticed that the curly haired boy had skidded to a halt, retracing his steps and stopping in front of one of the screens. "What is it?"

"Hundreds to one?"

She caught the note in his voice. "What's there, Dean? Is that a message from Ryan?"

"No. But come and look."

"My name is Mildred Winonia Wyeth and…" The message ended abruptly a few lines later, like someone had crept up behind Mildred and plunged a knife through her heart.

But somehow Krysty didn't get the feeling that anything bad had happened to their friend. Just that she'd been interrupted while leaving word to anyone coming along later.

"How long ago?" Dean asked.

"Can't tell." She looked at the keyboard, wondering if it could magically give a clue about the time that the message had been typed.

"If Mildred got through here…" Dean allowed the hopeful sentence to trail away.

"Then mebbe…*mebbe*…Ryan could also be in this redoubt." Another thought came to her. "Or, he might still be making a jump here."

0920.

Behind Krysty, the cherry-red chamber door whispered shut and a voice began to broadcast the warning that a matter transfer was taking place.

She drew the Smith & Wesson 640, conscious that the boy had pulled out his Browning Hi-Power.

They waited together.

Chapter Nine

It was just after 9:30 in the morning, and six out of the seven friends had arrived in the redoubt.

Krysty and Dean were helping Michael to recover from what had been a devastatingly unpleasant jump for him, supporting the teenager as he sat on the floor with his head between his knees. They knew that Mildred was somewhere ahead of them, but had no idea where she might be.

She had moved quickly away as soon as she realized that there was a matter transfer taking place, running until she reached the bottom of the elevator shaft.

J.B. was picking his way carefully along the main passage on the higher level, aware that there was at least one other person in the redoubt with him, but having no suspicion at all of who that might be.

The sickly meld of scents was an odd mixture of the familiar and the strange. There was the strong odor of a hospital, which he remembered having noticed in one redoubt at some other time and some other place. But there was also the unforgettable and overwhelming stench of death.

Set against these unseen factors was the fact that J.B. hadn't yet come across any sign of life in the redoubt.

RYAN FOUND THAT PROGRESS was becoming slower and slower. It wasn't that there was any visible threat to him, but his combat sense, honed for most of his life, screamed "danger" at him.

The corridor had forked two or three times, but Ryan stuck to the main core, walking up a gentle incline, the weird cocktail of smells growing stronger with every step.

Sec doors, all locked, stood on both sides at irregular intervals.

There was an open area directly ahead of him, with what looked like seven or eight passages. And Ryan thought he could also see another map, this time relatively undefiled.

He suddenly caught what sounded like the distant murmur of voices, sending him flat against the wall of the corridor alongside yet another closed door.

Which opened.

Two figures shambled out, both turning to their left, away from him. Less than a yard from them, Ryan could hardly believe that they hadn't spotted him.

He leveled the SIG-Sauer and considered blasting them down with a full-metal jacket through each spine. But he kept his finger still on the trigger, holding fire not from humanitarian concern, but from the probability that the explosions of the blaster would draw others to him.

The only thing that struck Ryan was that they were walking in a strange, slow way, as though they were slouching toward some distant Promised Land. Both carried something cradled in their arms, but he hadn't been able to see what it was.

They were male, he thought, with thinning, stringy hair pasted to narrow skulls. Both dressed in an assortment of ragged clothes. The one on the left wore what might once have been a uniform of dirty gray green, missing the left leg of the pants. The other had on what looked like a hospital robe that could once have been white, but wasn't anymore.

And smells floated around them like the miasma from a stinking swamp at midnight.

Ryan made the spot decision to follow them at a cautious distance.

As he eased past the open door he glanced inside— and looked straight into the face of another of the redoubt's occupants.

J.B. HEARD A MUFFLED YELL, echoing down the corridor from somewhere ahead of him, and then a number of staggered shots close together.

"Dark night!" He knew the sound of Ryan Cawdor's SIG-Sauer P-226 as well as he knew his own heartbeat.

Without a moment's hesitation the slight figure began to sprint toward the noise of the shooting, slinging the Uzi over his shoulder and grabbing at the folding butt of the Smith & Wesson M-4000 scatter-gun.

Mildred, just stepping out of the elevator, also caught the distant rumble of gunfire.

Not knowing what it might portend, she hesitated, licking her dry lips.

And finally began to walk up the main passage.

IT WAS 9:39, and Krysty threw the lever to close the double sec doors on the control room. Dean and Michael were standing close behind her, looking nervously around the blind bend of the winding corridor to their right.

"Let's go and see what we can see," she suggested.

Back in the heart of the deserted mat-trans unit, the cherry-red chamber door was just swinging silently shut for the sixth and last time.

THE TORRENT OF nuclear missiles that defiled the earth during the brief holocaust did more than cull most human beings on the planet. It also slaughtered a vast percentage of all living things, animal and vegetable. Food chains were destroyed or distorted, and the fragile ecostructure was tilted and changed for the rest of eternity.

Landscapes were altered. Volcanoes, long extinct, found ferocious new life and the earthquakes raged, tilting tectonic plates that raised valleys and leveled mountains. There were lagoons where there had been deserts, and forests where there had been flat plains.

Much of California slid into the Pacific, and cities fell and vanished.

After four generations, the underlying effects of the nuking were still running rampant. The first mutations had been more subtle, but the deviations from what had once been the norm grew ever more gross.

Plants, fish, birds and reptiles, everything that walked or crawled or burrowed or ran or swam or flew was altered.

Muties.

Most visible as you traveled through Deathlands were the humanoid muties.

Ryan had seen most of them, fought and killed plenty of them.

But he'd never come across anything quite like the creature that stood within the room, staring blankly back at him.

It was the eyes that drew his attention first.

The first impression was that they were melting in their watery sockets, that they'd been removed and boiled, then carelessly replaced. The pupils were almost invisible, and the whites were a muddy pink. And there seemed to be no spark of life within them.

Ryan had once stared at the closest range into the dead eyes of a great white shark, but they had teemed with turbulent energy compared to these dull, blank orbs.

The skin of the face was puckered and soft, like a peach kept in a bowl of water. It was pitted with open sores like one of the worst rad-sick cases. The mouth was half-open in surprise, showing only the stumps of a few crooked teeth, set among gums so rotten they were almost black.

Ryan took all of this in, also absorbing the fact that the mutie had a drooping mustache but was wearing a woman's flowered dress. There was no sign of a blaster, just a thin-bladed, bone-hilted knife stuck into the belt.

There was one other thing that slowed Ryan's usual lightning reactions.

The mutie was holding a human leg, severed neatly below the knee, the flesh snow-white. In the center of the calf a ragged half-moon had been bitten out.

"Hey…" The voice was deep, like a lowing steer. The hands, with filthy, jagged nails, dropped the leg and began to fumble for the knife.

But it was all done in ultraslow motion, as if the mutie were trapped underwater. Ryan was aware, out of the corner of his eye, that the other two muties had begun to react to the bewildered cry. As they started to turn, he realized that one was actually in the act of biting a chunk from a woman's severed breast, while the other was hugging an armful of unidentifiable meat, the glint of bone showing amid the bloodless flesh.

Ryan had once seen a vid that showed trick photography—films speeded up, with blowers blooming and dying in half a minute and a bullet bursting a water-filled balloon; an elephant dying and then being devoured by millions of maggots. A huge jigsaw puzzle completed in a flash.

The pieces of this puzzle all came together at once in his mind.

The smell.

The drained human flesh.

Not a hospital.

"A morgue," he whispered, putting a 9 mm round through the throat of the nearest of the ghouls. Switching his aim, he chilled the other two. One of the bullets burst the severed breast apart, splattering skin and gristle into the mutie's face. Another hit it in the chest, sending it into a clumsy, staggering dance along the corridor, slapping the wall with its bloodied hand, leaving crimson smears on the concrete.

Two more rounds kicked the last of the ghouls into an untidy heap on the opposite side of the passage, rolling on its ruined face, bare feet kicking in the last spasms of death.

The handblaster's boom would carry for miles through the vaulted sections of the redoubt.

Ryan shook his head and sighed. "Shit!" He quickly reloaded the SIG-Sauer, listening to try to hear if there were any more muties coming his way.

He could hear feet moving, combat boots clattering on stone, heading toward him.

But it didn't sound like an army of muties. More like a single sec man. Ryan eased back into the side corridor, stepping carefully over the corpse, his own boots slipping in the sticky lake of spilled blood from the torn throat.

Whoever came along would see the bodies, but they might figure the killer had moved on. And then Ryan could backshoot him from cover.

Best and safest way of doing the job.

J.B. RAN AS QUIETLY as he could toward the shooting, though he was aware of the steel tips on heel and toe of his boots clattering and echoing ahead and around him. Part of him knew that he was going to be too late.

One way or another.

Ryan would have won the brief firefight—and the Armorer hadn't caught the sound of any other blaster—or he would already be chilled.

He saw the bodies, one of them still scraping his bare feet on the stone in the insensate residual movements of the nearly dead, lying bloodily about thirty yards ahead of him.

Ryan heard the running feet stop and readied himself with the SIG-Sauer.

J.B. edged closer, alert for any threat. The powerful shotgun was braced at his hip, finger relaxed on the trigger.

He noticed the door on the left, slightly ajar. He moved away quietly to the opposite side of the corridor, giving himself a better angle.

Ryan sensed the intruder, very close. All of his attention was focused on the main passage, making the instant decision to take the initiative. Other enemies might be closing in, and time wasted was time lost.

He kicked the door open, finger whitening, checking the movement at the last splinter of frozen time as he recognized the crouched figure of J. B. Dix.

"I nearly..." Ryan began.

But J.B. hadn't stopped, swinging the gaping muzzle of the Smith & Wesson toward him and firing.

Ryan felt the blast of heat and noise.

Chapter Ten

Doc Tanner came to, finding himself lying on his left side, knees tucked up to his chin and a thread of spittle cooling over his cheek.

He knew better than to open his eyes too soon after a jump, aware of the sickening rush to the cortex that normally resulted.

Doc swallowed a few times, pleased he wasn't going to throw up. He coughed to clear his throat and spoke into the darkness around him.

"To make one jump is unfortunate but to have to make two jumps seems like carelessness."

He waited for someone to respond, expecting some waspish dig from the cantankerous black woman doctor with the beaded dreadlocks.

"Mildred?" he said.

There was simply the vast silence, a stillness so intense that the old man was aware of the sound of the blood coursing through his skull.

He opened his eyes and remembered.

IT WAS TWENTY MINUTES to ten in the morning.

Krysty was running as fast as she dared, Michael

and Dean struggling to keep up with her. Ahead of her she'd just spotted the entrance to the elevator.

"What's rush?" the boy panted.

"Trouble. Ryan, trouble." She had no breath to explain more. Not that you could explain the icy fingers that gripped you by heart and lungs, the feeling that in some limitless cavern on a barren star a hooded figure had opened its shadowy eyes and directed a ruby laser into the deeps of your soul.

MILDRED WAS HALFWAY between the top of the shaft and the scene of the killings, but she heard the unmistakable thunderous roar of the big shotgun.

"John," she breathed, and began to run up the slope of the corridor.

RYAN SLIPPED, losing his balance in the spilled blood, landing on top of the dead mutie. He came within a hairbreadth of putting a bullet through J.B. for the triple-stupe attempt to send him to buy the farm. Then behind him he heard the sudden noise of someone clattering to the floor.

"Ace on the line, Ryan," J.B. said, levering another round into the shotgun.

The mutie had been able to creep up close behind Ryan without him hearing, and it had been gripping a steel-shafted hatchet in its clawed fingers. If the Armorer hadn't chanced the risky passing shot, then the blade of the ax would have probably been buried in the back of Ryan's skull.

The Smith & Wesson scattergun fired eight rounds of Remington fléchettes, twenty inch-long darts in each shot. At any range over fifty yards the spread was so great that they were of little lethal value.

But the mutie had been only a dozen paces from J.B., and the fléchettes had, literally, ripped its heart apart.

As Ryan got to his feet, still holding his blaster, he noticed what lay on the floor a few steps behind the most recent mutie corpse—a severed human arm, so slender that it must have belonged to a dead child, with three fingers missing, gnawed off at the splintered knuckles.

J.B. was checking the bodies of the ghouls, whistling between his teeth as he realized what they'd stumbled on. "I caught the smell. Thought it was a hospital."

Ryan nodded, joining him in the main passage. "Same here. But the body parts have been emptied of blood. Preserved in some way. Frozen or pumped with chemicals."

"This redoubt must have been used as a graveyard."

"The word is 'morgue,' John." A pause. "Or, perhaps 'mortuary' would be more accurate. But certainly not a graveyard."

They both turned and saw Mildred watching them from way down the tunnel, her voice carried by the excellent acoustics.

"The others with you?" Ryan asked, walking toward the woman, his eye constantly on the watch for more danger.

"Haven't seen them." She looked past him to J.B. "Hello, John. Thought I might not ever see you again."

"Me, too, Mildred."

Ryan moved aside as they embraced, hugging each other, the woman burying her face in the man's shoulder. For several long seconds none of them spoke. When Mildred finally broke away she was sniffing, wiping her nose.

"Must be those bastard stinking chemicals. They made my eyes water."

Ryan glanced at his chron. "Nearly ten o'clock. I came out of the jump just after eight. There was a repeater on the wall in the control room."

J.B. was industriously polishing his glasses. "Eight-twenty for me."

Mildred's jaw dropped. "Eight-forty. Intervals of twenty minutes between each of us. You think . . ."

Ryan was trying to work it out, and he didn't answer for a moment. "If there's a twenty minute gap, then there's three possibilities. Everyone's ahead of us. Or everyone's behind us. Or they're split up."

"They could have wandered off down any of the other passages," Mildred observed.

"And run into these cannibal muties. Haven't heard any noise of a fight."

"Nor me," Ryan agreed.

"You didn't hear anyone behind you?" The Armorer was slipping another round into the shotgun.

Mildred shook her head. "No. Found the code for the elevator on the wall and came on up."

"Mebbe we should go back, Ryan. See if it's been used again by Doc or Krysty or someone."

"I don't understand why the shooting hasn't brought some more of the muties. Noise must've carried right through this part of the redoubt." Ryan looked at the four bodies and the sad, scattered remnants of human flesh.

J.B. repeated his question. "How about going to check the elevator, Ryan?"

"Why not?"

Mildred had stooped to examine the corpses, straightening, shuddering. "Bad sight of the week, friends. Sickest specimens I ever saw outside the covers of Japanese horror comics. If that's what eating human flesh does for you, then I think I might turn vegetarian."

Ryan looked down the gentle slope that would bring them back to the top of the deep shaft. "All right," he said. "Close together and on triple-red."

"I'M WANDERING as lonely as a... Perdition! I seem to have mislaid what I wandered lonely as. A flower? A cloud? No, I think that it wasn't that, either. But I certainly seem most damnably lonely here."

Doc had stepped out, past the surgical gloves and gowns, hardly noticing them. He walked around the control room, passing the screen that carried Mildred's message without it registering on his consciousness. He was humming to himself.

The wall clock was now showing just one minute shy of ten o'clock.

"You're a trained scientist, Theophilus. Exercise that rapier-keen intellect and work out just what the devil, what the Satan, what the Beelzebub, what the Hades, what..." He jerked his head to snap himself out of the pattern. "What has happened to the others? Where are they? What went wrong?"

He sat at a desk, close to the sec doors, and looked vaguely around him.

"Redoubt in Florida was about to be drowned. Something went wrong and got separated in the jump." He ticked off the points on his bony fingers. "All ended up in different places. Damn it, I'm starting to speak in some infernal telegraphese. Now, if everyone went elsewhere, then the probability is that they all tried again. I have ended here, wherever 'here' happens to be. Why should they not also have ended up in this redoubt? The answer is that they might." Doc laughed. "And then again, my dear old duffer, perhaps they might not."

He stood. "If you wish to make a practical test of the hypothesis, then that is what you shall do. I shall boldly go where somebody else might have gone before."

Doc walked to the door and moved the green lever to the "up" position.

KRYSTY, FEELING an overwhelming fear of disaster, was close to the ragged edge of panic. She arrived with Michael and Dean at the closed door of the elevator, seeing a light showing that the cage was at the top of the shaft.

"Gaia!" She banged a fist on the cold metal.

"There's a coded sec lock," Dean said, "but it looks real triple-grunge difficult."

"We'll never get it." Her keen mind felt as though it were trying to operate under water. "There have to be millions of combinations."

"If the others are ahead, they must've gone that way." Michael scratched his nose. "Unless they somehow got one of the side doors open."

"No. They're up on top. I can feel that. But I— How the fuck can we open it?"

"Krysty!"

"What, Dean?"

"I don't think I ever heard you say 'fuck' before. Wait till I see Dad."

She managed a part smile that didn't get within a country mile of her narrowed emerald eyes. "You do that, Dean. When we meet him, you tell him."

"What's this written here?"

Michael was pointing at some faint lettering on the pale cream wall by the control panel.

"Just some..." Krysty began, her eyes widening. "No! It's the code for the elevator, Michael." She hugged him, squeezing so hard it took the breath from his body. "Brilliant. Read it out and I'll punch it in."

"Green . . . C for Charlie . . . M for Mike . . . one . . . nine . . . blue . . . five . . . E for Echo . . . E for Echo . . . red."

They all heard the distant hiss of pneumatic gears operating. Dean laid his hand against the door and grinned. "I can feel it coming."

"Keep the blasters ready." Krysty suddenly began to regain control, aware that whatever danger had been threatening Ryan had passed.

For the time being.

"SOMEONE," Mildred said.

But they'd all heard the machinery slipping into action, watching the yellow light disappear from the *T* above the sliding door.

J.B. turned away, staring intently down the corridor to their right.

Ryan caught the movement. "What?"

"Company."

"Many?"

"Yeah. But . . . sounds like they're coming real slow. Not at the charge."

"Cautious," Mildred suggested, still watching the elevator door.

Ryan shook his head. "Mebbe not. When I chilled those three . . . Well, it didn't sort of register at the time, but their reactions were real slow."

"We best get ready."

"What if the elevator brings Krysty or Doc or Dean? Or Michael? They could run into an ambush." Mildred had her ear pressed to the door. "Just stopped."

The light was now on behind the *B* indicator.

"Time it gets up here again, we could have us a sizable firefight." J.B. glanced around. "Could be best to go meet them halfway, Ryan."

"Yeah. But one of us should stay here."

"You. Me and Mildred can go and fill the wags up for mutie hell."

"Right."

DOC WAS FEELING in surprisingly good spirits, striding out, taking in deep breaths of the oddly scented air, his lion-head sword stick rapping smartly on the stone floor of the curving passageway.

Twice he momentarily forgot that the others had disappeared, but each time he remembered, it plunged him into an instant gloom. The pendulum between manic and depressive was swinging more actively than usual.

NOW RYAN WAS AWARE of the sounds of the muties, a sullen, confused muttering, like the waves sucking at bare rock along a deserted coast. But it hardly seemed to be drawing closer. Certainly there hadn't yet been the noise of blaster fire from Mildred and J.B.

He stood with his back to the elevator door, listening to the powerful machinery that was hauling it up to the top, wondering which of the missing four it might contain. He was torn between hoping for Krysty and for his son.

There was the distinctive clunk of the cage reaching the top of the deep shaft, and the tiny, bell-like pinging of the signal. Ryan half turned, keeping watch on the dark mouths of the numerous passages running away in all directions.

"Hello, lover," Krysty said, planting a small kiss on his cheek, schooling herself to keep calm, just as though she'd known all along that he'd be standing there when the door slid back. "Good to see you."

"You, too...and you, son, and Michael. You haven't seen Doc, have you? He's the only one missing now. No?"

For a moment it looked like Dean was going to hug him, but he checked himself. Instead, he tugged at his father's sleeve.

"Dad?"

"What?"

"Krysty said 'fuck' down at the bottom."

Ryan smiled. "No! Then I guess I'll have to wash her mouth out with—"

Then it all started to happen.

Chapter Eleven

At that moment Doc had arrived at the bottom of the elevator shaft and was peering with a scholarly interest at the control panel.

"What a world of choice we have here. Colors, letters and numbers. If I had my calculator with me, I could work out the odds against reaching the correct code, which odds I believe must be positively astronomical. But since I do not have it, then I needs must return to the infernal gateway and... But soft!" He placed a melodramatic finger to his lips. "What sequence is writ on yonder wall?"

A touch of rheumatism in his fingers made Doc a little clumsy at punching in the key buttons. Twice he made mistakes and the display panel admonished him. The second time it warned that a third error would result in "Availability termination and security-force contact being made."

Tongue protruding between his lips with the effort of concentration, Doc carefully followed the handwritten instructions and became the fifth person in the past ninety minutes to use the ten-symbol code.

He leaned on the sword stick, feeling peculiarly nonchalant. Waiting for the elevator took him back to the time that he and his lost wife, Emily, had stayed at the luxurious hotel on Sixth Avenue . . . the name escaped him. That had been one of the first times that either of them had ever come across such an ultramodern invention, and they had ridden up and down in it for half an hour, giggling like children, to the considerable irritation of the hotel's other guests.

A dimly heard bell told him that it had arrived, and he waited for the door to open, rapping on the metal with the silver lion's head on the top of the cane.

"Come on, my good fellow." He noticed the Open Doors button and pressed it.

The large cage was empty and he stepped into it, looking back to make sure that no other elegantly attired ladies or gentlemen were about to join him.

But there was nobody.

"To Del Marco's excellent dinery at the top of the tower," he said, "where my wife and I propose to imbibe a bottle of your best Haut Brion and dine on the finest mutton with some of your famous wow-wow sauce."

He used the ferrule of the stick to press the button that closed the door and set the elevator off on its long climb to the upper level of the redoubt.

"Going up. First floor, soft goods and everything in draperies and bed linen. Second floor. The department for the layette and the trousseau. Babies and brides. Third floor, hunting, shooting and fishing. Fourth floor, toys for all ages." He grinned to himself, showing his amazingly perfect teeth, glittering in the dulled steel walls of the cage.

The steady upward progress continued.

"Going up for gentlemen's outfitting and the tonsorial department. Ladies' lingerie, going down."

A delicate blush crept across Doc's wrinkled cheeks, and he shuffled his feet like a little boy caught peeking through the outhouse door.

"Sorry, Emily, my dove," he whispered. "I suffered a slip of the tongue, dearest. I promise that such bawdry will not pass my lips again."

The ride seemed to have been going on forever, and Doc rocked back and forth on his heels, checking that it was still ascending.

"Why, here we are at our destination, Emily. I confess to being a trifle peckish."

He pushed the button to open the door, part of his mind expecting to find himself looking at an ornate lobby with red velvet curtains and crystal chandeliers, a throng of elegant boulevardiers parading before them, with a bewigged flunkey in a frogged brocade coat and knee breeches bowing unctuously to greet Emily and himself to the restaurant.

Doc was busy pasting on a patronizing smile, ready to slip a silver dollar to the man to make sure they got a really good table near the orchestra and a long way off from the door to the kitchens.

"Good to be here, thank—"

For a mind-freezing moment, Doc thought that he was facing a saffron-robed Buddhist monk.

But what would a monk be doing in Del Marco's eatery in upper-crust New York?

The man stared at Doc as though he were equally amazed at his appearance. He was barely five feet tall, with a pale complexion and a puckered scar that ran from the corner of his mouth down into his neck, vanishing beneath the yellow-orange sheet wrapped around his scrawny body. His head was totally bald and his sunken eyes were grossly bloodshot.

Though Doc was six feet away from the bizarre apparition, he recoiled at the appalling stench that was exuded through its sagging mouth, like an open sewer.

Why in the name of the Almighty would a Buddhist monk be carrying three severed and bloodless human hands strung around his waist?

And why would he be slowly drawing a rusted saber from his belt?

Doc's brain was in frantic overdrive, trying to rationalize what he was seeing and what was happening.

It wasn't a Buddhist monk in Del Marco's, it was a murderous mutie in a redoubt! Doc staggered away, until he was trapped at the back of the elevator, just dodging the ponderous swing of the sword.

"Fuck'n outland," the ghoul snarled, struggling to stop the weapon from carrying him off his bare feet.

Doc had his own sword stick in his right hand, which made it difficult for him to get at the Le Mat in its holster. But it only took a moment to twist the lion's head and cast aside the ebony case, freeing the blade.

"Have at you, damn your insolence, you verminous cur," he yelled, swishing the glittering steel in a dazzling maze of death.

But the mutie didn't even seem aware that its potential prey was miraculously armed. It had regained control over its own brass-hilted saber and was readying it for another haymaker slash at Doc's head.

Doc, at six foot three, was vastly taller than his opponent, with a vastly superior reach, which he immediately used to its full advantage.

He dropped one knee slightly, his left hand lifted to shoulder height, like a lithographic illustration from a nineteenth-century manual on the proper use of the foil. His right arm was held straight so that the slender rapier became an extension of his body, and he lunged beneath the clumsy attack of the slobbering mutie.

"Touché, mon brave!" he exclaimed.

The needle tip of the slim sword drove into the creature's neck, splitting the Adam's apple. Doc's timing was so perfect that the point slid off the cervical vertebrae and emerged three inches out of the back of the ghoul's neck. A twist of the wrist at precisely the correct moment ripped the sides of the throat apart, sending a cascade of choking blood into the lungs.

The saber fell with a clatter, and the mutie started to lift its hands to the penetrating rapier.

But Doc had already withdrawn it, standing and watching, knowing that the wound was fatal.

"Tapped your claret, you evil-looking piece of near-human ordure," he said, finding that he was not even panting from the brief fight.

"Fuck'n outland," it spluttered, falling to its knees, its white severed hands trailing on the floor.

"So you said before," Doc observed, delighted at his successful duel.

Blood was pooling on the metal floor of the elevator as the mutie slithered facedown and died.

Doc stooped and wiped his scarlet-smeared blade on the saffron robe then straightened, picking up the ebony shell that surrounded and hid the Toledo steel.

He stepped confidently out of the elevator, finding himself in an open area with a number of corridors opening off. In dying, the mutie had lost control of bowels and bladder. But Doc was aware of a different, more sickly smell.

"Like an operating room. Or..."

Doc's train of thought was interrupted as he emerged in the upper level of the redoubt, to find himself surrounded by dozens of the muties. Many had portions of partly devoured human bodies in their hands or strung about them, and all held knives, axes or spears.

"Fuck'n outland" came from one throat.

Then another.

And another.

Soon it became a roar of inarticulate hatred of this intruder into their world.

Doc knew that this was the end.

There was no Ryan or John Barrymore Dix to come to his rescue with blasters blazing.

He threw the ebony stick behind him and fumbled with his left hand, ignoring the ring of brutish loathing that was beginning, surprisingly slowly, to close in around him. The Le Mat seemed stuck, but he eventually freed it, cocking the hammer over the single, central .63-caliber shotgun round, aware that there would be no time to shift it to utilize the nine .36s the gun also fired.

One roaring explosion that would take out several of the pressing muties, then his dancing blade for a few more seconds. Then they would overwhelm him.

"I pray for a swift passing, Lord," he whispered.

He stepped carefully over the body, back into the elevator. If only there had been a moment's warning; he could have pressed the button to close the doors and been safe.

Now it was too late. They filled the doorway, grunting and jostling one another, waving their knives at him.

"Watch the manner of a gentleman's passing," he shouted.

And pulled the trigger.

Chapter Twelve

Ryan had never met any muties quite like those that infested the redoubt.

He'd come across forms of cannibalism before. Hell, everyone in Deathlands knew someone who knew about it. Krysty had once told him stories about something called the Donner Party, way back in the old 1800s. Somewhere up in the high Sierras, trapped in winter. Nothing at all to eat except each other.

There were tales of stickies that ate human flesh, roasting it over open barbecues.

Occasional whispers of a group of inbred "cannies," way up in the Shens or hidden deep in the festering depths of the bayou country.

But nothing...*nothing*...on this kind of scale.

The threatening gang of thirty or forty muties that were confronting J.B. and Mildred all seemed to have bits of drained corpses about them.

Krysty, Dean and Michael had barely walked out of the elevator to greet Ryan when they heard a shout from the Armorer, sounding like he was only about fifty or so yards away, up one of the shadowed tunnels.

"Got us a lot of company, Ryan!"

The other odd thing about this particular tribe of grossly mutated creatures was their slowness.

Ryan had seen stickies, crazies, dirties and swampies, most of them with a feral hatred of norms that was made manifest by vicious and often cunning attacks.

Trader's rule of thumb on dealing with muties had been implacably ruthless, and based on a lifetime of frontier experiences with the breed.

"Chill them. Chill them today and tomorrow. Chill them fast and chill them good."

But there was something about these brutish, ponderous entities that was thoroughly disgusting and malevolent. Yet somehow too stupid to be a heart-stopping menace.

The six friends stood together in a narrow line of resistance, facing the mob.

All with blasters drawn.

At first Ryan couldn't catch what was being shouted at them, the words blurred and overlapping. It was a string of what had to be threats or insults, but there was no attempt to unite the bedlam of cries into a chorus.

He glanced down at his son. "You got sharper ears than me, Dean."

"Calling us fucking outlanders, I think." A moment's pause. "Why don't we chill them all, Dad?"

"Don't see a blaster among them."

He'd checked them out with a single, raking glance—far more men than women; usual ragged clothes, mainly barefoot; cleavers, axes, homemade spears and knives with crude wooden hilts, bound with strips of sinew.

And the extraordinary amount of human flesh. Most had laid down their burdens, and Ryan could see flayed skulls and hunks of ribs with splintered ends of bone protruding from white flesh. One of the muties had shaped up to throw the spear he held in his right hand, but his coordination was exceedingly fallible and he finished by chucking a pair of feet, joined by a cord inserted through the ankle bones.

Apart from the animallike bellowing and the waving of their blades, the line of muties was notably reluctant to advance toward the blasters.

It was the sort of situation that Ryan particularly hated.

A standoff.

It would be easy enough to butcher the gang where it stood. A burst of fire from J.B.'s Uzi alone would put half of them down on the concrete.

Yet Ryan had never been a believer in slaughter for slaughter's sake. All he really wanted to do was to try to track down Doc Tanner, whether he was ahead or behind them, then get them all out of the redoubt to explore the locality.

But he had no way of knowing just how many of the cannies there might be infesting the complex.

"We could go back to the elevator and try one of the other passages," J.B. suggested, showing that he was thinking along the same lines at Ryan.

"Looks best option."

"What about Doc?" Krysty shouted, raising her voice as the noise from the muties swelled suddenly to almost deafening proportions.

"Don't know. What time did you all come through?"

"Me and Dean together at nine, more or less on the hour. Michael came through twenty minutes later."

Ryan nodded. "That's the interval. I was here at eight. J.B. twenty minutes after that, then Mildred the same period after him. So Doc has to be either a little way ahead of us, or mebbe following on."

The dull explosion of the blaster roiled up the corridor behind them.

The Armorer spun. "The Le Mat," he yelled.

"He's behind us." Ryan made an instant calculation, trying to determine the balance of terror. "Krysty, come with me. Rest stay here."

EVEN AS HE FIRED the pistol, feeling it buck against his wrist, Doc's mind wasn't totally on his imminent demise at the hands of the muties.

Part of him was distracted and amused by the similarity between the hideous face of the leading attacker and the ghastly appearance of Lon Chaney in the flickering old vid of the *Phantom of the Opera*, the same staring bloodshot eyes and stretched rictus of a nightmare leer.

The face disappeared into a spray of flesh, bone and splattered brains as the .63-caliber shotgun round struck it though the middle of the porcine nose.

It bought Doc a few moments more of life, the effect of the single shot paralyzing the huddle of muties, silencing their continual cries of hatred. There was just barely enough time to stick the Le Mat back into its holster and ready himself, the rapier on guard.

"'We who are about to die salute you!'" he shouted, flourishing the sword into a hissing circle of polished steel. "I will rejoin you, Emily, my dear!"

Ryan, sprinting toward the elevator, heard Doc's defiant voice. He rounded the corner with the sound of Krysty's boots clattering at his heels and saw the murderous mob, all with their backs turned, oblivious to his arrival.

His first impression was of the scarlet mist that dappled the heads and shoulders of the muties, as well as spraying the ceiling and walls of the elevator.

Boots slipping a little on the cold stone, Ryan skidded to a halt ten yards from the mob, standing with feet spread, his 9 mm SIG-Sauer pointing like the flaming sword of the angel of vengeance.

Krysty stopped at his side, steadying her own 5-shot .38.

He began to shoot a heartbeat before her.

Doc was awash with sweat, his hand and right sleeve sodden with spilled blood. It had been a lifetime since he'd been coached by Adelmo Sicilio at the Boston Athletic Club in the fine points of épée, foil and saber, and he had been so much younger then.

His arm was exhausted.

The muties hardly even tried to parry his repeated lunges, and three more were down on the floor, being trampled on by their fellows. One was choking, pink froth bubbling from the narrow wound in his chest.

Despite all Doc's endeavors, they still pressed forward against him, knives flailing as they tried to peck at him. Their efforts were so clumsy that he noticed several had cuts on hands and arms from the weapons of others.

But none of that counted.

When he heard the snap of gunfire, Doc could hardly believe it, not until the press of bodies seemed to weaken, heads turning to stare behind them.

The shots were calm and measured.

"Not head shots," Ryan shouted to Krysty. "Might ricochet and hit Doc. If he's still alive in there."

"Hang on, Doc!" Krysty yelled.

"By the Three Kennedys! Is that the Seventh Cavalry coming over the hill in the last reel?"

The guttural bellowing of hatred for the white-haired outlander had almost stopped, replaced by a thin, anxious piping. Those at the head of the crowd were aware of the attack from the rear and were trying to push out of the death trap of the steel elevator, while those caught helplessly at the back were seeking cover from the remorseless hail of lead by elbowing their way toward the front. It was bloody chaos.

Ryan leveled his blaster, picking his targets with great care. At such close range it was impossible to miss, but it was important to try to make every round a killing shot, going for the center of the spine, level with the heart and lungs. Or, if the muties had turned, to drill them neatly through the middle of the chest. Of his first eight bullets, seven were instant clean kills. The eighth was just ducking away and got hit under the left arm, the full-metal-jacket round angling up off the ribs, exiting through the side of the neck.

Krysty was equally careful.

Her Smith & Wesson 640 held only five rounds, so she used four, taking out four cannies, obeying the great Deathlands rule that Ryan had drummed into her, about not using your last bullet unless you had to.

Doc leaned against the scuffed wall of the cage, watching the miraculous dissolution of his enemies. Bodies tumbled and, literally, gallons of blood poured across the floor, lapping at the toes of his boots.

The muties cracked and finally turned to run, moving with exaggerated clumsiness, their arms flapping like penguins, heads wobbling on weak-muscled necks. They dropped their weapons as they lumbered from the killing ground, scattering, disappearing down the other passages.

"Reload," Ryan instructed, watching them flee. He waved a hand at the figure of Doc Tanner, towering above the mound of twitching corpses that blocked off the entrance to the elevator. "You all right in there?"

"Never better, my dear fellow."

From behind Ryan he heard the voice of J.B., raised in concern. "Need help?"

The Armorer would never use three words when two would do the job.

"No. Chilled some. Rest gone." He smiled as he matched J.B. at his own game.

Doc had wiped his rapier, picking up the polished ebony sheath that converted it into a walking stick. He climbed carefully over the bodies, unable to avoid stepping on the chest of one of the two mutie women chilled, forcing a gasp of crimson froth from between her blue lips.

"Do I assume that we are all united again, Ryan? Then that is the finest news a man could have. My thanks to you and the exquisite Mistress Wroth for your well-timed rescue." He hesitated. "Though, if I may be forgiven for nitpicking, I would appreciate it next time if you could arrange to save my life a little more quickly. It was a damnably close-run thing, friends."

Ryan grinned, clasping him by the hand.

Life, which had seemed unbearably bleak and desolate only a couple of hours ago, was now filled with the warmth and affection of good companions.

And the love of his son.

And Krysty.

Chapter Thirteen

They all stood together, ringing the map of the redoubt that Ryan had noticed earlier.

Mildred pointed at the various sections, delineated in different colors, shaking her head. "The whole of this floor and the one above it, toward the main entrance, seem to have been one great big mortuary. If all of them were filled with bodies, a century ago, then—"

"What is the difference, pray, Dr. Wyeth, between a morgue and a mortuary?"

She stared at Doc. "The one good thing about this redoubt was that it looked like you weren't in it. But, if you really want to be educated, Dr. Tanner, then I can enlighten you, though I admit the distinction is a touch subtle."

"I can scarcely wait to hear you exhibiting subtlety, Madam," he countered.

"A morgue has the connotation of a place where the bodies of the unidentified dead, or the victims of some accident, are first taken. While a mortuary is more generally the building where bodies wait before being taken to the cemetery for burial or on for cremation."

"What's the difference between a cemetery and a graveyard, Mildred?" Dean asked.

"One's enough for today, young man. I'll have to think about that and tell you some other time."

"We going to hang around in here?" Michael asked. "The smell makes me feel like throwing up. It would be good to breathe some fresh air."

"I will second that. It seems a most pleasant idea to be able to use this—" he flourished his sword stick "—as a walking aid for my frail old legs rather than to spill the unclean blood of the ungodly."

"Show it to me, Doc," Dean begged.

"We've got to move on, son," his father said.

"Just a quick look. I never saw it properly before, and Doc chilled them so well."

"Doc, save him from making himself a pain in the ass, would you?"

"Surely." A twist of the lion's-head hilt released the blade of Toledo steel. The rapier flashed in the stark overhead lamps of the redoubt.

Dean touched it delicately with the tip of a finger. "Thin, ain't it, Doc?"

"But very resilient, springy, and powerful, my boy. Its strength lies in its very lightness."

"What's that lettering?" The boy lowered his head closer. "Can't read it."

"It is an old language from Europe, called Spanish. In the original it says '*No me saques sin razon; no me envaines sin honor.*'" He traced the floridly engraved words along the narrow blade.

"What's it mean, Doc?" J.B. asked.

"Do not draw me without a good reason and do not sheathe me without honour."

"Shit or get off the seat," Dean said.

Doc shook his head, replacing the ebony cover. "Not exactly, dear boy, not exactly."

J.B. HAD AN EIDETIC MEMORY for maps. Once he'd looked at one it would be printed permanently in his mental files.

"Guess we might as well take a look at one of the central storage sections," he suggested. "Then we can easily get out of the main entrance."

"What about the cannies?" Krysty asked.

"From what we've seen, I don't think they'll be a threat." J.B. looked at Ryan. "I never saw such poor, slow-moving bastards in all my life."

"Long as we don't get ourselves bottled up in a dead end, we should be fine. Don't know how many of the tribe there are, but we've already dented their numbers some."

Krysty touched him on the arm. "Still can't properly believe that we all made it. Not after all going off on jumps to other places. Thought I'd lost you, lover."

"Me, too. First chance we get, I'll try to make it up for you." And he kissed her softly on the mouth, the tip of his tongue pushing gently at her lips, parting them for a moment.

She broke away from him, her green eyes bright, cheeks slightly flushed. "Let's go and take a look at this morgue or mortuary, shall we?"

"GETTING COLDER, DAD."

Ryan was walking with his son at the head of their little party. It was more or less the usual triple-red skirmish line, with J.B. and his Uzi bringing up the rear and the others strung between them.

"Yeah. Only way those bodies could've been kept fresh was if they were chilled right down."

"How many you reckon?"

"How long's a piece of string, Dean?"

"Can't answer that, can I?"

"No. Because you haven't got enough information even to make an intelligent guess."

"And it's the same here?"

"Yeah."

J.B. had told Ryan that he figured the redoubt hadn't been broken into by the muties all that long ago. "Certainly months and not years."

"Could be weeks and not months." Ryan based his opinion on the fact that the main nuke gens were still running, controlling the temperature throughout the main part of the redoubt. The mat-trans gateway section normally had its own, totally self-contained power unit.

Given enough time, the sort of brutish muties that they'd encountered would have done something to wreck the whole comp-control system, then everything would have rotted. But the coolness as they drew nearer to the main blocks, and the fact that the cannies had been holding untainted meat, supported the theory about a recent invasion, possibly from some long-established mutie camp, not far from the redoubt.

Now the drop in temperature was even more marked, making everyone walk more briskly.

They'd spotted the muties only twice during the long progress through the silent corridors, moving deeper into the heart of the abandoned complex. Each time the creatures had been standing at distant corners, staring in their direction, but making no effort at all to either flee or to fight.

"There," J.B. called from the back. "That section to the right, where the passage forks."

"Looks like some kind of air lock," Krysty observed. "Double doors with seals on them."

Ryan had noticed that the floor had, for some distance, been smeared with gobbets of ripped flesh and occasional splinters of bone.

Krysty had been correct. Through the first set of doors the air was decidedly colder, making Dean shudder. And, directly in front of them, was another pair of swing doors with dark rubber sealing strips at their center.

"Everyone ready?" Ryan asked, the SIG-Sauer in his fist.

Mildred waved a hand. "I'd just like to say that this is not likely to be a pretty sight. If those things have broken into a death house as big as this one, then..." She allowed their imagination to take over.

IT WAS WORSE.

Michael stared for a dozen, endless seconds, then

spun on his heel and ran straight back out, hand clasped firmly over his mouth.

In their different ways, the other six were somewhat inured to the horrors of Deathlands. But, even so...

The room that they'd entered was like an enormous warehouse, at least two hundred feet in length and about eighty feet wide. The ceiling, the better part of fifty feet high, was partly obscured by a faint mist, caused by the extreme air-conditioning, a freezing atmosphere so bitter cold that everyone's breath was hazing around them.

The whole place was filled, top to bottom, end to end, side to side, with what looked, at first glance, to be like a massive filing system: towering flights of drawers, mostly closed, all painted white, with handles of dark green metal.

Many of the lower ones had been opened, and their contents strewed around the place.

Their contents had been, as Ryan and the others had suspected, human bodies.

The redoubt had been an unthinkably huge, postmodernist, high-tech catafalque, designed for a single purpose, probably not long before the murderous times of skydark. With the possibility of a worldwide nuke war, the American leaders, linked to Overproject Whisper, had built the redoubt as a temporary base for stacking the expected dead.

But the expected dead had utterly overwhelmed the fragile living, a megacull that was measured not just in hundreds of thousands, millions or tens of millions.

It was damned nearly everybody.

Ryan guessed that this redoubt had been used in the first hours and days of the nuking, well before the long winter snuffed out the lives of most of the handful of survivors, back when it would still have been called the United States of America.

At first the bureaucrats would have rejoiced at their foresight and their careful planning.

Each body was stacked in its own deep-chilled capsule, having first eviscerated it and drained away all the blood. Notes were made of name, sex, age and weight, and everything was filed away ready for...

Ready for what?

"All this," Mildred said, "just so a bunch of inbred crazies can come and use it like the frozen-food section at the local market."

The vaulted roof contained the dreadful silence.

Everywhere the eye turned, there were corpses. Bits of corpses. Hands and feet and many, many skulls, stripped of eyes and tongues and the delicious soft tissues that the cannies obviously considered delicacies.

"Looks like they never figured a way of getting to the top layers," Dean said in a small, breathless voice, unable to hide his own shock.

"There's a big forklift down there." J.B. pointed with the muzzle of the shotgun. "Guess the cannies are so triple-stupe they never got round to using it."

It was only the bottom six or seven layers of drawers that had been opened, their contents ravaged.

The shelving didn't just line the walls. There was row upon row, all up and down the vast room, like an old-fashioned public library.

Doc had strolled away from the others, to a section in one corner, where the intrusive damage was less marked. He called out to his friends.

"Come and see."

He'd opened one of the drawers, finding how easy it was with the greased runners. Inside, as they gathered around, he revealed a most beautiful young woman.

Her hair was as fine as silk spun from threads of pure gold, and her naked damask skin was flawless. It seemed as though she were a fairy-tale princess, not dead but simply sleeping. At a word, or a kiss, she might waken and smile, and stretch and tell them of the wonderful riverbank dream of a white rabbit that she had been enjoying.

"Her name..." Doc coughed, clearing his throat. "Her name, from the card, was Emily...the same as my dear, dead wife. She... I am sorry, my dear friends, but I cannot cope with this horror. It is not right that those ghastly and blasphemous entities should be able to feast upon such sweetness." There were tears brimming in his eyes. "It has no grace. No dignity. It is as though life and death are both suspended here, like some Stygian limbo. Mr. Poe and his nightmare vision of the facts about Monsieur Valdemar were as nothing compared with this."

He turned and walked away, vanishing around the corner of the row of body units, the sound of his heels diminishing into the distance.

"I don't know what that Valdemar was," Krysty said, "but Doc's right. It's gross. There must be something we can do to sort this out, Ryan."

"What?"

"Find how those sickies broke in here and seal it off. At least we can leave the dead with some . . . what was Doc's word?"

"Dignity?"

"Yeah."

"Let's take a look around first," J.B. suggested. "Might be something else in the redoubt, except for thousands of snow-white bodies."

"WHERE DID DOC GO?" Michael asked, when they came out of the wintry depths of the morgue. "He ran by me a few minutes ago, stared at the map, muttering, then went off like he had a devil on his shoulder."

"Got upset," the Armorer said. "Which way?"

"There." He pointed to the widest passage that gaped ahead of them.

"Main control area and the entrance." J.B. sniffed. "Might as well follow him. It'll take us through two more of those big rooms."

"Terrific." The teenager was still paper-pale, beads of sweat frosting his forehead, despite the intense cold that seeped out of the morgue.

"SOMETHING..." Krysty stopped dead, looking around, her eyes showing her puzzlement.

They were halfway across the second of the vaulted mausoleums, the scattered corpses seeming more numerous.

"What is it?" Ryan glanced around. He couldn't remember ever being in a creepier place than this dreadful redoubt of frozen death. There was no sign of Doc, and Ryan was beginning to worry that the disturbed old man had fallen victim to a gang of marauding muties.

If he'd been taken, then his fate was too appallingly certain to be thinkable.

"It's getting warmer." Mildred stood with her mouth slightly open. "You can feel it."

Dean touched the door of one of the cabinets at his side, showing them his finger, "Wet."

"Listen." Krysty held up her hand. "Can you hear it? The deep sound of the main nuke gen."

"I can't hear it," Michael said.

Ryan nodded. "Right. You can't hear it now, but you could hear it up to a few minutes ago. It stopped, but it was such a far-off, background noise that none of us even noticed." The penny dropped. "Of course. Doc!"

"What?" Mildred asked. "You mean the troublesome old fart turned off the switch?"

The temperature seemed to be rising faster. The mist across the roof had vanished, and worms of moisture wriggled down the walls.

Ryan sniffed the air. "Fireblast! You can already smell it. They can't be rotting that fast, can they? It's not possible. Mildred?"

"Been frozen a hundred years or so, Ryan. You only have to push the temperature up a couple of degrees above zero and corruption sets in."

"Then the sooner we're out of here the better. Let's move it, people."

They passed through the sealed doors into a stretch of open corridor, where the increase in heat was even more marked.

Just before they reached the final death house before the road to the entrance, J.B. spotted a few of the cannies. They stood thirty yards away, to the left, looking utterly lost. He waved the shotgun toward them and they cowered.

But one, bolder than the rest, took a few unsteady steps toward them. "Hot," it said. "Got hot."

"Ignore them," Ryan ordered. "Come on."

He led the way through the double air-lock doors, recoiling with a gasp of choking horror.

The miasma of rotting flesh was horrendous, like a fist gripping at his throat, stretching its fingers to twist in the bottom of his stomach.

Their feet splashed through a lake of condensation, a couple of inches deep, with segments of peeled skin floating on the scummy surface.

"Don't stop!" Ryan shouted. "Try and breathe through your mouth and try not to puke. Run!"

It was almost unbelievable how fast the thousands of corpses were decomposing. The bodies that had been ravaged and then discarded on the floor were already blackening and turning into a thick gruel that seemed to be melting off the bones.

Ryan found his concentration was wonderfully focused on not falling into the hideous soup.

A child's skull had been lying on its side, just in front of him and, even as he hurdled it, the lower jaw fell away with an audible plopping sound, revealing the rotting, blackened stump of the tongue.

Behind him, he heard Michael muttering a prayer as he ran. "... now at the hour of our death."

The farther doors were closed.

Suddenly they were thrown open, and there stood Doc, a smile of triumph on his face, his silver hair on end, waving his sword stick to encourage them.

"Faster, my brave friends. There is God's good air not far beyond here! Have I not done wonders?"

Nobody answered him.

The fetid heat was like the throbbing heart of a tropical jungle, making Ryan realize that Doc had done more than just switch off the refrigeration. He must have turned the heating up to maximum, speeding the process.

The doors swished shut behind Mildred, the last of the seven, closing off the larger part of the vile scent of mass death.

"The entrance is only a hundred yards ahead," Doc said. "Looks like a recent earth slip opened it up and let those foul charnel creatures in."

"You could've warned us what you were planning, you revolting old pervert," Mildred gasped.

"I am truly sorry, madam." He offered her a deep bow, his left hand on his heart. "But seeing the name of Emily drove all thoughts from me."

"What was that Valdemar character you talked about?" Krysty asked as they walked together toward the sunshine and bright, clean air.

"A character in a story of the neurasthenic and marvelous Edgar Allan Poe," Doc replied. "About a man who is artificially kept alive when he should be snug and dead. In the end the process is stopped and he is allowed to pass mercifully to the release he sought."

"I think I know that," Mildred said. "Saw an old midnight vid of it. Vincent Price?"

"I wouldn't know." Doc stopped and pointed back to the bowels of the redoubts. "But it ends in a most apposite way. If I can recollect it... Yes." He struck a dramatic pose. "It ends 'There, before the whole company, lay a nearly liquid mass of loathsome—of detestable putridity.' Did I not do the right thing?"

Mildred touched him gently on the arm. "Yeah, Doc. The right thing."

Chapter Fourteen

"Kansas."

"Bullshit."

"I tell you it's somewhere in the middle of Old Kansas. Sextant can't be wrong, Mildred."

"And I tell you that Kansas wasn't covered over with pine trees, thicker than fleas on a groundhog."

J.B. took off his glasses and polished them. "This is now, not then."

Mildred turned to Doc, hands wide in appeal. "Tell John Barrymore Dix that Kansas is plains, and wheat as high as an elephant's ass. Not a sea of dark trees."

"Waving seas of... of something or other."

"Thanks a lot, Doc. Look, I'm sorry, but this really *can't* be Kansas."

Outside it had been precisely the way Doc Tanner had described it.

The redoubt was hidden in the side of an enormous bluff, a couple of hundred feet high, almost completely buried. Some combination of weather and an earth shift had brought down hundreds of thousands of tons of rock and dirt, exposing a narrow gap at the side of the main sec doors that had guarded the place successfully for the best part of a century.

As they made their way out, blinking in the bright sunshine of late morning, the air tasted like nectar. There was no more sign of any of the muties.

"Guess they'll starve within a few days," Ryan said to his son, who'd asked him what would happen to the cannies.

"But they must've got along okay for a long time before they found the human bodies."

"Sure. But it looked like they'd been munching their way contentedly through the shelves for some weeks. From what we saw they had triple-small brains, even by the low standards of muties. Probably gotten used to easy meat. I wouldn't be surprised if they hung around until even they can't stomach the rotted flesh. Eat each other for a few days. Then die."

The argument had begun the moment that the Armorer checked his tiny pocket sextant and announced that as far as he could tell they were smack in the heart of Kansas, somewhere, he thought, between Wichita and Topeka.

But Mildred chose to disagree.

"I know what Kansas is supposed to look like. I come from Nebraska, remember. When I started shooting in serious competition I often came south. Kansas City, Topeka, Dodge City, Hutchinson and Wichita." Her voice was growing louder as she became more angry. "And I tell you that it didn't look like this."

Doc coughed. "For once I find myself having to agree with the good lady."

"I'm not your goddamned good lady, Doc!"

He sailed on, ignoring her outburst. "The landscape that offers itself to us is wonderfully reminiscent of Oregon or parts of northern Montana. No prairies here." He shaded his eyes and posed. "Lo, the poor Indian would get lost in the trackless forests we see here."

It was a slight exaggeration.

From their elevated position, it was possible to see that the forests were far from trackless.

But the predominant color of the plains wasn't golden. It was a dark, dusty green. The conifers had advanced to the foot of the slope below the seven watchers, a mix of larches, ponderosas and lodgepoles, with a scattering of beeches and live oaks to lighten the palette.

There was the unmistakable line of an old highway, running arrow-straight from the left to right, from southwest toward the hazy distance of the northeast. And there were several other minor tracks and trails cutting raggedly through the limitless swath of the forest.

"I don't much remember coming this way with the Trader," J.B. said.

"Me, neither." Ryan stared out across the rolling land. "Way I recall it, there were plenty of nuke hot spots around the old Midwest. Big places for siting our missiles, which made it a real big place for those sites getting severely swatted. Not a good region, even in the war wags."

"Think Abe found Trader?" Krysty was gazing blankly out into the day, eyes turned northwest. "I keep getting feelings that...real faint." She smiled. "One thing you have to watch with 'feelings' is not imposing what you want on what you feel. Could be I just hope that Trader is alive someplace, and that Abe gets to him."

"Hoping doesn't butter any parsnips," Doc said mournfully. "Speaking of which...does anyone else among our number share my feeling that something to nourish the inner man would not come amiss?"

"Do you mean am I hungry, Doc?" Dean grinned from ear to ear. "Double hot pipe! Yeah."

"I saw what looked like deer down there." J.B. put away his folding spyglass. "And there could be a ville beyond the trees. Past the highway. Where you can see the sparkle of the sun off water."

Everyone looked where he was pointing. Most could make out the silvery glint of what might be a small lake, but nobody could swear to seeing a ville.

"Venison," Ryan said. "Now that sounds like the best ace on the line since we left the Keys."

"Think those muties are around here?" Michael still looked pale from the horrors behind them.

Ryan shook his head. "Doubt it. If we return to the gateway in the next day or so we'd best walk triple-red. Out here, who knows what there is? So, we'll go take a look. Unless anyone fancies a third jump? No? You all agree?" Nobody said anything. He laughed. "Well, you don't disagree. Let's go."

THE WALK DOWN the sloping bluff was pleasant, with none of the danger that they'd so often experienced with redoubts set in the high country. The land below was visibly rich in game, and the woods were honeycombed with narrow trails. Birds sang in the high branches while narrow streams bubbled clean and pure over quartz-veined pebbles.

They all refreshed themselves, despite Mildred's warning that there might easily be some sort of unpleasant organism lurking in the water.

"You won't know its burrowed into your guts until you get unstoppable shits," she said. "And by then it's way too late to do anything."

But she also flopped belly-down, along with the others, and drank deeply from her cupped hands.

"If there was a ville off to the west," Ryan said, wiping his mouth with the back of his right hand, "then it could be that this is all part of some baron's domain."

J.B. sat with his back against a slender beech, polishing his glasses. His fedora lay in his lap, and he was smiling, his face turned to the sky.

"Tell you the truth, Ryan, couldn't give a flying fuck about any baron. Warm sunshine and clean water." He reached out to Mildred, who was dozing at his side, and touched her cheek. "Less she's right about the bugs. There's a good breeze."

It was an idyllic moment.

Ryan sat and sharpened his panga on the sole of his boot, watching as his eleven-year-old son lay flat on the overhanging bank of the stream, fingers dabbling in the shadowed water, trying to gudgeon a trout for them. But the speckled fish was too alert for him and slithered away between the boy's hands.

"Nice try, son."

"Nearly had him, Dad."

"I saw."

Michael was doing some of his stretching exercises, balancing first on one leg, then on the other, hands probing out with a supreme delicacy, as if he were a blind man seeking to touch a single invisible feather.

"This is good, Ryan," he said. "Used to be like this up at Nil-Vanity. Specially in the greening and in the quiet days of the early fall."

"Look," whispered Krysty, who'd been washing the scent of death and corruption from her brilliantly crimson hair. "Just on the other side of the stream."

It was a pair of roe deer, a doe, hesitant, but oddly unafraid of the proximity to the group of humans, and her little fawn, nuzzling at her flanks with its velvet nose.

"Looks like Bambi," Mildred said. "They're really cute, aren't they?"

Ryan drew the SIG-Sauer. The range was a little long for the automatic, but it had the advantage over the Steyr rifle of the built-in baffle silencer. The thought that they might be making a kill on the hunting land of a local baron made Ryan even more cautious than usual.

"Must you?" Doc asked, answering his own question. "Needs must when hunger drives, I suppose."

The silencer was beginning to lose its efficiency, as they mostly did, but it still muffled the explosion as Ryan squeezed the trigger.

The fawn went down in a heap, as if it had been struck by a thunderbolt, its skinny legs kicking and scrabbling, the blood marking its pale brown coat just behind the shoulder. Its mother looked around as though she couldn't believe that death should leap so suddenly from a clear sky.

"Take her out as well," J.B. suggested.

"No. Enough meat on the baby. More tender. We already seen spoor to know the woods are teeming with food. No need to jerk it, then have to carry it around with us. Just pick up what we want, when we want it."

The mother stooped her head on its slender neck and touched the twitching body, pushing as if the fawn were teasing her, trying to make it rise and run off with her.

"Oh, that's heartbreaking." Mildred looked away from the tragic pastoral scene.

Eventually Dean threw some stones at the deer, forcing it to scamper off into the trees, leaving the young one behind, its blood staining the grass.

RYAN GLANCED AT HIS CHRON, seeing that it was only a couple of hours past noon. The ashes of the fire still glowed, and the stripped carcass of the little deer lay to one side.

Mildred got up and nudged the blackened bones with the toe of her boot. "Poor little Bambi," she said, barely managing to stifle a belch. "But it sure tasted good. Maybe an onion and ginger sauce would have gone well, along with a puree of creamed carrots, snow peas and a piping of whipped potatoes. Followed by some of my mother's hot apple pie and a slice of cheese. Still, mustn't grumble."

"We moving on?" Krysty asked. "Explore a little more of this garden of Eden?"

"Not the best of metaphors, my dear Krysty," Doc mumbled sleepily.

"Why?"

"Have you forgotten the cunning snake that tempted Eve with the fruit of wisdom, and thus brought about the total ruination of mankind?"

Krysty smiled. "One thing I haven't seen around here is a snake. Mebbe we'll be all right, Doc."

Ryan stood and brushed leaf mold off his pants. "Enough talk. Time to walk."

THOUGH THE LAND had looked to be fairly flat from near the entrance to the redoubt, it flowed up and down in a number of gullies and dry washes. Ryan had glanced behind them, trying to locate the actual sec doors, but the angle of the hillside defeated him, keeping them hidden.

There was the occasional oasis of meadow, spotted with lupins and asters, but it was mainly mixed forest, with the tall pines having the edge.

Twice during the next half hour they all heard distant rumbles of thunder, far off to the east. From a grassy knoll Ryan saw that the sky in that direction was darker, streaked with the pink and purple flares of a major chem storm. The light breeze was coming in from the northwest, so there was no great danger of the storm moving their way.

From habit he checked the miniature rad counter clipped to his coat, seeing that the shading was a pale yellow, indicating some minor problems in the vicinity, but nothing serious enough for them to worry about.

They traveled on for a half hour, making their way up a gentle slope, with the predominant conifers giving way to groves of oaks. The sun was hot, throwing pools of light among the leafy shadows.

It was a heaven of a day.

Chapter Fifteen

Ryan dozed, lying on his back, his eye closed, relishing a time out of war, a time of relaxation in a gentle and safe environment. There were no venomous muties or ravening animals or thuggish sec men. Just the wind soughing through the leaves and the afternoon sun declining slowly to the west.

Krysty lay fast asleep at his side, and Dean whittled with his turquoise-hilted knife at the stump of a broken willow branch that he'd picked up along the trail.

Michael was climbing a chestnut tree on the far side of the clearing, a tree so massive that it must have dated from well before skydark.

J.B. was more restless. He sat for a while, then unloaded and reloaded the shotgun with the Remington fléchettes. Then he reached out for a handful of desiccated pine cones and juggled two of them, introducing a third and then trying for four, dropping the whole lot. He stood again, moving to watch the teenager making steady progress up the tree.

"See if you can spot anything toward where I thought I saw that ville," he called. Michael waved a hand to show that he'd heard him.

On a stretch of level ground, covered in fine leaf mold, Doc and Mildred were arguing over the Battle of the Little Bighorn.

Using twigs, they'd marked out the winding course of the river, making small hills from the dust to represent the bluffs and steep-sided coulees.

Mildred had once studied the social groupings of Native Americans and was vehemently taking the side of the massed groups of Sioux, Cheyenne and Arapaho who had ridden out over the Greasy Grass to face Long Hair and his bluecoated Seventh.

Doc was trying to make a case for Custer having been betrayed by his Crow scouts.

"No way. No way, Doc. Look." She pointed with her finger. "He splits the command here. Already knows there's one of the biggest camps in the history of the universe. Seen a trail a mile wide, for God's sake! Benteen up here and Reno going down along the Little Bighorn to... to about here."

"I met Libbie Custer," Doc said, recognizing he was on a loser and trying to change the subject. "Must've been some time in the early nineties. She'd already been a widow for fifteen years or more. She still turned the head of every man when she walked into the room."

"She always blamed Reno and Benteen, didn't she?" Mildred said. "Harried them to their graves. And beyond."

Doc nodded. "So I believe. I visited the scene of the fight in the late eighties. Walked the ground. One of the most mysterious and haunted places I ever saw."

Mildred nodded. "I went there in the summer be-fore . . . before I got ill. Local people call it the place where the ghosts walk in the midday sun. That's about right."

Doc stared down at their crude plan. "Nearly made it, you know, the son of a bitch. Got close to the crest of the hill and then Gall and the rest wiped them away."

"You got a theory why so many officers were in that last stand and not with their companies, Doc?" Mildred flapped a hand at a brilliant purple butterfly that was trying to settle on her shoulder. "How come they weren't with their men? Getting final orders from Autie?"

"Ah, now this is a particularly vexatious riddle that I have always found fascinating. One of so many about the battle. My own theory is—"

"Hey!"

Michael's voice attracted everyone.

"What is it?" Ryan called, sitting up quickly.

"I can see horsemen about two miles away, moving toward us."

"Fast?"

"No. Spread out, like they're looking for some-thing. Could be hunting, I guess."

"How many?" J.B. was looking up at the teenage boy as if he were considering climbing up to join him.

"Twenty or so. Can't see that clearly. They keep moving in and out of the trees."

Ryan glanced around. "We go into the brush over there." He pointed to a dense thicket of lush ferns. "Look out across the flat land below us."

"Want me to come down?" Michael shouted.

"Stay as long as you reckon's safe. Best they don't see us unless it looks like there's no danger."

J.B. kicked out the ashes of the fire, spreading them with his boot, cooling them. Ryan looked quickly around the clearing, scuffing his foot over Doc and Mildred's model of the Little Bighorn.

"If they got any trackers with them, they'll follow us easy," he said. "Mebbe we should run."

The Armorer ran his finger down the line of his jaw, head to one side, thinking.

"No. If they got trackers, then they'll pick us up. Not like steep mountain country where a man on foot has the edge. Horses'll run us down in minutes. Best we hide. Get ready for a firefight."

Carried on the breeze, they suddenly heard the sound of a distant horn, short urgent notes, repeated a number of times. And the barking of hounds.

"Fireblast! Michael, you didn't mention them having dogs!"

"Couldn't see them, Ryan. Sorry."

It changed things.

Ryan had encountered barons, particularly in frontier villes, who kept packs of dogs, often crossbred rottweilers, used to hunt down enemies. The animals were notoriously vicious and unreliable, and had been loathed by the Trader.

"Only thing worse than a baron with a dog," he said, "is a baron with two dogs."

Now the idea of hiding seemed much less attractive.

And the idea of running was impossible.

If the horsemen had been spotted a couple of hours ago, there might have been sufficient time to retreat to the redoubt and jump out of trouble.

"If they come this way, we're done," J.B. commented.

"Mebbe they'll make their kill before they get close enough to pick up our scent." Krysty beckoned to Michael, almost hidden in the branches. "Best come down now."

"Still can't see what they're hunting. They're well spread out. I think they're all carrying guns."

"Hand or long?" the Armorer queried.

"Rifles, and I think some shotguns."

"Come down now. Might as well hide in those ferns and see what we can see."

"Might it not be possible to ambush them from the cover of the forest?"

Despite the potential danger to all of them, Ryan found himself grinning. "You bloodthirsty old... If they were fewer and more bunched together, then we could."

"But they aren't and we can't," J.B. added, trying to judge from the noise of the dogs and the hunting horns just how much time they had left.

Michael scrambled down from the chestnut tree, jumping the last fifteen feet and landing with a casual elegance and ease that Ryan envied. "Less than a mile," he said.

"Just our luck if the deer comes straight through here." Mildred had her Czech blaster drawn. "What if you try and spot it first and take it out with the rifle, Ryan? Could keep them away from us."

"I fear that such an act might also bring the ungodly down upon us like the Assyrians on the sheep in the fold, with their cohorts—"

"Shut up, Doc!" Ryan snapped. "But he's part right, Mildred. At the crack of the Steyr they're going to get real interested in us. Best chance is hide and hush. Everyone down and everyone real quiet. Those tracking dogs can hear a flea farting at three hundred yards."

The ferns were growing on the site of the small stream, the cool water seeping from beneath the roots of a lightning-scarred beech tree. They were so tall and luxurious that they had to be some kind of genetic mutation.

But they provided excellent cover. Ryan wriggled in last, wishing that there had been more time to try to conceal their trampled tracks all about the clearing. But if the dogs were that close, then they'd scent them anyway.

"Can see down here, Dad," Dean whispered.

"What?"

"Sort of open place at the bottom of the slope where it's double-oozy. I can see quite a way through the trees. Three trails all meet up."

The seven friends huddled close, snug in the moist green cavern of the ferns. Ryan had eased himself to the front, alongside Dean, picking his way with great care as he became aware that the little spring had made the muddy earth loose and treacherous.

"Don't get too close, son," he warned. "If this lot gives way, we're all in it, good and deep."

Now the riders were much nearer, enough for Ryan to be able to catch the bright jingle of harness and the occasional crack of a whip.

Someone shouted, either man or woman, it was hard to say. The voice was distorted by the surrounding trees.

The horn blared again, longer notes, fading away at the end, seeming to send the pack of dogs into a frenzy. They barked louder and more fiercely.

Ryan waited, watching between two of the fibrous, saw-toothed leaves, wondering if he'd catch a sight of the prey, hoping that he wouldn't. Perhaps it was the mother of the fawn that he'd shot down earlier.

He glanced behind him, seeing, as he'd expected, that J.B. was sitting with his back to the action, looking the other way, making sure they didn't get cold-cocked by someone creeping up from their rear.

"Dad." Fingers tugged at his sleeve to attract his attention.

But Ryan Cawdor's keen eye had already spotted what his son had seen. The racketing fluster of a covey of ring-collared pigeons rose from a thicket about two hundred yards away, in a direct line from the noise of the hunters.

Something, presumably the prey, was heading straight toward them.

Through a gap in the trees, Ryan caught a glimpse of a blur of movement, dark brown, running fast.

"Deer," he said quietly.

There it was. Not the small doe that they'd seen earlier. This was a magnificent full-grown stag, carrying at least twenty points on its spread antlers. It entered the open space below the hidden watchers, head turning from side to side, nostrils flaring, as though it could almost scent the watchers. The brazen horn shrieked out triumphantly and the animal turned and bounded away to the south at great speed.

For a moment Ryan was puzzled. Michael had said, when he had first seen them from the tree, that the hunt had been moving slowly, well-spread. So, how could they hope to ring down something as fast and powerful as the stag?

Seconds later it all became clear.

Dodging between the pines, head down, panting and stumbling, came the figure of a middle-aged man. His brown jerkin was torn and he had nothing on his feet, which were streaked with mud and blood. As he ran he kept looking fearfully over his shoulder toward the crescendo of barking and shouting.

"Dad?" Dean's tone was shocked and puzzled.

"Yeah. I reckon that he's the prey for the hunters. Not the stag. Him. It's a manhunt."

Chapter Sixteen

It was instantly obvious that the wretched man was in the last stages of exhaustion, overlaid with terror that had robbed him of all his senses. From less than fifty paces away, Ryan could see the blank horror in the eyes. The man's mouth hung open, his fingers plucking at the sleeve of his tattered shirt. There was a damp patch on the front of his light brown pants, showing where fear had loosed the control of his bladder.

Dean leaned farther forward, nearly slipping in the loose earth. But Ryan grabbed him by the belt, heaving him back into the ferns, only letting go when he was sure his son had recovered his balance. "Careful!"

The end of the hunt was very near.

The hallooing of the riders was deafening, and the belling of the hounds was right on top of them.

The man dropped to his hands and knees, his stomach heaving as if he were trying to be sick.

He hadn't moved when the first of the rottweilers came bounding into sight.

"Sweet Jesus," Mildred breathed, leaning against Ryan's shoulder to watch the last act of the drama.

It seemed for a moment that the huge dogs, all wearing spiked brass collars, would tear the helpless, cringing figure apart. But they'd been well trained. One or two snapped in a ferocious excitement at the man, but the rest formed a tight circle around him, keeping him there. Heads up, they bayed their triumph to the following hunters.

"Sec men. Coming." J.B. was alongside Mildred, his eyes screwed up behind the lenses of his spectacles.

Within half a minute the clearing was filled with riders, all well mounted. Twenty-four was Ryan's quick count. And well over half of them were unmistakably sec guards for some powerful local baron, perhaps from the distant ville that the Armorer thought he'd seen.

Their uniform was a dark maroon, so deep a hue that it almost seemed black in the shadows. Most carried rifles slung over their shoulders, the blasters looking like the Armalite that the Trader had always carried.

There were five people in civilian clothes, four young men and a woman.

But it was the woman that took the eye.

Like the guards, she was wearing shirt and pants in dark maroon. But in her case they were made of fine, soft leather, gleaming with a rich sheen in the late-afternoon sunshine. Her boots were the same color, low-heeled, with savage Mexican spurs. A silver-hilted quirt dangled from her gloved right hand.

Her face was pale, though Ryan could see two hectic spots of bright color on each high cheekbone. She had narrowed, almost Oriental, eyes and the most beautiful hair that Ryan Cawdor had ever seen.

Krysty's flaming mane was staggering in its brightness, but this woman's hair was a tumbling cascade of purest black. But "black" seemed a totally inadequate word.

The softness of midnight velvet.

The edge of a raven's wing.

The still depths of a woodland pool.

Ryan vaguely remembered once hearing Doc talk about a book or a vid called *The Heart of Darkness*. That was the nearest phrase he could think of to describe the waist-length hair of the woman on the gray mare.

In passing, he also noted that the flanks of the animal were specked with blood, behind the high-pommeled saddle.

Three of the sec men swung down from their mounts, approaching the kneeling man, one of them beating the eager dogs away with a short-thonged whip.

"Bring him to his feet."

Her voice was soft and gentle, yet it carried the unmistakable caress of total authority.

The hunted man didn't make any effort to struggle as he was heaved upright, standing between the guards, who each held him by an arm.

Ryan and the others knew, without a shadow of doubt, that they were looking at a dead man. Mildred wondered what crime he could have committed to be chased like an animal. Dean's private guess was that he was an escaped prisoner. J.B. was studying the blasters, impressed by their condition. Michael was feeling sick. Krysty had closed her eyes, the certainty of murder bringing a wave of sudden faintness. Doc was chasing a residual memory of some ancient story he might once have read, about someone hunting human beings with a pack of dogs. No, a pack of hounds. But it slipped elusively away from him and he decided it probably didn't much matter.

Ryan watched the woman, almost overwhelmed by the palpable and oddly sensual aura of power that surrounded her.

The clearing had become almost silent.

Most of the rottweilers had thrown themselves on the trampled turf, tongues lolling. The horses were still, with only an occasional shift of movement.

From their hiding place, the watchers could hear the harsh breathing of the captured man.

"A disappointing chase, friends." The woman heeled the mare closer to the prisoner. "But you have had your chance at saving your life, have you not?"

There was no answer. The sec man with the whip lashed the man across the face, making him cry out.

"Answer Mistress Marie when she speaks, you bundle of shit in a skin!"

The woman shook her head, her long hair glittering in sinuous movement, like a nest of countless black snakes.

"Don't waste any more time. The sun is on his way to his bed, and we should return to home for food and rest. Do the necessary to him."

The "necessary" was brutal and mercifully swift, carried out with such a casual expertise that Ryan knew it had been done by these sec men on many previous occasions.

Off came the mud-splattered shirt, tossed down in the dirt. The sec men on each side took a half step away, pulling the man's arms straight. His ribs stood out like a picket fence against the pale skin of the chest.

The man with the whip drew a heavy blade, like a Bowie knife, fifteen inches in length, tapering to a needle-point. He glanced toward the woman on the horse, who nodded.

Though her face was partly in shadow, Ryan caught the gleam of teeth and realized that she was smiling.

The knife was thrust in hard, just below the man's navel and was drawn up to grate against his breastbone, then to the left, toward his armpit. Back again, repeating the deep gash to the other side.

"The flying eagle," Doc whispered. "It was a Viking way of butchery."

The doomed man had given an inarticulate cry of agony as blood flowed thick and dark from the cuts, across his trousers, puddling at his feet.

"Now," the woman called in a high, clear voice. "Finish it now!"

The sec man immediately plunged both of his hands, wrist-deep, into the white-lipped gashes, fumbling for a moment, then pulling them out, holding the man's lungs, froth coated and dripping, in his fingers.

The other guards let go, and the dead man slumped to the bloodied earth.

There was a round of polite applause from the four male civilians, while the woman merely tugged sharply on the reins of her mare, swinging it around.

"Home again, I think," she said. "Leave the offal where it lies."

Ryan felt a release of tension.

It was going to be all right.

The wind was carrying their scent to the east, well away from the pack of hunting dogs, and it was obvious that not one of the riders had any clue that they were being observed from only a few yards off.

If this was the way of life in the nearby ville, then it seemed that a better option for them all would be to return to the redoubt and face the unpleasant challenge of a third jump.

Ryan had been around Deathlands long enough to know that there might be a reasonable explanation for the way the man had been chased and butchered.

"Man who jumps to conclusions sometimes ends up jumping into his own grave," Trader had said.

One of the sec men had a short copper bugle that he put to his lips and blew a series of brief, yipping notes. The dogs all jumped up and began to bark.

The woman they called Mistress Marie had heeled her mare across the clearing until she was directly beneath the bunch of ferns, some twenty feet above her.

Ryan could have spat into her hair.

The pack of hounds was already leaving, streaming along the trail toward the north, the powerful force of sec men readying themselves to follow. The four elegantly attired men, all of whom Ryan saw were only in their early twenties, were still talking excitedly among themselves, carefully avoiding the eyes of the woman.

Nobody was taking any notice of the corpse, lying discarded on its face, arms spread like a supplicant. From above, it showed no signs of the hideous injury to the abdomen. The puddle of congealing blood was already attracting the interest of a number of mottle-winged blowflies.

The woman sighed. "I'm bored already," she said. "An hour or so of exercise and then a few seconds of delight. And then . . ." She snapped her fingers. "It's over. Just like that."

She kicked the spurs into the mare's flanks, making it rear. Dean had been leaning farther and farther forward and the sudden movement of the horse made him jump. The loose, wet earth gave way and, before Ryan could snatch at the boy, Dean rolled helplessly down the slope, landing almost under the hooves of the woman's horse, flat on his back, arms lifted to his face to protect himself.

"That tears it," J.B. said.

Chapter Seventeen

If Dean hadn't been winded by the fall, there might have been some hope. Slender, admittedly, but there could have been the possibility of escape. A quick burst of shooting to bring down some of the armed sec men and panic the horses, then up and away into the surrounding woods.

But even that had drawbacks.

It would mean keeping together at the speed of the slowest member of the group, which was Doc, by a goodly margin. And there might be other hunting parties around the forest, all on their home turf, knowing the shortcuts and the streams.

A man on a horse could easily ride down a running man, even in a woodland like this one. And the sec men looked disciplined and tough.

Half a dozen blasters were pointed at the breathless boy, and Ryan knew that this was one of those times for talking rather than shooting.

He stood, showing both empty hands.

"No danger," he said. "There's six of us here. Okay if we come on down?"

The woman seemed least affected. She had looked up in surprise as the boy appeared from thin air and spooked her mare. But she had regained control, pulling on the bit, again using her spurs. Now everyone waited for her to speak.

"Why didn't you kill us, outlander?"

"Not our way."

She smiled thinly. Now that Ryan could see her more clearly he realized that she was older than he'd guessed, possibly a couple of years into her thirties. Her eyes were a dark brown and looked curiously up at him.

"That's a nice rifle and a quality handblaster at your belt. SIG-Sauer. The rest of you got weapons of that quality?" Dean had managed to stand and was staring intently at his father, waiting for a signal to dart for cover. The woman touched him with the braided tip of her quirt. "Don't, lad. Don't even think about it for... Ah, I see the resemblance."

She looked at Ryan. "Your son?"

"Yeah."

"I see. I could have shot him, just by nodding my head. And you, too."

"Then you'd be chilled in less than a heartbeat, and half your pretty sec men with you." J.B. had shuffled silently a few yards to his right, still keeping in the dead ground behind the brow of the small hill.

"And the other half wouldn't last long." Krysty had her blaster leveled, just out of sight.

"More and more. You know you're on the hunting land of my father, Baron Nathan Mandeville?"

"No."

"Does it make a scrap of difference now that you know, outlander?"

"Not really."

One of the young men spoke up. He had a shallow, spoiled face and was, Ryan could almost swear, wearing women's makeup. "Why not just shoot them all, Mistress Marie? Or simply take them all prisoner?"

"I have long believed that all of your brains dwell in your cock, Anthony. And from what I hear of your more recent 'performances,' it means they aren't too profuse. Don't think of speaking again unless I tell you that you can. Which will not be until we're all back at Sun Crest."

"Want us to leave your father's lands?"

"Possibly. But no, outlander. You look more interesting than most of the border scum that come crawling up here from the mud of the Sippi."

"Then can we all come out?"

"Yes."

Ryan turned. "Stay on triple-red," he said quietly. Louder he added, "Everyone out when I give the word."

He turned back to the self-possessed woman. "After your sec men shoulder those Armalites, if that's..."

"Of course." A wave of the gloved hand brought instant obedience.

Ryan led the way down the slope, leaning back to keep his balance in the loose earth. He was followed by Krysty, then Mildred and Doc. Michael came next, with J.B. cautiously bringing up the rear.

Ryan made the introductions, explaining the usual story they used. They'd been traveling around Deathlands, looking for any sort of work, leaving the suggestion that the "work" might have some connection with hired blasters.

"Our wag broke down five days ago. Gearbox just about dropped onto the highway. Been walking since."

He had the feeling that the woman on the horse, looking down at him with a cool disdain, didn't believe a word of it. But, oddly, it didn't seem to matter.

"Very well, Cawdor. My name is Marie Mandeville. My father is the Baron Nathan Mandeville, and he owns Sun Crest and all the land as far as you can see to west and north."

"That the ville over that way?" J.B. asked, pointing behind the riders.

"Yes, Dix, it is."

It was bizarre that they were having a civilized conversation within ten feet of the stiffening corpse of the hunted man, butchered in as brutal a manner as Ryan had ever witnessed.

There was a long silence, broken by Ryan. "Well?"

She lifted her head, glanced at the four young men, silencing their whispering. "I am not used to having anyone speak to me in that tone of voice, Cawdor. My father is a baron of considerable wealth and power."

"That's good for you, lady. Doesn't impress me all that much. Guess he eats and shits just like I do. Like he did." Ryan pointed at the body.

"This person broke a number of rules and was legally tried and sentenced. And executed."

"Sure. Now, you want us to come with you or go our own way? Just tell me."

He could almost hear the wheels spinning in what he figured was a sharp little brain.

"This isn't a place of dramatic landscapes," she replied. "You sit down and the land seems to surround you like a bowl. My father has always been a man to try to relieve this monotony in any way he can. Outlanders like you and your companions might inspire him. Come and be our guests."

Ryan glanced around at the others. None of them showed any great enthusiasm for the idea. But none of them showed any marked resistance, either.

"Sure," he said.

FOUR OF THE SEC MEN reluctantly gave up their mounts, trudging disconsolately along behind the hunting party.

Ryan rode with Dean perched in front of him. Mildred and Krysty doubled on a tall gelding. Michael clung on with extreme unhappiness, arms locked tight around J.B.'s waist. And Doc rode in solitary splendour on a fine Appaloosa, grinning back at the four dismounted guards.

"Story of warfare through the ages," he called to Ryan. "Cavalry never much cared for ending up with the poor bloody infantry."

ONCE THEY WERE EN ROUTE for the ville of Sun Crest, Marie Mandeville virtually ignored them, riding ostentatiously at the front of the column, surrounded by the quartet of sycophantic and elegant young men.

The trail was well marked, though it occasionally narrowed among the trees, forcing them into a meandering single file. But most of the time it was possible to ride in pairs or threes.

Ryan found himself alongside the most senior of the sec men, a grizzled veteran with three golden stripes on his sleeve.

"Name's Harry Guiteau," he offered. "I seen you someplace, Cawdor."

"Could be. I been most places. Looks like that could be true for you as well."

The man nodded. His left cheek was badly scarred, as though he'd once been on the wrong end of a charge of buckshot, and two fingers were missing from his left hand. He noticed Ryan appraising him.

"The hand was a woman. Hunkpapa, up in the high plains. I was sixteen years old and drunker than a skunk. Pain woke me up, but she got away. I always wondered what it was that I'd done to make her so sore."

"How about the mark on your face?" Dean asked, unable to quench his insatiable curiosity.

"I rode a time with Gert Wolfram."

Ryan glanced around to see if J.B. had picked up on the notorious name from their joint past, but the Armorer was arguing with Michael about not holding on so tightly.

"You knew him?" Guiteau asked.

"No. Know the name. Used to run a kind of mutie freak show around some of the northern pestholes. Must be ten or fifteen years ago. Mebbe longer."

They were moving steadily down a gentle slope, with clumps of stately cottonwoods on both sides of the trail. Somewhere not far ahead Ryan could hear the sound of fast-flowing water. The sun was sinking rapidly, and the shadows clustered more closely around the riders.

Guiteau heeled his mount through a narrow gap between a pile of jumbled stone and a fallen pine.

"Used to be a vacation cabin," he said, gesturing with his thumb at the ruin. "Some vid star. Locals say she topped herself with a straight razor when her tapes stopped selling. Supposed to be triple-famous. I can't remember what she was called."

"How long before we reach the ville?" Ryan asked.

"Hour. Got to cross the south fork of the Antelope. Had some rain lately, so it's up at the ford." He looked back at the one-eyed man. "I've sure as shit seen you before. You was saying about Gert Wolfram?"

"No. You said you rode with him. I said I'd heard the name before. Years before."

The sergeant had a chew of tobacco in his cheek, and he loosed a thin stream of dark liquid onto the trail. "Yeah, that's right. Your kid asked me about this." He touched the deep scar tissue that disfigured his cheek, tugging the corner of his mouth up into a perpetual quirkish grin.

"Shotgun?" Dean offered.

"Yeah. One of Gert Wolfram's fucking star attractions done it to me."

"Mutie?"

"Right, Cawdor. Kind of half-breed. Stickie mother and a swampie father. Least, that was the story."

"Bad mix." Now the noise of the river was growing much louder, making it more difficult to hear the sergeant's story.

But Ryan wanted him to keep on talking so Guiteau lost interest in whether or when he might have seen him. There were places with long memories where the Trader and his men and women were concerned, places that had encountered the iron fist inside the iron glove.

"Bastard got hold of a sawed-down. Wolfram used it in part of his show. Only loaded with rock salt. Fired it at the muties when they pretended to attack him from right across the cage. Course, it made a hell of a bang but it didn't do no harm. Not at that range from a sawed-down. This mutie had a woman, and I was younger and I'd have fucked anything that didn't have hooves." Guiteau laughed. "Fact is, even that's not totally true. Long nights our riding the lines and that little sheep starts looking about the prettiest thing you ever... But that's not the point."

Now Ryan could glimpse the river ahead of them, about eighty feet across. Upstream, the water was swollen, dark and deep, tinted crimson by the setting sun. Below the point of the shallow crossing was a long run of menacing rapids, white water over jagged stone.

Behind them, Doc was having increasing trouble in controlling his horse, shouting at it and trying to punch it across the top of the head.

Guiteau turned in his saddle and his grin widened. "That Comanche's a vicious sun-bucking star-fishing bastard. The old man best watch her across the ford."

"The mutie and the shotgun?" Dean shouted, leaning half off the back of the horse.

"Oh, it weren't nothing. When he seen the body of the woman . . . I didn't mean to, but I was wild then. That night he decked old Gert and grabbed the scattergun. Might've been salt, but it nearly took my fucking head right off my shoulders, kid. Hurt like a bastard."

"You kill him after?"

"No."

"No?"

"No. Not *after*. Killed him right then and there. Broke his neck. Then passed out. Wolfram said it got the biggest cheer he ever heard from an audience. When I got better he wanted to try and work it into a regular sort of act. That was when him and me parted company. Well, here we are at the Antelope. Best make sure that Mistress Marie gets over without her pretty little boots getting splashed."

Everyone reined in and Guiteau spurred on to the front. Dean nudged his father.

"He seems kind of all right, Dad."

"Seems to me to be one of the coldest-hearted bastards I ever saw."

GUITEAU CAME BACK to rejoin Ryan. "Taken a look and there's a shitload of water going down the pike right now. I suggested to Mistress Marie that we could go a few miles upstream where there's an old stone bridge across the Antelope."

Ryan smiled at the expression on the sergeant's face. "And she didn't warm to that idea?"

"You're all right, Cawdor. No, you could say she didn't take to the suggestion."

"So?"

"She ordered Anthony to go first."

"Who is he? All four of them look like preening pretty boys. Are they—"

Guiteau held up his disfigured left hand to silence Ryan. "One thing you'd best learn right here and now, Cawdor. Worst enemy a man can have at Sun Crest is Mistress Marie. Sure, Baron Nathan runs things tighter than a beaver's ass. But you know where you are with him. Word gets back to her—" he jerked a thumb to the woman, who was watching the young man picking his way into the river "—that someone spoke wrong or looked wrong, then they'd do well to swallow their Armalite."

"I get it."

"No, you don't, Cawdor. You think that you've talked to me and you and me are a lot similar. Sure we are. I can judge a man, and you and me ridden a lot of the same trails. But that don't mean I'd piss on you if you were burning to death. Understand me? I ride for the baron. And all that means.''

Ryan nodded. ''Sure, Guiteau. I understand.''

''Be sure you do.'' He rubbed a hand over his cropped scalp. ''I know I seen you before. But it's so long ago. This scar of mine makes folks remember me. Same with that lost eye of yours. How did you lose it?''

''Stupe way. Taking a rabbit from a snare. Wasn't dead. Kicked back and popped my eye out of its socket as neat as any doctor's knife.''

Guiteau gave a roar of laughter. ''Good one, Cawdor! Nearly as good as my waking up to find my fingers missing. Only good part of that was she didn't slice off my dick.''

Anthony had finally succeeded in getting his mount across the Antelope, with much splashing and squeakings of alarm. He now sat on the far side of the ford with a complacent grin on his soft, vacant face.

Marie didn't hesitate for a moment. In went the spurs and the horse shot forward in a clumsy, spread-legged leap. For a moment Ryan thought that the woman had lost it, as she vanished in a welter of brown spray. But it was no surprise to see her emerge, hair dripping wet, breasting the river and emerging alongside Anthony. Her face showed no sign of any emotion, as her eyes locked on Ryan.

Doc was close to the one-eyed man, still battling his stubborn horse. ''By the Three Kennedys! I would rather make a dozen mat-trans jumps than face this, Ryan.''

"You'll be fine, Doc. Look, I'll come in with you. Get alongside and then, if anything happens, you can leap off and hang on with me."

Doc managed a smile that was more a rictus of trepidation. "The graveyards of history are littered with those poor souls who were persuaded to change horses in midstream, my dear fellow. And you want me to do the same."

"Just in case. Come on, everyone's going for it."

There was shouting and cursing as the hunting party began the fording of the south fork of the Antelope.

One of the sec man nearly lost it as his gelding stumbled, going clean under water. But the man was good, staying with the horse, rising with his arms clasped tight around its dripping neck. He eventually made it to the far shore amid a chorus of ironic cheers.

Guiteau had remained with the outlanders, possibly to make sure they remained safe, possibly to make sure that nobody changed their mind about accepting the invitation from the chatelaine of the ville of Sun Crest.

"Over you go," the sergeant said, his finger not all that far from the trigger of the Armalite.

Krysty went first, Mildred holding her around the waist, followed by J.B. and Michael. Ryan watched anxiously, but both horses were strong and had no trouble with the crossing.

Now there was only Ryan, with Dean at his back, Doc and Sergeant Guiteau, who shook his head at the worried look on the old man's face. "I'll lead your horse and you can swing off and grab on my stirrup. I'll drag you over safe."

"Safe, perhaps, my good fellow. But with some concomitant loss of my precious dignity. No, I shall pay the price to live with myself on my own terms. Come on!"

He went so fast that Ryan was taken by surprise, heeling his own horse in a little behind the frothing wake of the spirited Appaloosa.

There was time to shout a warning to his son to hold on tightly, then the cold water was foaming around his thighs, the horse bucking and rolling as it fought desperately for a footing in shifting stones.

Ryan was aware of Guiteau, pushing confidently along a little to his rear, holding the Armalite above his head in his mutilated left hand.

The danger was very real, with the sawtooth rapids only a few yards to their right.

But it was exciting, and Dean gave a sudden piercing rebel yell of delight, slapping their horse on the flank with the flat of his hand.

"Don't let go!" Ryan shouted, half turning in the saddle—in time to see the threatened disaster become a reality.

It might have been that Doc's horse was already nervous of the surging water, or it might have been the old man's own fear communicating itself to the animal.

The reason didn't matter.

Ryan saw the mount rear, as though it scented danger. Doc's cracked boots slipped from the irons and he went over backward, vanishing under the dark river.

The horse recovered its balance and galloped out onto the opposite bank, where it stood trembling.

But Doc hadn't surfaced.

Ryan caught a fleeting glimpse of a clenched fist, breaking through the white froth at the brink of the rapids.

Then it disappeared.

Chapter Eighteen

Ryan's first gut impulse was to go straight in after the old-timer, but his combat reflexes saved him from what could have been a suicidally foolish move.

If he dived off the back of the horse, the Steyr rifle on a sling around his shoulder could snag and drown him. It would also leave Dean perched on the withers of the animal, with no hope of controlling it or reaching the safety of the shore.

Ryan reached behind and grabbed the boy's arm. "Take the reins!"

He turned to Guiteau. "Watch for him."

He unslung the rifle as his boot slipped from the left stirrup, his leg swinging over the pommel. He threw the blaster to the sec man, not even waiting to see if he caught it clean.

The raw power of the Antelope as it surged along the valley astonished him. For a fraction of a moment Ryan recalled one of his earliest times with the Trader. Not far from Four Corners some renegade jolt peddlers had set up a gaudy in the White House ruins at the bottom of the sacred Canyon de Chelly, and Trader had been paid by the Navaho to go down and scour them out.

It had been an easy job. "Swatting a few flies away" had been Trader's description. But it meant descending the steep bluff opposite the shell of the Anasazi buildings and wading the river, all done on a moonless night.

Okie had been scouting for War Wag One and reported the river wasn't too deep and not too fast.

Ryan had been in charge of the cleansing party and had gone first. He could still remember his shock at the relentless gripping power of that river that had very nearly taken him by surprise, off balance, and dumped him on his ass.

That memory flashed past as he hit the Antelope in a clumsy, facedown dive.

Icy water gushed up his nose and into his open mouth, making him choke and splutter.

The next minute or two was a tumbling, helpless montage of mental and physical confusion. Something struck him a crunching blow in the small of the back, just above the kidneys. In odd moments his head was above water and his eye was open, but he perceived only a blurred, darkening world.

He had no hope of seeing Doc, or even knowing where he might be.

All Ryan could do was to kick and push himself with the current, figuring that this might be his only chance of catching up with the old-timer.

His right arm wedged between two boulders, stopping him up with such a wrench that he feared his shoulder might have been dislocated. But he freed himself.

A large fish, scales glittering like a thousand rainbows, forced its way up the stream, passing Ryan as he rested a moment in a quiet stretch of the Antelope, before another spinning rapid greeted him.

The water buffeted and boiled, making him lose all sense of direction and time. He might have been in the river for fifteen seconds or fifteen minutes, traveled a mere quarter mile or five miles.

He experienced a drop, so deep that Ryan became disorientated, not even knowing which was air and which was the grinding cold of the river bottom.

His outstretched hand touched wet cloth.

The one-eyed man kicked with all his might, erupting out of the river like Neptune from the ocean, shaking water from his eye and looking all around.

He noticed something white, like torn linen.

Ryan vanished again.

A breaking voice, screaming out over the remorseless thunder of the Antelope, caught his attention. He saw Dean, perched on a jutting rock, finger pointing to his left.

Ryan looked again, spotting the patch of white, able to see now that it was Doc Tanner's hair.

Plunging for it, arm at full stretch, he felt the brush of clothing against his fingers again. Snatching it, losing, holding once more.

Ryan found himself pushed up against a large wall of sheer rock, as slick as ice. He managed to brace his boots and power away, keeping hold of Doc's coat, heaving him out of the main flood of the Antelope toward the quieter shallows.

It was as though a deafening noise had been suddenly made still.

There was a gentle slope of gray boulders, with Dean and Krysty to help him. He saw the anxious face of J.B., who furiously wiped spray from his spectacles as he peered down from the bank to see if all was well.

Ryan lay on his back, his feet still trailing in the gentle water, fighting for breath, becoming conscious of the numerous bruises and scratches that he'd suffered during the rescue.

"How is he?" he panted, sitting up to see the worrying sight of Doc, arms spread, face like ivory, with a livid bruise across his right cheek, lying quite motionless alongside him. Krysty knelt by him, reaching into his open mouth and pulling out sand and strands of weed, making sure his tongue was free of the air passage.

"Want a hand, lady outlander?"

For a moment Ryan wondered whose voice it was, booming from the fringe of trees above him. Then he remembered Guiteau and the woman with black hair and the nearby ville.

And the butchered fugitive in the clearing.

"No." Krysty was intent on what she was doing, pinching Doc's nose and breathing deeply into his mouth. She beckoned to J.B. "Come and press on his chest when I tell you."

Ryan sat up, finding that the sergeant was now at his side, steadying him with a hand.

"Mistress Marie was impressed, Cawdor."

"Couldn't fucking care less whether she approves of what I did or not."

"Mebbe it could mean more than you know."

"How?"

"Ah." He placed a finger along the side of the nose. "Careless talk can get you chilled. Fancy a drop of a warming cordial?"

"Sure."

The sec man produced a small glass flask, bound in silver and leather, with a screw top. It was beautifully made by the hand of a craftsman, and was part-filled with a scented, fiery liqueur that Ryan didn't recognize. But it flowed down his throat and into his stomach, carrying its heat to every part of his body.

"Thanks." He handed back the flask. "You collect predarkies like this?"

Guiteau laughed. "No. Baron does. Sometimes he gives a present to someone if he's pleased with them. Gave me this for chilling an assassin, couple of years back. Bunch-backed half-breed, hopped about like a bottled spider." He slipped the flask back inside his jerkin. "Looks like your friend is recovering. I thought that was well done, Cawdor."

Doc was spluttering, coughing up what looked like half of the south fork of the Antelope.

"Take it easy," Krysty cautioned. "Just lie still awhile, Doc. You came close to the last train to the coast."

"I blame...blame Master Cawdor for his foolish lack-brained advice for me...for me to change my horse in the middle of the stream."

Ryan grinned. "Sorry about that, Doc."

The rheumy eyes considered him. "By the soggy and disordered state of your clothing, I draw the deduction that, once again, I owe you my life, do I?"

"Sort of, Doc."

The old man sat up, supported by Krysty on one side, the Armorer on the other. He was badly shaken by his ordeal and touched his bruised face with fingers that were trembling.

"The angel of death came damnably close this time, did he not?"

Mildred had appeared at the top of the bank, with Michael and most of the hunting group. Sitting her mare a little away from everyone else was the mistress of Sun Crest, her face quite blank, showing not a hint of any emotion.

"Oh, perdition!"

"What's up, Doc?"

For some quite inexplicable reason, Ryan's question made Mildred giggle, sticking out her front teeth as though she were impersonating a rabbit.

"My gun!"

"The Le Mat?"

Doc was right. The dark leather holster that had held the enormously heavy old blaster for so many adventurous months was empty.

"Fireblast!" Ryan himself had always felt great affection for the archaic weapon.

Doc gestured to them to help him to his feet, seeing Mildred picking her way over the muddy ground.

"I am well, madam, and have not the least need of your dubious professional skills."

The black woman favored him with a wry smile. "If you can still talk to me in that waspish way, Dr. Tanner, then I guess you haven't been much harmed by your unscheduled dip." She turned to Ryan. "Next time it happens, try to let him go around for one more spin cycle, will you?"

J.B. was staring at the fast-flowing river. "If we could rig up a grapnel and cast for it, we might manage to snag the trigger guard of the Le Mat."

Ryan patted him on the shoulder. "Seen any pigs flying by, lately? No? Nor me, J.B., so I reckon we can forget about trying to find the blaster."

"I feel lost without it at my hip." Doc was gradually reassembling a form of control over himself. "I shall no longer have that macho gunfighter's swagger that made me irresistible to the ladies."

"That's the way the prune wrinkles." Mildred grinned. "And that's not a bad metaphor for you, Doc."

The cold voice of Marie Mandeville cut across their teasing. "My father will not be pleased if we arrive late. We will move now." She looked at Doc. "I suggest you avoid falling off your horse again, outlander."

Ryan was about to snap at her when he caught the look on Harry Guiteau's face, a look that said to let it lie and not argue with her.

So he kept quiet.

AFTER THE WILDERNESS of the forest, they soon found themselves riding paths much more traveled, trails that widened, eventually turning into a well-tended black-top.

Evening had come creeping quickly across the plains on Kansas. By the time they finally came within sight of the outer walls of the ville of Sun Crest, it was full dusk.

But Mandeville had built well and skillfully, choosing the top of a hill for his mansion, so that it caught the last crimson rays of the setting sun.

"Gaia!" Krysty exclaimed as they all rounded a bend from within the forest and saw the ville for the first time.

It was one of the grandest baronial homes that any of them had ever seen, rising in towers and pinnacles and endless Gothic crenellations. The rich green of copper sheathing and silver and gilt danced in the fading glow of the western sun.

Doc leaned on the pommel. "'In Xanadu, did Kubla Khan a stately pleasure dome decree,'" he said softly.

Dean put it even better. "That's the hottest piping house I ever saw."

Chapter Nineteen

"Reminds me of San Simeon," Mildred said.

Michael nodded. "I saw pictures of that place. It wasn't all that far away from Nil-Vanity, close to the coast. The home of... I forget."

"William Randolph Hearst." Doc, now fully recovered from his ordeal, sat with them all, reined in a few yards from vast double gates of iron-studded wood. "A man who owned dozens of newspapers and thousands of people. He built himself the biggest and richest home in America. So he said. I must agree with you, Mildred. This ville does have certain similarities." He lowered his voice so that none of the surrounding sec men could hear him. "Particularly with regard to its gross and baroque bad taste."

Seen close up, Sun Crest was a staggering building. Ryan's knowledge of architecture could have been written large on the head of a pin, but even he could see that it was a bizarre mixture of styles.

A moorish minaret towered from a black-and-white, half-timbered Tudor hall. One end of the ville was a heavily ornamented Gothic spire. The opposite flank to that gargoyled monstrosity was a grossly mismatching copy of a Norman keep. Sturdy and plain, decorated only with arrow slits and a lowered draw-bridge across a decorative moat filled with blue-tinted water.

"If this is the outside, then what on earth can the inside be like?" Michael wondered.

The main gates had swung open, revealing an inner courtyard. Harry Guiteau had walked his horse into the group, hearing the teenager's comment.

"Inside is quite something," he said. "Real contrast to this dull and commonplace outside."

Ryan gave him a polite laugh, joined by the others. All of them assumed that the sec sergeant was joking.

But he wasn't.

THE HORSES WERE LED AWAY by a number of grooms, all dressed in the same muted red livery of Baron Mandeville. Without a word or a glance, the daughter of the ville strode toward a small door set at the bottom of one of the towers, which opened when she was only a step away, as if someone had been waiting patiently for exactly that moment, and then closed behind her.

The sec men also filed off, presumably to their quarters to wash and eat, leaving the seven friends standing on the cobbles, with only Sergeant Guiteau for company.

"What now?" Ryan asked.

"What indeed?"

It was full-dark, but the yard was well lighted with yellowish electric bulbs. Ryan had noticed that they'd crossed another river, much narrower than the Antelope, a half mile back, which was probably used to power a generator.

"We staying here all night?" Mildred was becoming angry. "We're all tired and hungry, and Doc here is an old man who's been through a dreadful experience. He's still soaking wet."

Guiteau shrugged. "Nothing I can do until I get some orders."

"Sure. Your kind always shuffle off behind that excuse. 'I was only obeying orders.' Must be one of the most convenient lies in all history."

"Soften it, Mildred," Ryan said quietly.

"But it's—"

One of the entrance doors to the central block of the ville opened, spilling a great flood of golden light over the stone yard.

Silhouetted against it they could see the figure of a man. Guiteau made a half bow, laying his gloved right hand across his heart in a sort of salute.

"Baron."

Nathan Mandeville's voice was friendly, deep and warm, the sort of voice you might associate with a winter's evening in front of a roaring log fire.

"Sergeant Guiteau, my daughter tells me we have some welcome guests."

"Aye, sir."

The baron looked to be close to six feet tall, very well built, possibly running to fat. But with the bright lights behind him, it was impossible to make out any details. There was a silver halo floating around his head, making it look as though he could be white-haired.

"Our evening meal will be served within the hour," he said, waving a hand to include them all. "We hope that you'll join us. Perhaps stay a day or two. I would relish the opportunity to show my little ranch to some fresh eyes."

Ryan nodded. "Kind of you, Baron. We've had a hard time of it coming here."

Mandeville clapped his hands together and actually did a clumsy little jig of pleasure. "I am delighted, Cawdor. But the doctor there is trembling with cold and wet. Yes, I heard of your brave rescue, but I shall expect to have a personal account of it while you share my humble repast."

Ryan thought that Guiteau gave a quiet snort of amusement at that, but he couldn't be sure.

"Sergeant."

"Aye, Baron?"

"West wing for our new outlander friends. Rooms are being prepared and we shall eat—" he glanced down at something that flashed golden on his wrist "—in fifty-eight minutes from now. That is at thirty minutes after eight, if you have a chron. Hot water is in each room." He started to turn away, then changed his mind. "My dear child, who is notably observant in such matters, tells me that you, Cawdor, and the beautiful lady with hair like flame are...what had they used to call it? An item. Yes. That was it. And Dix, who has *such* an unusual line on scatterguns, and the black lady are also perceived as a couple." He paused. "Two double rooms and three single ones."

"Baron?" Ryan said.

"Yes, I'm aware that the boy is your son. And his room will be adjacent to yours, Cawdor. That was what you were going to ask, was it not?"

"Yeah. Thanks."

Mandeville spun on his heel and took a step back into the dazzling light, the door closing immediately behind him. Once more Ryan had the feeling of servants waiting for precisely the right moment.

Guiteau let his breath out in a long, silent whistle. "So far so good, outlanders. Follow me and I'll show you to the west wing and your rooms."

"Thanks."

"One thing, Cawdor."

"What is it?"

"Sun Crest really is not a good place to wander around. Stay where you're put and move when you're told. And if the baron or Mistress Marie tells you to jump, your only question is 'How high?' Understand?"

"Clear as crystal," Krysty replied. "Now. Can we go find that hot water?"

GUITEAU SHOWED THEM into a vast, galleried hall, where other servants took over.

Ryan would have appreciated some leisure to admire the furnishings and the astonishing richness of the ville, but they were whisked up a wide stone staircase and then hurried into a maze of narrower passages and corridors, all lined with paintings and with ancient arms and armor hung on the oak paneling. The servants bustling about them were all female, in maroon blouses and surprisingly short maroon skirts, and low-heeled boots of soft red leather.

They looked to be mostly in their early twenties or late teens, and there was one young woman to each of the guests. None of them spoke.

After going up and down three separate flights of stairs, even Ryan's excellent sense of direction had been thoroughly spun around and confused.

An older woman, in a longer skirt, was in charge. A bunch of large keys dangled from a ring at her broad leather belt. She had been in the lead, feet pattering on the deep carpets, and she occasionally glanced behind to make sure they were all keeping up with her.

"Here," she finally said. "These are the rooms arranged for you outlanders."

"Arranged by who?" J.B. asked.

"Mistress Marie."

She had a small notebook on a piece of cord, also attached to her belt and she consulted it, reading out numbers and names, watching with an eagle eye to make sure the young servants obeyed her instantly.

"Cawdor and Wroth in sixty-eight. The boy in sixty-seven, next door. Do you wish to have the connecting door unlocked or kept bolted?" she asked Ryan.

"Unlocked. Please."

"Ah." The woman revealed surprise and veiled pleasure at the second word. "Then in sixty-four is Dr.

Tanner, and Master Brother in sixty-three. Those rooms also have a connecting door.''

"Locked, I think, dear lady, if you please. That would be most awfully kind."

Flustered by the sight of the old man's large and perfect teeth grinning at her, she automatically dropped him a curtsy. "Pleased to serve, sir. And sixty-one is for Dix and Wyeth."

She clapped her hands at the other servants. "Show them to their rooms, quickly, or you'll find some skin missing from your backs, and blood down to your ankles." The woman turned once more to Ryan. "Anything you want, just ask them. If you find any difficulty, then ask for me. My name is Mercy Weyman."

"I'VE DIED AND GONE to heaven," Krysty said, sighing.

The bathroom was lined with tapestries and filled with steam. The heavy scent of pine had flooded into the main bedchamber after the servant had poured it into the white enameled tub from a bottle of dark green liquid.

She had shown them the closets and the toilet in the corner by the bath, folded back the layers of bedclothes and pointed out an oak chest that held more blankets.

"Bellpull goes direct to us in the cellars," she said in a breathy little voice. "Ring if there's anythin' you want and I'll come runnin' for you. My name's Laura."

Once they were left alone, Krysty raced Ryan for first to go at the bath. He was ahead, then one of the laces on his combat boots got snagged and she was an easy winner. He sat on the floor, picking at the knot, watching her lithe, naked body, the burst of hair between her thighs matching the flaming mane on her head.

"Don't take too long," he said, finally stripped off, walking into the bathroom.

She was lying down, almost invisible behind a cascade of white bubbles, smiling up at him.

"Good to be real clean, lover. And it'll be good to have you real clean for a change."

He knelt down at the side of the tub and held out his hand for the soap.

Krysty gave it to him, closing her eyes, smiling. "Start at the top and just sort of work your way down, lover."

He rubbed the back of her neck, then around to the front, feeling the taut muscles relaxing under the massage. The soap smelled of fresh lilacs. Krysty wriggled as his hands reached her breasts. Ryan used the soap to run tiny circles around a nipple, bringing it instantly to a soft firmness. He lowered his head to lick the soap away.

"Ryan," she protested. Very weakly. "We both have to bathe and then get ready to eat. I don't think this baron is the sort of man who'd appreciate lateness. And if... Oh, you shouldn't do that, lover, or I'll..."

Her hand snaked over the edge of the tub, reaching down for him.

He gasped as her fingers tightened, bringing him to full, hard readiness.

"Thought you were worried about getting something to eat," he said.

Krysty grinned and kissed him on the mouth, her tongue snaking between his lips. She broke away for a moment, looking down at his erection. "Something to eat?" she whispered.

THEY FOUND THE BEST WAY of enjoying each other's body as well as getting clean was to make love in the bath.

Krysty moved over so that Ryan could get in and lie down on his back, head and shoulders out of the water. She stood astride him, while he reached and caressed her thighs, hands sliding soapily between them, touching her.

As she lowered herself toward him, Krysty used her hand to guide him inside, sitting down with a gasp.

"That is ... something else, lover."

They both started to move, but this created such waves in the narrow tub that pine-scented water immediately began to slop onto the long Persian runner.

"Mebbe I should give you one up for every two downs," Ryan suggested, making her giggle.

"Better still," she said, kissing him hard on the mouth again, while her fingers pinched his nipples, making him writhe, "you don't move. You had a tough day. Now it's become a *hard* day. So you relax and let me do the work. Lie back and think of supper."

After they'd finished, to their mutual satisfaction, they both carefully eased apart, got out and dried each other with the warm, fluffy towels that hung on the radiators.

"What do you make of this place and the baron?" Krysty asked.

"Can't say. Got more jack than most other barons in Deathlands put together. Daughter isn't one to turn your back on. And the sec men are well trained. Not sure I'd want to go up against Harry Guiteau."

There was a knock on the door, a nervous little voice said, "It's Laura, sire and madam. They'll be servin' supper in the main dining room in just five minutes. Miss Weyman says it's best not to be late."

They were on time.

Chapter Twenty

"You're all thinking that I look like a Currer and Ives portrait of Father Christmas. Don't deny it, my friends. Everyone says it."

Ryan had never heard of Currer and Ives, but he had certainly seen pictures of Santa Claus, knew that he had been a mystical figure from way before sky-dark who was a sort of patron saint for children and who gave presents to them.

Nobody could argue with Baron Nathan Mandeville about the way he looked. He even dressed in a loose red shirt and red trousers to augment the impression.

He looked to be in his late fifties, burly running toward fat. His red cheeks spoke of a liking for alcohol, or high blood pressure. Perhaps both. A shock of thick white hair ran down past his ears and turned into a startling full beard and mustache. He had soft lips, like a young woman's.

Mandeville sat at the head of a long table, with his daughter at his right hand. Marie was wearing a floor-length dress of black leather, perforated with hundreds of tiny holes, so that it shimmered like a fishing net. It wasn't *quite* possible to tell whether she was naked underneath the gown.

There were seats for twenty or thirty at the refectory table, but only Mandeville and Marie were seated there. Ryan noticed another table, close to the entrance to the kitchen, where half a dozen young men were crowded together. Among them were Anthony and the others from the hunting party.

"Come, join me, ladies and gentlemen. I keep a poor table, with only the most humble of food and drink, but you are most welcome to it. As is any traveler." He gestured to Krysty, pointing to the seat on his left. "Here, my dear, and make an old man happy with your beauty. Rest of you, take what places you find best."

Ryan sat next to Krysty, with Dean on his left. After some shuffling and hesitation, Doc found himself seated alongside Mistress Marie Mandeville, who pointedly ignored him, with Michael on his right. J.B. placed himself next to Michael with Mildred opposite.

The "humble" food and drink was as good as any of them had ever eaten.

They began with a mousseline of salmon and juniper berries, served on a bed of diced fresh salad vegetables. Enormous trouble had been taken, with tiny carrots carved in crocus shapes, and tomatoes that looked like flowering roses.

With it, the maroon-clad sommelier offered a light white wine, with a hint of quince and nettle in its palate.

Following was a choice of carved meats: a side of beef or a loin of pork, with rosemary and clove sauce, and a monstrous turkey, deliberately undercooked a little, so that a fine pink juice trickled from the carver. There were also succulent ribs of lamb, served with a red currant jelly or a plate of plump pigeons, stuffed with foie gras.

Everyone's plate came with a delicate piped ring of creamy duchess potatoes and a brown earthenware dish of seven tiny portions of different vegetables, including broccoli and a puree of cauliflower.

The dinner wine was a foreign one in a green bottle that Nathan Mandeville insisted on serving himself, taking it from the pudgy hands of the sommelier with as much reverence as if he were holding the Holy Grail.

"There is no label on this, guests. All I can say with confidence is that it is a wonderful claret. The man who sold it claimed it came from thirty years before the nukings. In the olden days before skydark there were men who could have told you the château. The year. Even which side of the hillside it came from. Just sip at it, friends, and you will, I think, appreciate its full majesty."

Ryan tasted it from a large-bowled glass. "Not bad," he commented. "Not bad."

"Tastes bitter to me." Dean pulled a face.

Nathan Mandeville's kindly face was turning as sour as a lemon. "Not too bad! Bitter! Marie, what kind of—"

Doc Tanner saved the day.

"It has a wonderful bouquet," he proclaimed in a boomingly confident voice. "A *premier cru,* unless I miss my guess." He poked his beaky nose inside the glass and inhaled deeply, watched with some admiration by the sommelier. "Oh, excellent. Where are the summers of yesteryear? There was once a marvellous Haut Médoc, back in Paris in—" He caught Ryan's warning glance. "I disremember. But this is truly a remarkable wine, Baron Mandeville. I would consider it a great honor to be allowed to visit your cellars at some convenient time."

The chubby cheeks had softened again, the little blue eyes losing their icy coldness. "A man of taste and distinction, I can see, Doctor."

There was a choice of desserts: meringues as crisp as snow castles, rich, sticky puddings of dark chocolate, flavored with the zest of oranges. Cakes that were layer upon layer of fruit sauces and whipped cream. Fresh fruit salad, covered with a potent, clear liqueur that Doc whispered was probably something called *"eau de vie framboise."*

For the first time during the meal, Marie Mandeville spoke. "You're right, Tanner," she said. "How come you know so much about good food and drink? Ragtag assortment of hired mercies like you lot?"

"Not mercenaries," Ryan corrected quickly. "Seen some mercies, a month ago, up toward the Shens. We have good weapons, that's true. But we don't offer them for hire."

"I have the finest collection of blasters east of the Pecos," the baron boasted. "Tomorrow, during my guided tour of Sun Crest, you shall admire them."

"Look forward to that," J.B. said.

The wine that came with the desserts wasn't like anything that Ryan had ever tasted before.

Even Dean licked his lips and asked for more.

"More? More, boy?" The baron nodded. "This bottle, here in my hand, is quite possibly the last bottle of this vintage left in the entire world. Not just in Deathlands, but in the *world*. It is from the late 1970s and is called a Muscat de Beaumes-de-Venise. From the Domaine de Durban. For once, the label has survived the holocaust."

"Well, it tastes like..." The boy considered for a moment, head to one side. Krysty thought at that moment how like Ryan he looked. "Like a mixture of snow and honey."

Baron Mandeville clapped his hands approvingly. "You have redeemed yourself, young man."

Platters of cheeses were brought in by some of the silent women servants, with fresh-baked biscuits and pats of salted butter. They were accompanied by a tray of crystal decanters, each filled with a different colored drink—dark green, light green, gold, cherry-red, orange and even blue.

While they tried them out, in tiny waisted glasses, the baron became more expansive.

"Your weapons were mentioned earlier. Indeed, they were one of the first things that my dear daughter—" he blew a kiss to the stone-faced Marie

"—noted about you. I have a profound interest not just in blasters, swords and daggers, but in all forms of weapons and all forms of fighting. Do you have any special skills among you?" He positively twinkled. "I cannot believe that such a sturdy group is without combat talents."

Everyone looked at Ryan, waiting for him to give them a lead.

"Most of us can fight some," he replied guardedly, uncertain of what lay behind the question.

But he was always aware of another of the Trader's aphorisms, this time relating to how you dealt with any baron, particularly in the heart of his own ville. "Trust half of what you see and nothing of what you hear."

"Cautious, Cawdor. Very cautious. Every now and again we have small contests, competitions, games . . . Call them what you like. Just within Sun Crest. Helps to keep everyone on their toes, you understand."

Ryan felt a slight pressure against the side of his thigh as Krysty moved her knee to touch him. They had been together long enough for him to be fully aware of the hint of a warning in that moment.

But her feeling that something wasn't quite right simply complemented his own concern. Here was this amazingly wealthy ville and this jolly, outgoing baron. In Deathlands the two things simply didn't go together. How, for instance, had Baron Mandeville obtained such wealth?

"Look forward to watching these games," he replied.

"And taking part?"

"Perhaps."

"Good, good. Now, I have some special genuine coffee shipped up to me from the Blue Mountains of the western Indies. Can any of you be tempted?"

Everyone around the table nodded enthusiastically. What generally passed for coffee sub in Deathlands had its origins in acorns or burned sugarcane or any of a hundred other bizarre concoctions.

The servants shimmered into sight again. Ryan had noticed that Harry Guiteau had joined the fops at the lower table and thought he caught an exchange of glances between the sec men and the lady of the ville. He wondered whether Guiteau had been checking out their rooms, and guessed that he probably had.

But he wouldn't have found anything potentially harmful to their cover story. Nobody carried documents or identity cards to prove who they were.

The coffee was served from what Mildred told him were Georgian silver pots, into tiny, paper-thin cups of the finest Oriental porcelain.

The sugar had been so processed that it had turned almost white, and the cream was fresh.

"Can I ask you a question, Baron?" Ryan asked.

"Anything you want to know?"

"All of this." He gestured to the vaulted dining room around them. "This ville. Didn't come cheap, did it?"

"No." The man's belly laugh was so deep and infectious that everyone around the long table found themselves grinning. Except, Krysty noticed, the Mistress Marie.

"You rob the bank in jack city?"

"Something like that, Cawdor. Now, more liqueurs? If not, then perhaps it's time for us all to withdraw to our beds. Busy day tomorrow."

The question had come and gone, unanswered. But Ryan had seen the drop in temperature in those merry little eyes, the narrowing of the lips under the magnificent white beard, the visible tightening of the knuckles around the handle of the silver cream jug.

Mandeville's wealth was obviously an off-limits area.

It was also clear that the evening meal was at an end.

The baron rose quickly, but his daughter was already gone from the table, the heels of her shoes clicking over the gray flagstones as she disappeared without a word.

THE YOUNG WOMEN APPEARED to shepherd the guests to their rooms, with Mercy Weyman leading the way.

As they all paused in the main corridor before splitting up for the night, she clapped her hands together, the sudden movement making the keys at her belt jingle softly.

"One thing I must tell you, ladies and gentlemen. Baron Mandeville is, like all men in his position, sometimes subject to threats from the lawless elements without the walls. As a consequence there is stringent security within Sun Crest. There is a strict curfew operated, and the ville is ceaselessly patrolled by armed and vigilant sec men.''

''Wouldn't expect it to be patrolled by sleepy, unarmed sec men,'' J.B. muttered, getting a freezing glance from the woman.

''If you die because you have not listened to my warning, Mr. Dix, then I hope you will not blame me.''

''Course not. Can you get on with it?''

''These guards have orders to shoot on sight without the formality of a challenge. You must not leave your rooms.''

''Sure,'' Ryan replied.

''To help ensure your safety, Baron Mandeville has instructed me to lock your rooms after you are within them. They will be opened in good time for tomorrow's activities.''

''What if there's a fire?'' Michael asked.

The boy got a wintry smile. ''That has all been taken care of. Emergency procedures will liberate you safely.''

It occurred to Ryan that there was an awful lot of ''safe'' and ''safety'' being talked about. He wondered just whose safety was really involved.

Mercy Weyman looked at the group. ''Of course, if there should be any problem during the hours of curfew, such as a sudden illness, then you all have the bells within your room to summon assistance.'' She paused a moment. ''Which will, of course, arrive with a full security presence. Now, good night.''

Ryan had planned to talk with the others as soon as they were left alone, but the curfew, confirmed by the turning of the key in the heavy brass lock, canceled that. He went straight to the windows, pulling aside the maroon velvet drapes.

It was pitch-dark outside the ville, and the leaded windows were locked shut. High-grade steel bars had been set deeply into their stone frames.

"Those'll stop anyone getting in at Mandeville," Krysty commented.

Ryan tested them, finding they didn't budge at all. "Or stop any of us getting out."

Chapter Twenty-One

Ryan had always found it difficult to fall asleep in a strange bed, particularly when the bed was as vast and luxurious as this one in the west wing of the ville of Sun Crest. Krysty prodded the mattress, shaking her head. "I swear that it's goose feather, lover."

"Goose feather! We had one like that back home in Front Royale. Great in winter. In summer you lay on it and it kind of enveloped you, like a sucking pit. All you could do to fight your way out of its embrace."

"I think it's romantic. Like in that old folk song about the princess who runs off with the gypsy into the forest. You know it, Ryan?"

"Yeah. Think so."

He walked across the deep-piled carpet and pressed his forehead against the chill metal of the bars that closed off the window. "Guess we didn't have a lot of free choice coming here."

"I can't get a true feeling about it. There's a sort of softness in the ville, but hard underneath. Like... Well, like this mattress but with barbed wire hidden at the bottom."

"We could have opened up and blasted them away when Dean fell."

"Sure we could, Ryan. And one of those sec men could easy have blown the boy's skull apart. You said yourself they were well trained."

"I guess. Still, let's go to bed and catch up on sleep. Then see what the baron has to show us in the morning."

RYAN FOUND the immensely soft mattress was just like his worst childhood memories. Wonderful for the first five minutes, then it became too hot, wrapping itself around his body, so that he seemed to be sinking slowly into a quagmire.

He tossed and turned, trying not to keep Krysty awake. But she had used the meditation techniques taught by her mother and was fast asleep, lying on her back, breath clicking faintly in her throat.

Eventually, grudgingly, he slithered into a shallow, fitful darkness.

THE SUN, directly overhead, had the pinkish-purple hue that threatened a serious chem storm. Only a few torn fragments of maroon clouds marred the perfection of the bowl of the sky.

The ground beneath Ryan's boots was bone dry, shifting as he moved his feet, composed of the finest dust. A tiny tailless lizard, its scales an iridescent turquoise, scuttled from one shadowless rock to another.

The landscape was featureless, stretching around Ryan, making him feel like a man sitting at the bottom of a soup bowl, the gray desert seeming to rise all about him.

Here and there he could make out the jagged shapes of cacti, though not like any he'd seen before. They were a leprous, sickly yellow white, with narrow spines a foot long, tapered like the sharpest needles.

"Christina doesn't mind the desert, you know, Ryan. But the brightness hurts my eyes."

It was no surprise to find that Jak Lauren was walking at his side. The vivid sun flared off the deathly white of the albino teenager's hair, deepening the ruby coals of his deep-set eyes.

"You should wear dark glasses, kid. Sorry, Jak. Forgot you don't like being called that. Been such a long time since we last met up."

"Yeah. Tomorrow is the yesterday you worried about before we met, Ryan."

"Or you could try blinding yourself in one eye. I did that, and it cuts the pain from the sun in half. Why don't you give that a try, Jak?"

"Sure. Or could pluck out both eyes and then have no pain at all."

Somewhere in the brazen fastness above them they heard the raw screech of a hunting falcon, but neither of them could quite make it out.

Jak laughed and threw his skinny arms out wide. "Happiness is being happy, Ryan," he shouted, his voice seemed to echo back from the edges of the land.

Far off, toward the distant horizon, there was a single vivid flash of lightning that appeared to stay frozen in place, like a jagged strip of silver. Ryan turned and stared at it, but it eventually faded away, leaving only a faint dark memory imprinted across the retina.

The building to his right, a quarter mile away, seemed to be falling into a dark tarn, its ivy-covered walls crumbling like stale bread. At one of the golden, lamplit windows, there was the shape of a woman, with long hair, watching them across the wilderness.

Jak had started to run, spinning like a dervish, his bare feet kicking up clouds of dust that threatened to envelop and overwhelm him.

"Careful, kid. Watch out for the big, bitching cactus behind you."

"Don't…call…me…because I'll call you, Ryan." A screech of eldritch laughter erupted from the center of the dust devil.

"Of course you call me Ryan. That's my name, Jak. I've got my identification on my belt."

The white-haired boy stopped suddenly, deathly still, both hands making a strange flicking motion. Ryan felt something tug at his right shoulder and almost simultaneously at the left. A jabbing, stabbing pain.

When he glanced down, Ryan saw that Jak had hurled two of his leaf-bladed throwing knives, showing his usual unerring accuracy. Each of them pinned Ryan's coat to the barn wall behind him, the honed tips also nipping a fold of skin. A tiny trickle of blood ran down each arm.

"Good throwing, Jak. But why did you do that?"

"Stopping you stopping me, Ryan, old friend, old comrade, old look-after-yourself-first."

Jak resumed his whirling dance, nearer and nearer to one of the murderous cacti.

"Keep an eye out, Jak," Ryan called.

It was extremely difficult to understand exactly what happened next.

Jak stumbled over an eyeless human skull that lay half-buried in the sand and fell, facedown, into the cactus.

He screamed, rolling over and over, feet kicking in the air, his hands pressed to his face, pressed to his eyes, over his eyes. He squeezed tight, the slender, bloodless fingers clamped close together, but that didn't stop the blood coming through.

Not white, like his hair and skin.

Red.

Vivid, brilliant red.

A venous, arterial red.

It oozed into a trickle, into a sticky, steady rush of blood that dripped over Jak's hands and onto his neck and shirt and pattered into the dust, drying instantly into small clotted lumps, like dark popcorn.

Ryan ran to him, his feet slipping. Three paces forward and then two paces back.

Behind him he heard a rumble and turned for a moment to see that a huge crack had opened in the flank of the house, and it had fallen into the bottomless lake.

"Can't see. Once could see but now blind, Ryan. Was free but now lost."

The boy was sitting up now, his face still hidden behind his hands, the blood still pumping out from the unseen wound. Ryan knelt and gently pulled away the hands, surprised how soft and unresistant they were, feeling his own hands become instantly clotted with Jak's blood.

Seeing now the wound.

The spike of the cactus had penetrated clear through Jak's crimson eyeball and speared it out, leaving only a raw and empty socket.

But what added to the horror, and made Ryan cry out in shock and despair, was that the wound was so deep it had gone right through the teenager's head and out the other side, leaving a neat round hole the size of an old silver dollar, through which Ryan could see the desert and the bright blue of the sky.

Jak was smiling up at him, as though God were in his heaven and all was right with the world. "Nothing too bad, Ryan? Said, nothing too bad?"

Ryan said nothing, staring at the wound, from which a flood of wriggling maggots was beginning to crawl.

IN THE MOMENT OF WAKING, Ryan found that his entire body was streaked with sweat, rigid with the paralysis of the horrific nightmare.

His mouth was open, lips dry, the muscles in his jaw aching as if he'd been chewing forever and a day on a raw hunk of inedible meat.

Krysty stirred in her sleep, right arm thrown across her eyes. She'd pushed the cover down below her breasts, which glistened with perspiration in the cold moonlight that speared between the draperies.

Ryan stood, careful not to disturb her, fighting his way clear of the fetid embrace of the goose-feather mattress. He padded naked to the window and peered through the gap in the velvet curtains.

The steel bars were icy to the touch. He gripped them tight, consciously trying to steady his breathing after the dream, aware that his heart was still beating fast.

The land outside was thrown into sharply contrasting patches of light and blackness, with the river gleaming like polished glass and the trees stretching away across Kansas, farther than the eye could see.

He looked at it with the keen eye of a combat veteran, noting the care that had gone into the defensive placements of the powerful ville: the high wall, topped with impenetrable coils of razored antipersonnel wire; gun positions, some of them with a shadowy figure behind an LMG; the trees and bushes hacked away to clear lines of fire.

Ryan was suddenly conscious that he was being observed, and he looked to the right, seeing that there was someone standing in the shadows of the turret roof on the next block along, staring directly at him.

It was difficult to tell, because of the thickness of the glass, but he was reasonably certain that it was the mistress of Sun Crest.

Marie Mandeville.

Ryan closed the draperies and went back to bed, to sleep dreamlessly until the morning.

Chapter Twenty-Two

Neither Baron Mandeville nor his taciturn daughter appeared at the breakfast table.

Ryan and the others had been roused and unlocked from their chambers at 8:15 by Mercy Weyman, accompanied by a discreet but powerful force of a dozen sec men, all carrying Armalites.

She explained that the baron was often a late riser and that Mistress Marie had followed her usual practice and gone riding in the forest.

They all ate at the same long table as the evening before, in the galleried dining room, served by a dozen silent women. The only other member of the staff of Sun Crest who appeared was Sergeant Harry Guiteau.

He nodded to them and sat at the bottom end of the refectory table, helping himself to a jug of coffee and making no effort to join in their muted conversation. Ryan felt that the sec man was there merely to observe and listen. And then to report back to his master.

The food was varied and excellent: fresh apples and oranges and some more exotic specimens of fruit, in heavy, sweet syrup; several brans and flakes with foaming milk; platters of eggs, some over easy and some sunny-side up, with ham and bacon and link and patty sausages; the finest, fluffiest hash browns that Ryan Cawdor had ever eaten; a copper dish of fragrant refried beans; trout, as fresh as the sunrise, on and off the bone, and some delicious smoked salmon; a dozen or more different breads and biscuits, all warm from the ovens, with twice as many jellies and preserves.

And plenty of the wonderful coffee.

Nobody said more than a few words, everyone concentrating on the rare sybaritic pleasure of eating fine food in the finest surroundings.

As they'd walked down from the floor with the bedrooms, Ryan had been sharply alert, trying to work out the lay of the land, the strengths of the ville. And the weaknesses.

So far he hadn't managed to spot any weaknesses.

Just as Doc was draining his fourth cup of strong sweet coffee, Baron Mandeville made his appearance. The first clue to his arrival was the scraping of the chair legs on the flags as Guiteau stood upright.

He was wearing a crimson cap of fine wool, perched on top of his snowy curls. The Father Christmas outfit of the night before had gone, replaced by a dark green jacket over a pair of tailored black pants that were tucked into neat ankle boots. Ryan noticed what tiny, trim feet he had. A small pearl-handled revolver in a holster was at his belt.

It crossed Ryan's mind how often frontier barons went in for ostentatious blasters, rather than selecting dull and functional weapons.

"No, sit down, sit down," he said, beaming and waving his pudgy little hands. In fact, the only person to stand had been his senior sec man.

"Thanks for the bed and lodging," Ryan said. "Couldn't have been better."

There was a chorus of agreement from all around the table. Doc wiped his mouth with his swallow's eye kerchief, barely managing to stifle a belch.

"I think that your table is as fine as any in the history of man," he commented.

"Very welcome, Doctor. All of you—" he spread his arms wide "—are most welcome."

Ryan stood. "If you want us to go, then we'll move along, Baron."

"No, no, no!" Each repetition rose up the scale into an anguished squeak.

Guiteau broke the sudden silence that followed. "Baron wants you to see his collection of predarkies this morning. Then, after you take a break for some more food, there'll be the postnoon combat skills."

"We can watch these tests?" Mildred asked.

It seemed that Mandeville hesitated for a moment. Then his smile returned like the sun from behind a cloud. "Of course. But better than that. All of you can take part in any of the events that take your fancy."

"Are there prizes?" J.B. queried.

Guiteau laughed, smothering the sound behind a cupped hand, trying to turn it into a cough. The baron turned toward him as though he were going to say something. He changed his mind. "Prizes for those who do well and please me."

"And those who do badly and do not please us will also get their own reward."

None of them had been aware of her entry. But Marie Mandeville was leaning over the rail of the minstrels' gallery above them, her hair falling straight down on either side of her pale oval face. She was in shadow, but Ryan again got the uncomfortable feeling that the woman was staring directly into his face, trying to stare into his soul.

Nobody asked her what she meant, but the sense of the unvoiced threat hung in the air like the remembered hiss of a venomous reptile.

"Good morning, my dear. Did you enjoy your ride?"

"No. The bitch of a mare nearly foundered under me. I had to spur her and lash her until the blood flowed to the ground to get her home."

"Will you eat?"

"After you've gone. Guiteau."

"Lady?"

"Remain behind."

"Lady."

Mandeville was still near the main doors, and he beckoned to them. "Come then. I shall show you my pictures and my weapons. I am proud of both."

Ryan was standing close to Guiteau, who whispered softly, "I remembered where I seen you before. Long years ago, in another place. Trader's man."

"That a problem?"

"Not for me. Nothing's a problem for me. Nothing in Sun Crest touches me, Cawdor."

The rest were filing after the baron. Marie still watched, motionless, from above.

Ryan smiled at the sec man. "You can't be a diamond swimming in a sea of shit forever, Guiteau."

"No?"

"No. Doesn't take long before you're just another shit-covered diamond."

"MY PICTURES FIRST. I was always a lover of the art of painting. Even before I was able to...to obtain some for myself. Now I have them here in this gallery."

He had led them out of the dining room, along a broad passage with three flights of stairs opening off it. Ryan noticed the sec men posted at the angles of the corridor, none of them showing the boredom and indifference that he'd seen from guards in other, sloppier villes.

They tracked the stout figure up a wide staircase, each step made from a single block of rose-tinted stone. The banisters were marble, and some sort of heraldic animal stood guarding at top and bottom.

"This way."

The baron acknowledged the salute of a sec man. "Morning, Brandt. Wife better?"

"Much, thanks, Baron."

They moved on, Mandeville turning and speaking over his shoulder to his following guests. "One of the best in the ville at hand-to-hand until he dislocated his right knee a year ago. Broke his heart he couldn't compete anymore. Any of you people much good in that field?"

Eyes darted toward Ryan, who nodded at Michael. There didn't seem much risk in showing their skills to Baron Mandeville. If he'd wished it, they could all have been sent off to buy the farm at any time since they reached Sun Crest.

"I'll give it a try," Michael said.

"You? Tad young for a rough-and-tumble. Still, like your courage, young man. Brother, isn't it?"

"Yeah."

"Don't suppose any of you have a way with a knife? Throwing?"

Ryan answered for them. "Used to know a boy. Could put a knife in your eye at fifty paces."

"Hope that isn't how you lost your eye, Cawdor." A bellow of laughter filled the hall. "Course. You said that it was a rabbit, didn't you? Rabbit! Like that, Cawdor."

They turned a corner, finding themselves facing an immensely long gallery.

The morning had been cool, and fires burned in six hearths measured along the length of the gallery. A little smoke had drifted out as the wind veered easterly, and the room was so long that it was impossible to make out the far end through the woody haze.

The ceiling was fifteen feet high, and there was not a single window in either of the endless walls. It was lit with strings of hand-cast light bulbs that flooded the walls with a golden glow. Ryan noticed that a significant proportion of the lights had malfunctioned.

But what caught the eye were the pictures.

At that first startling glance, it seemed to Ryan that there wasn't a single inch of space on the walls, from floor to ceiling, that wasn't covered by pictures. All had been hung haphazardly, some of them overlapping.

Many were in ornate frames of rococo gilt, while some had plain frames of unvarnished beech or elm. Some had glass over the paintings, but most were uncovered.

"By the Three Kennedys!" Doc stood stock-still, the ferrule of his sword stick rapping very softly on the polished wood-block floor.

"Gaia! You must have all the paintings left in Deathlands, Baron!"

"Far from it, Krysty. I may call you by your first name, may I? Good. No, there are many other barons throughout the world who have collections every bit... Well, honesty makes me admit that their collections are not *quite* up to the quality of my own gallery. Not quite."

"Quality or quantity?" Mildred whispered to J.B. "He's sure got the quantity."

"Perhaps I should take you through, picture by picture," Mandeville said doubtfully. "Though that would take us all day and most of the night. I want you also to admire my collection of weapons this morning. And there are the games this afternoon. No, we will move along the gallery and I will comment on any that are specially dear to me."

Ryan found the next hour or so lurched past him in a blur of names and colors, giving the cumulative effect of staggering boredom.

There were more paintings in that single room in Sun Crest than he'd seen in his entire life. But after the first couple of dozen they all started to merge in his mind.

He remembered the first one clearly.

The small brass plate on the bottom of the frame said it was by Eric Bailey R.A., though Mandeville wasn't sure what the initials meant. Possibly "Royal Artist," as the man had been English.

It was a large portrait of a modest young woman conversing with a canary in a cage. She wore a dress like a puritan's, with a white collar and cuffs, and her hair was smoothed, nunlike, into a low chignon. Though it was impossible to ignore the nubile curves of her body. On her face was an expression that struck Ryan as rapturous imbecility.

The title of the picture was *The Pretty Maid*.

"She looks double-stupe," Dean whispered to his father. "Like she was going to eat that jaybird."

Mandeville didn't hear him, striding on ahead, hands locked behind his back, beaming with a proudly proprietary air.

Mildred and Doc boggled in amazement at some of the paintings, which they said were very famous, though both of them, making sure that Mandeville didn't hear them, suggested that they thought that quite a lot of them were either fakes or prints of the original pictures.

Ryan couldn't find many to admire, though he enjoyed a large canvas of a fallen tree with dark, jumbled branches, against a field of bright rapeseed. The signature looked like "Alan Burgess," but he couldn't be certain.

One of the few pictures from the over-the-top collection that everyone liked was an impressively plain painting of a rectangular adobe building, with a shadowed door, against a reddish-pink Southwestern landscape.

Mandeville said he didn't know who it was by, but had traded a pair of matched Navy Colts for it a few years earlier.

Doc and Mildred were in agreement that it had been painted by a woman artist called Georgia O'Keefe.

Names flowed by Ryan as the pictures blended into a mosaic of multicolored wallpaper.

Hopper, Alma Tadema, Picasso, Winslow, Warhol and Remington—one of the few names that prompted any interest at all from J.B.

"One of your relatives, Mildred?" Michael asked, peering at the name beneath a portrait of a sturdy naked woman with a plait of reddish hair.

"Andrew Wyeth? No. No relation."

The smoke settled on Ryan's chest, making the atmosphere more oppressive.

The talk had been fairly desultory at the beginning, but by the time they'd all joined the baron at the distant end of the gallery a gloomy silence had descended over them all.

Mandeville was sitting on a brocaded chaise longue, waiting eagerly for them.

"Well?"

"Amazing," Ryan commented after a moment's consideration. "Double amazing."

"Yeah," the Armorer echoed. "Never seen so many pictures all in the same place."

"Beautiful." Krysty looked back at the diminishing perspective of the gallery, its distant entrance quite invisible in the dusty haze.

"No criticism? Just unstinted praise?" Baron Mandeville beamed.

"I thought there was too many of them," Dean said. "I liked some, like that desert house and that woman lying on the hillside. And I thought the one was a hot pipe with the raft and everyone chilled. But there was just too many all at once. Sorry, Baron, but you asked."

"Too many pictures," Mandeville repeated. His merry little face had gone cold, as though a mask of ice had been slipped into place. "You think—"

"Mozart, the great composer, was once told by his noble patron, the emperor, that a piece of music contained too many notes." Doc looked to make sure he had the baron's attention. "Mozart asked the emperor which particular notes he thought that he might profitably remove." And he gave a great bellow of laughter to underline the fact that it was supposed to be a joke.

"Yes, yes, I see. Too many notes. Too many pictures! Of course."

Mandeville threw back his head and joined in Doc's merriment, the ice vanishing and his rosy Father Christmas cheeks and smile returning. But Ryan noticed that the meltwater look never left the eyes.

RYAN HAD GLANCED at his chron several times during the interminable visit to the ville's art gallery, watching the digits tick over with agonizing slowness.

Yet, somehow, it was already close to noon and a faint rumbling in his stomach warned him that some more of the baron's excellent food would be welcome.

It was a fact that had also impressed itself upon Mandeville himself.

"Damnation and blast it!" The baron stamped his foot in a strangely childish temper. "I wanted to show you my guns and swords before we ate. But now it's the mid of the day and the games are set for two o'clock."

"Do you collect anything else, Baron?" Krysty asked.

"Pictures and weapons are—" He was suddenly suspicious. "Why? What have you heard about my private— What?" His eyes blinked and he tugged at the white beard, trying for a strained, false laugh. "What am I— Of course you didn't know. Couldn't, unless that unnatural bitch has been—"

He had a gold hunter watch in a pocket of his vest, on a golden fob chain. It suddenly started to play a tinkling, melodious little tune, which, oddly, reminded Ryan of an antique Western vid, but he couldn't recall what it was.

It broke the thread of Mandeville's anger.

"I think that every one of you probably possesses some sort of cunning in fighting. I feel that, Cawdor. Yes, oh, yes. The ladies will watch, if they wish. And the bright little boy. But the rest of you will amuse us."

"If you like," Ryan said casually. "But if you have anyone who reckons themselves with a handblaster, then I'd back Mildred against them."

"Back the woman? Sergeant Guiteau is the best I've ever seen. Mildred can shoot against him if she wishes."

She smiled. "I wish, Baron. I really wish."

ONCE AGAIN THE REFECTORY table groaned under an assortment of cold meats, salads and pastries, with jugs of chilled fruit punch to drink.

J.B. sat next to Ryan, picking at a plate of sliced roast beef with some cold potatoes and pickles.

"Think going in for these combat games of his is a good idea, Ryan?"

"I don't know. Just have to wait and see. They start in an hour, so we won't have long to wait."

Chapter Twenty-Three

Andromeda lay behind Trader and Abe, and they were now resting on a hillside overlooking the dull waters of the Cific Ocean. The ghostly ruins of the old ville of Seattle were about a hundred miles to the east of them, overlooking Puget Sound.

"I never lost the pleasure of looking at the fucking sea, Abe."

"Yeah. Me, too."

The smaller man was still unable to believe that he'd really done it.

Done it on his own.

Everyone had believed that the Trader was dead, that he had simply walked away from the war wags when the rad cancer that had been chewing his guts for years had finally flared up past the level of tolerance.

"Look—" he pointed with his right hand, away to the north "—see them?"

There was a cold mist drifting off the bleak shore, and Abe couldn't make out at first what Trader was indicating. Then he saw them.

"Whales."

"Gray whales, Abe."

"Yeah."

They watched in silence. The sun was setting away to the west, beyond the farthest edge of the sea, pouring a torrent of blood toward them across the coppery water.

The leviathans were moving through the crimson alley, rolling and dipping. Abe's sight was erratic at any great distance, but he counted five or six of the adult whales, with three or more calves gamboling around their mothers.

"Ain't they the greatest?" Trader said. He stifled a cough, biting at his lip.

Abe turned to look at his former boss, seeing that the old lines of pain were more deeply etched around the mouth and eyes, and that his hair was whiter and thinner. The man himself was markedly leaner.

And the Trader hadn't ever been known as a man who carried a lot of surplus weight.

"All right, Abe."

"What?"

"Man who has too many questions is going to get too few answers."

"I know that."

"But you want to know. Know about where I went and why. And what's been happening since then."

"Sure do, Trader."

"Man says a thing once won't say it twice. That true?"

"Yeah."

"True of me?"

Abe grinned. "Sure. Truer of you than any other man living, Trader."

"So, you figure we should try and contact those two miserable sons of bitches? Ryan and John B. Dix?"

As they'd strode together over back trails and quiet green highways, Trader had pumped the former gunner from War Wag One about what had been happening since he'd dropped out of life. What Ryan had been doing. And the rest.

He hadn't passed many comments.

Until the subject of Ryan's son came up.

"Sharona was the mother? Well, I'll be hung, quartered and dried for the crows!"

"She died about three or four years ago. Got the rad sickness real bad, so Dean says. And she—" Abe had suddenly realized what he'd said and stammered, looking away from the cold eyes. "Not that rad sick means you all die or... Just that..."

But Trader hadn't picked up on the hint to talk about his own gut-gripping illness.

Now, lying together on sheep-cropped turf in the cool of the evening, Trader looked like he was about to open up about his own mystery.

"We get word to them, they'll want to hear what's happened to you, Trader. Course they will."

"Like I said, I'm not a man to chew his meat twice, Abe. When we all meet up, I'll tell what went down. Not until. Now we should find a camp for the night. Wolves around here. Four-legged and two-legged."

ABE WASN'T ALL THAT GOOD with words. He knew what he felt, but he was never confident in expressing it.

There'd been the three hundred pound widow woman near Canon City who'd asked him if she thought she was mebbe a little on the large side. Abe had happily told her that he really liked very fat women.

She'd broken both fists in beating up on him, and he'd never understood why.

Now, sitting by the crackling fire, with a skinned rabbit roasting on the willow spit, Abe wanted to tell the hunched figure opposite what he felt.

That he felt safe.

Secure.

Like he'd found the father he'd never known.

He decided to try.

"Trader?"

"Yeah, Abe?"

"Just that . . . Fucking nice night."

Trader sounded puzzled. "Yeah. Guess it is."

From near the cliff top, they could hear the pod of whales making its mysterious way through the deep waters. Their unique belling calls to each other echoed around the misty valleys that arrowed down to the coast.

"They reckon they can talk to each other cross hundreds of miles," Trader commented.

Abe nodded, then realized that he couldn't be seen in the moonless dark. "Yeah."

"Next day or so we'll move on to Seattle. Big center for the travelers passing through. Men and women call themselves the traders." He laughed shortly. "So soon they forget. We'll persuade some of them to carry a message for us to the one-eyed man. It'll likely take a good long time, but they'll find him in the end. And we got the time to wait."

Abe stretched, suddenly burrowing under his bedding and scratching furiously at his ankles. "Fucking lice," he moaned. "Can't get them out of this old blanket. Might as well burn the son of a bitch."

He heard Trader sitting up. "Don't you remember how we coped with lice back in the war wags?"

"No."

"Think it was O'Mara taught us. Said it was a trick from the Apaches near the Grandee."

"Oh, yeah. Something to do with ants."

"Right. When you get up you spread the blanket over the nearest anthill. Red ones was bestest." The wind rose and ruffled the leaves on the grove of live oaks near where they'd camped. Trader listened for a few moments before carrying on. "The ants think it's free-lunch time and swarm over the lice. Eat all the little boogers in sixty minutes flat."

Abe laughed. "Then you get the blanket and give it a real good shake and all the ants fall off and you start clean."

"That fat kid...cook's assistant on War Wag Two. What was his name?"

"Ray. Always used to ask 'who?' when anyone shouted at him. Gotten called 'Hooray' after a bit."

"That was the guy. He tried out the blanket treatment, but he couldn't find his ass with both hands. Forgot about shaking off the ants after they ate the lice and got bit worser than anyone I ever saw." Trader's voice was shaking with laughter. "Funniest thing I ever saw since that breed whore master in Nogales slammed a drawer on his cock and cut it off."

Abe remembered at that moment that the Trader had always been a man with a dangerously dark side to his character.

THE NIGHT PASSED uneventfully, ending in a dazzlingly fresh dawning.

Abe got up and wandered into the edge of the trees, squatting to relieve himself, using a handful of dew-damp leaves to wipe himself clean.

By the time he got back, Trader was up, busying himself in reviving the smoldering ashes of the fire.

"It's good to see you, Abe," he said, not looking up, not seeing the beam of delight on the mustached face of the little man. "Part of me still wishes I'd stayed unfound. That was the idea. But a part of me is pleased you tracked me. And it'll be good to meet up with Ryan and John B. and the others."

Chapter Twenty-Four

Guiteau had shown them a handwritten list of the events that they'd be seeing during the afternoon.

"Baron'll be happy if you go in for some of them," he said. "More the better." He spoke in a flat, measured way, but the implicit threat was very clear.

They all gathered around, Krysty reading it out loud to the others.

"Starts with some wrestling on the lawn out back. Then we go to the butts for archery, followed by rifle shooting and knife fighting demonstration with muffled blades."

"They tie rags around them and smear paint on," said the sec sergeant. "So you can see when a hit's made."

"Pistol shooting is last." She glanced at Mildred. "Oh, no, there's something at the end. Just called a 'special final.' What's that, Guiteau?"

"Sort of a grudge fight, Krysty. Last thing of the afternoon is when the Baron Mandeville and Mistress Marie get to give out the rewards."

"Prizes?" J.B. asked.

"You could say that." He looked at the big pendulum clock at the end of the passage. "Let's go, outlanders. How many of you going to compete?"

Ryan had managed to talk to the others during the lunch, agreeing they might as well put up the best show they could, as long as it didn't involve any serious risk to any of them. From the list, nothing looked too hazardous.

"Michael for the close combat. J.B. in the long-blaster shooting. Me with the knives. And Mildred with the pistol."

Harry Guiteau looked curiously at the black woman. "I heard you thought you was good. You know you'll shoot against me. Well, couple of others as well, but they couldn't hit themselves, even with the barrels up their asses."

"You want a side bet, Sergeant?" Mildred asked.

"Wouldn't take your jack, lady."

Mildred stepped in closer, pushing her face at the grizzled veteran. "Wouldn't be that you're frightened of losing to a woman, would it?"

He took a half step away, holding his hands up, palms out, trying to calm her. "Hey, take it easy. It's nothing personal. Back off."

She nodded. "Doesn't really need a side bet, does it, Guiteau? We both know what we're shooting for."

He looked like he was going to say something, then thought better of it and turned away.

"Dangerous bastard," Ryan said. "I know most sec men don't have the brains of an outhouse shovel. Guiteau's good. Anyway, let's go take part in the games. Michael, you're going to be on first. Do your best but try not to chill anyone."

It was intended as a joke, but the teenager didn't even crack a smile.

"EACH FIGHT WILL BE ENDED by a submission, a knockout or a fall, both shoulders pinned to the grass for a count of three." The sec man looked up at Mandeville. "Are you ready, Baron?"

"I think so. Will young Michael be prepared to take on the winner, or should I ask Guiteau to pick out a boy from the kitchens to tumble with?"

The teenager answered for himself. "I'll take the winner. No trouble."

"Good. Let them come on to it."

The lawn lay out at the back of the ville, defended by a high stone wall, the river flowing just beyond it. Considering the general dryness of that part of Kansas in the summer, the grass was amazingly green and lush.

Guiteau had explained. "Watered and rolled every day for the last fifteen years. Hand weeded. You could have grass like that if you took the trouble, Cawdor." He drew closer. "By the way. Whatever happened to the Trader? Heard so many rumors. He really go up to God in a golden war wag?"

"I heard rumors. Far as I know, Trader's dead. Been gone a couple of years now. You know different?"

The sec man shook his head. "Nothing to prove, Cawdor. Lot of cheap talk. Nothing else."

Baron Mandeville was seated on what was close to being a throne, set on a dais, above everyone else. He was wearing a loose jerkin of soft green wool fringed with sable. The rich fur was so dark it had a coppery sheen to it, reminding Ryan of the wings of blowflies.

Next to him, in an identical seat, was his daughter.

Marie was leaning back in her chair, tapping her fingers on the arm. She wore a short dress of white fringed leather, with a wide belt of brilliant red. There were rings on all of her fingers, some of them unlike anything Ryan had ever seen. One was a silver skull with an opal set in the forehead. Another held an unnervingly accurate glass replica of a human eye. Ryan hoped it was only a replica. Her ankle-length boots matched the belt and had tapering, slender heels.

The baron waved a hand to them. "We can begin now. Find yourselves somewhere to sit." He gestured to a row of chairs ranged on both sides of him.

Ryan noticed that the preening fops were conspicuously absent from the gathering, though three sides of the lawn were lined with male and female servants from the ville.

Marie beckoned to him. "By me, outlander."

Ryan sat where she pointed, with Krysty beside him. The others all found seats to watch the wrestling.

It was almost immediately obvious which of the wrestlers Michael was going to have to face.

Guiteau had positioned himself directly behind Ryan and Marie Mandeville, giving him a whispered commentary on the fighters. One was a butcher, heavily muscled, but slow and clumsy. Another worked in the forest, slimmer, but visibly worried about getting himself hurt.

"Jericho'll take them, one hand behind his back, won't he, Mistress Marie?"

She didn't turn to face the sec sergeant, contenting herself with a nod.

Jericho appeared in the third of the opening bouts. Unlike the others, he fought stripped to the waist, and Ryan noticed that he was greased across the shoulders, chest and arms, making it harder for any of his opponents to hold him. He wondered whether Michael had spotted the trick.

"He a sec man?" he asked, the question intended for Harry Guiteau.

But Marie answered. "Jailer."

"Jailer? You got a jail in the ville?"

She turned and stared at him. "You don't look triple-stupe, Cawdor. Man who rode at the right hand of the Trader can't be a stupe. So, why pretend to be surprised that we have a prison here at Sun Crest? You measure the power of a baron by the number of his enemies."

He nodded. "Yeah. Yeah, you're right."

It was fair comment, even though it had been put a little more bluntly than he'd liked.

Jericho the jailer was well over six and a half feet, looking to be around three hundred and twenty pounds. He was very strongly built, despite the suggestion of a beer gut hanging over his maroon trousers.

He won both his bouts with absurd ease, his opponents unable to conceal their fear of him.

Justified fear.

Krysty leaned toward Ryan. "Not just big and powerful, lover," she said quietly.

"No. Also fucking mean."

"Will Michael . . ."

He cut her off, knowing that Marie and Guiteau were both listening to them. "We'll see."

The second of Jericho's opponents was being helped away, bleeding from nose and mouth. The first had only just recovered consciousness after a bone-numbing knee drop, performed with a grinning ease by the jailer.

"Will your boy fight this giant of mine, Ryan Cawdor?" the baron asked.

"Ask him yourself."

Michael stood and peeled off his black denim shirt, taking several deep breaths. Ryan watched the crowd, seeing from their muttering that they felt the slender teenager had no hope at all. There was a ten-inch difference in height and nearly two hundred pounds in weight.

Jericho was stomping around in steel-tipped boots, hands clasped above his head, trying to psych the boy out. But Michael ignored him. He looked out above the tips of the trees, his dark eyes half-closed, his black hair, which betrayed his Crow ancestry, gleamed in the afternoon sunlight.

"No contest," Mandeville said loudly.

"Wrong, Father."

"What? You think that stripling boy has a chance, Marie? Seriously?"

"A wager, Father?"

"What?"

"If the outlander wins, then he dines with me in my rooms tonight."

"And if he loses?"

Marie waved a slender hand dismissively. "Then let him dine alone with Jericho."

Guiteau muffled a laugh.

Michael heard the noise and half turned. Ryan caught his eye and nodded slowly. The young man responded with a broad, confident smile.

"On with it," Mandeville ordered, "or the day will be gone. Both ready?" Jericho saluted his master, and Michael dropped into a fighting crouch.

"A moment."

Mandeville looked at Ryan. "What is it?"

"If my friend damages your man?"

"Then the fool deserves to be damaged, outlander. But I wouldn't worry about that. Worry for the skinny boy once Jericho lays hands on him."

But Jericho never really laid hands on Michael.

He moved in with all of the leering confidence of the successful bully, fingers crooked, intending to pull the younger, lighter, shorter man into his grasp and then rend and utterly destroy him.

During his lifetime at the reclusive monastery of Nil-Vanity, Michael had become an advanced master of the esoteric Oriental martial art of Tao-Tain-do, a skill that had turned him into the fastest fighting machine that Ryan or J.B. had ever seen.

He moved in a blur of action, feinting to duck away from Jericho, then closing with him and dropping beneath the gripping hands. The watchers gasped as the slightly built youth appeared behind the blundering jailer, snatching at his left arm and wrenching it behind the man's sweating, oiled back, bringing him to his knees, crying out in pain, face whitening.

"Submit?" Michael asked, as calmly as if he were asking whether Jericho would perhaps like more beans with his pork.

"No, no. . . fuck you! Yeah, yeah. I give in. You're breaking my fucking wrist."

The teenager stepped away, turning toward Ryan and the others, unable to conceal a small smile of triumph. Marie Mandeville tapped her father on his arm.

"I win," she said.

"I guess . . ."

While Michael's back was turned, Jericho lunged at him, driving up from his beaten position on his knees, smashing a huge fist into his ribs.

Ryan jumped to his feet, the SIG-Sauer drawn and cocked.

But Guiteau was faster, almost as if he'd second-guessed Jericho and anticipated Ryan's reaction. He had his own blaster out, the barrel pressed into the one-eyed man's spine. "Sit down," he said quietly.

In the brief time that the exchange took, the fight had moved on.

The cowardly punch sent Michael staggering to his right, away from the furious jailer. The boy's face had gone sheet-white, except for a spot of crimson on each cheekbone. He rubbed the spot where the blow had landed, turning to confront his opponent.

"Stop it, Baron," Mildred called, but Mandeville ignored her.

"Tricked me, you little shit heap," Jericho hissed.

"You gave in."

"Sure. Just to make you let go my arm. No submission this time, outlander."

"No," Michael agreed, his color returning. "No submission this time."

He started to skip lightly on his toes from side to side, jigging back and forth. Someone in the crowd giggled and Jericho frowned. "Stand still and take it, you brownholin' little bastard!"

Ryan was watching intently, but it was so lightning-swift that he missed it. The young man darted in, seeming to flick contemptuously at the jailer's face. There was a light crack, as though someone had slapped a naughty child across the back of the legs.

"Blessed Jesus!" The voice belonged to an elderly woman, bursting out of the crowd in shock.

Jericho had sunk slowly to his knees, both hands gripping his throat. His mouth gaped open, and he seemed to be battling to draw breath. The only sound in the sudden stillness was the harsh cry of a peacock, near the water.

"Smashed his voice box," J.B. said.

It was like seeing a freeze-frame on a flickering old vid. The giant figure of Jericho, blood trickling from his mouth, looked helplessly up at his slim young destroyer.

"Submit?" Michael called, the raw edge of ragged anger clearly audible. "Can't hear you, Jericho?"

"Put the blaster away, Guiteau," Ryan said, not looking around. "Not needed."

"I can see that, Cawdor. The boy's going to chill him, ain't he?"

"I guess he is."

"I don't hear you saying anything, Jericho." He mocked the injured man's whispering, painful attempts to speak.

"Do it, boy," Marie shouted, standing up, her hands gripping the arms of her carved oak chair, her knuckles white as chiseled ivory.

Tiring of his revenge, the teenager swiveled, putting all his weight on his left leg. The right foot shot out like a power hammer, the heel driving into Jericho's face, just below the bridge of the nose.

Ryan heard a noise that he'd heard a few times before in his life.

The noise like a grown man treading square on a large, ripe apple.

A soft, crunching sound.

"Done him," J.B. commented unnecessarily.

Marie Mandeville was breathing hard, one hand now pressed against her breasts.

"Yes," she whispered.

The kneeling man fell backward, vivid blood gushing from his mouth. The blow had pulped his nose, driving splinters of bone into the brain.

Jericho lay very still, just one leg kicking for a few seconds in a postmortem neural spasm.

"Well done, outlander!" shouted a young man, wearing the outdoor uniform of the ville.

"Take that person's name and deal with him, Sergeant," the baron said, not even bothering to conceal his anger at the overwhelming defeat of his champion.

"Right, Baron."

Standing close to Marie, Ryan was aware of the tension in her body, her thighs squeezed together in a paroxysm of excitement. Suddenly she relaxed with a great sigh, opening her eyes and smiling at him.

"I shall enjoy dining with that fast boy, outlander," she said.

Ryan simply nodded, moving away to congratulate Michael on his victory.

Mandeville was on his feet, struggling to readjust the beaming, good-natured mask. "A surprise, there, friends. But more for Jericho, I believe. Now, let us go to the butts for the shooting."

Chapter Twenty-Five

The shooting range was actually outside the fortified walls of Sun Crest. It lay a quarter mile to the east, across the wooden bridge over the narrow river and through a copse of elegant silver birches to an open area that had been painstakingly cleared from raw forest. The rifle butts ran for a full half mile, ending in a high bank of sandy earth. A number of round, colorful straw-padded archery targets stood ready.

"I can't hardly believe that this is Kansas, bloody Kansas," Doc muttered. "Granary of the world. Wheat from sunrise to sunset."

"More like northern Montana or Washington State," Mildred agreed. "Endless forests."

Guiteau had deliberately fallen in to walk with Ryan. It was noticeable that the sec presence was much greater once they were outside the ville, all carrying their standard Armalites. All of them were alert.

"Never seen the like of that breed kid of yours," the sec sergeant commented.

"Not a breed. Think he had a Crow grandfather. Wouldn't think about calling him a breed, Guiteau."

"Where'd he learn to fight like that?"

"Don't know." Ryan wasn't about to get himself tangled up in the complex realities of time trawling.

"Jericho never had a chance. Like a spitball up against a gren launcher."

"Man shouldn't have tried to blindside the boy."

Guiteau laughed. "You can sure as shit say that again, Cawdor." They were near a row of seats set out along a raised dais at one end of the butts.

"Archery first?"

"Yeah. You outlanders don't have anyone who can put six from six in the gold, have you?"

Both J.B. and Ryan were a lot better than adequate with either longbow or crossbow, but it seemed a good idea not to lay every card down on the table.

"Guiteau!"

"Coming, Baron." He paused a moment. "Letting that ball-of-fire kid chill Jericho might turn out one of the worst moves you ever made in your life, Cawdor."

Krysty caught the last words, registering the venom that lay beneath them.

"What was that about, lover?"

"Guiteau shooting his mouth about how Michael could've made a bad move for us."

"He didn't have to chill the jailer."

Ryan sniffed. "Mebbe. I'd have done it in his place."

THE ONLY SURPRISE in the archery came when one of the young bedroom servants beat a bearded sec man in the shoot-off, scoring two golds, three inners and an outer with her last six shafts.

The man stalked angrily off, the mocking shouts of his fellows and the watching crowd ringing in his ears.

Twice Ryan had glanced along the row of seats to where Marie Mandeville had insisted on Michael Brother being next to her. For the first time since they'd encountered the woman, she was showing animation, talking in a low urgent voice to the teenager, constantly laying her hand on his arm.

Or on his thigh.

Baron Mandeville ignored his daughter, but Harry Guiteau was also keeping an eye on what was happening.

J.B. TOOK THE STEYR RIFLE from Ryan, who hung on to the Uzi while he competed in the long-gun target shooting.

"Like taking candy from a baby," he said, his eyes glinting behind his glasses.

When it came to anything linked to weapons, the Armorer wasn't often wrong.

It *was* like taking candy from a baby.

The three sec men who reached the last round to go against J.B. were the best of the mediocre bunch. All of them handled the targets at fifty and one hundred paces without any trouble, slamming bullet after bullet from their immaculate Armalites into or very near to the bull.

"Want to come in, outlander?" Mandeville shouted, much of his good humor restored.

"I'll wait until it gets harder, thanks, Baron. I could spit at the target at this range."

The Father Christmas smile disappeared like September frost off a meadow.

Once the range went up to two hundred and fifty yards, the cracks started to appear.

At the announcement of the progression to five hundred paces, J.B. stood and slowly made his way to lie down alongside the maroon-uniformed sec men, wrapping the sling on the rifle around his forearm for extra stability.

Guiteau nudged Ryan. "You got some of the best blasters I ever saw, Cawdor. That a legacy from your days with the Trader?"

"Some are, some aren't. It's been awhile since Trader took his last walk, you know, Guiteau."

"Sure. What was it the Indians called him? Oh, yeah. 'The Man Who Walks without Friends.' You and Dix think of him like that, Cawdor?"

"That was a name given Trader by those who weren't his friends. He had some good friends." He paused. "And he didn't have many enemies."

"Not many enemies?" A disbelieving grin split the grizzled sec sergeant's face.

"Alive."

J.B. never allowed the shooting to be anything approaching a contest.

The Steyr SSG-70, firing the uncommon 7.62 mm full-metal-jacket round, had the powerful Starlite night scope and a brutally efficient laser image enhancer.

Working the bolt action with fluid ease, the skinny Armorer pumped all ten rounds into a group less than a hand's span across, each hit being greeted by a wave of the green flag by the servants acting as markers at the far end of the butts.

None of the sec men got more than half their shots on the target.

They all stood, but J.B. lay still, looking up at them. "What's happening?"

"You won, outlander," one of them grunted ungraciously. "Beat us out of sight."

"We not going on to the half mile?"

"No fucking point, is there?"

Mandeville gave the signal to Guiteau, who clapped his hands together. "Let's hear it for John Dix, winner of the long-gun shooting."

The applause was scattered and hesitant.

None of the workers from the ville wanted to seem too enthusiastic in supporting the victory of any outlander. Not with the baron watching them so closely.

Marie Mandeville hardly seemed to be noticing what was happening.

Nor did Michael, whose left hand was clasped firmly in her long-nailed fingers.

NATHAN MANDEVILLE WAS becoming distinctly unhappy and decided that the knife fighting would have no preliminaries. He ordered Guiteau to pick his best man to go against Ryan Cawdor.

But there was something vaguely puzzling and disturbing about the baron's reaction. Despite his obvious unhappiness at the easy wins for Michael and J.B., there was something else going on behind the white beard and cheery smile.

While Ryan stripped off his coat and gave the Uzi to Dean to look after, Guiteau ghosted up to him again. "That's two bad mistakes, now."

"Want to explain?"

The sec man touched his scarred left cheek in an unconscious movement. "No."

It was like the sort of "safe" fight that Ryan had seen in dozens of frontier pesthole drinkers, where an argument had been fueled by jolt or gut-rotting whiskey but hadn't become serious enough for blood to be spilled.

Ryan and his opponent were each given a long-hilted dagger, the blade nine inches long. But the steel was well protected with layers of thin muslin tied tightly in place, and then soaked in paint—traditionally red—so that any hit would be marked.

It was yet another sec man. This one was young, barely out of his teens, slimly built and light on his feet, wearing tight pants and bare to the waist. He carried a star-shaped scar above his right eye. Ryan was impressed with the catlike balance and ease of the youth, guessing that he'd be both quick and cunning.

"Want some free advice, outlander?" The sec sergeant had joined him again.

"No, but you're going to give it to me anyway, aren't you, Guiteau?"

"Sure."

"Well?"

"Be easy to slip on the grass. Late afternoon. Could be getting greasy. Take a streak of paint and then everybody's happy. Know what I mean?"

"If I lose, it's because that wet-behind-the-ears kid's better than me."

Guiteau spread his hands. "You don't know what good advice that was, too."

"Will I find out?" He tried to work out what precisely was going on.

"Sure. Keep winning. But it might be your friends have gone too far down the road."

But Harry Guiteau wouldn't say any more about the enigma and walked slowly away to settle down on the turf near his baron's throne.

"Watch him come in low," J.B. said, strolling casually over to where Ryan was getting the feel of the knife. "Went to take a leak, and a couple of those fop bastards were jawing. Reckon the boy's fast and clever." He turned, then checked himself. "What did old Harry want?"

"Nothing."

"Go!" the baron snapped, his hand cutting down as the signal to them.

The crowd immediately began to bay for a success for the ville. Ryan sensed that the young man was genuinely popular with the watching servants and that this time their shouting wasn't inspired by fear of their baron.

The sec man grinned nervously, coming in toward Ryan in a slow crabbing circle, the paint-smeared knife held, as J.B. had predicted, very low.

For a minute or two they fenced, the sodden cloth making no sound as they thrust and parried, almost like swordsmen. Twice the younger man tried to duck and step in, aiming for Ryan's lower stomach and groin, in a classic knife-fighter's move. But each time the one-eyed man spotted the attack coming and easily stepped away from it.

Mandeville's champion was very good indeed, making Ryan aware of a passing relief that they weren't going at it for real with naked steel.

Once, as Ryan dodged back, his feet slipped on the damp grass and he nearly went over, but the youth held off, suspecting a trick to lure him in. Guiteau had half risen, sitting down again, catching Ryan's eye with a wry grin.

The climax came, as it would in a true combat, in the flickering of an eye.

The young sec man feinted low and then gambled all on a cut at Ryan's throat. The one-eyed man had nearly fallen for the ruse, starting to drop his guard, only checking himself at the last splinter of a second, driving instead for his opponent's stomach.

He felt his knife land, hard, and a moment later had a sensation of cold across the front of his neck, realizing that the counter had come close to working.

Ryan stepped back smiling, holding out a hand. "That was good, son. Nearly had me."

There was a smear of crimson just above the sec man's belt, dead center. Ryan touched his own neck, fingers coming away stained red.

The crowd of watchers were all cheering, but it took a few seconds for Ryan to realize that they all thought that the ville had won. They hadn't properly seen his own lunge and believed that the cut to the neck had been decisive.

"I beat you, outlander." The young man scowled.

"You know you didn't. And I know you didn't. Talk won't change that, son."

"Fuck you."

"It was a draw!" Guiteau shouted, but nobody heard him above the hubbub of yelling.

Mandeville was up, punching one hand into the other, laughing triumphantly.

Ryan saw that even J.B., Krysty and the others were doubtful. In the close whirl of the combat, the two blows had come too close together for the onlookers to be sure. But he knew, and the other man knew.

He remembered Guiteau's warning and smiled ruefully. "Yeah. Guess I could probably be wrong about it. You might just have shaded me."

"Fuck you." The cloth was ripped away, and the late-afternoon sun glowed scarlet on the cold steel.

Ryan didn't hesitate. He dropped his knife to the trodden turf and drew the SIG-Sauer P-226 from its holster, leveling it at the young man's chest.

"Don't," he said, having to raise his voice over the roar of anger from the crowd.

From the corner of his good eye Ryan could see that J.B. and Krysty had also drawn their blasters, the Armorer swiveling to cover Mandeville and Guiteau with the Uzi.

For a single heartbeat, he thought that the youth was going to call his bluff and come at him with the dagger.

Because, of course, it wasn't a bluff.

He was totally prepared to pull the trigger and blow a hole clean through the sec man's chest.

The voice that rang out belonged to Marie Mandeville.

"Put that knife down and stand back, or you're a dead man. Now!"

The crack of command was unmistakable, and the youth responded to it. He opened his fingers and allowed the paint-blotched steel to fall to the dirt, spitting on it and turning his back, walking away from Ryan to cheers of sympathy and support from the crowd.

The blaster slid into its holster, and Ryan took his seat again, acknowledging the squeeze of Krysty's hand.

Mandeville was on his feet. "A draw!" he called. "I say it was a fair draw. Before the special fight that will end the afternoon, we have the handblaster competition. Your own, your very own, Harry Guiteau against . . ." He gestured toward Mildred. "Against her."

"Careful, love," J.B. whispered.

Chapter Twenty-Six

Guiteau vanished while servants were bustling around, setting up targets for the handblaster shooting.

Human silhouettes had been pasted onto hardboard, life-size, painted like charging muties, suckered hands stretching out. They were fixed along the butts at thirty paces, seventy-five paces and one hundred paces.

"What kind of blaster is he going to turn up with?" Mildred was waiting for J.B. to give a final once-over to her ZKR 551, the Czech revolver.

"Don't forget the baron reckons to have a good gun collection," the Armorer replied. "Could be anything from a flintlock onward. Might be shit. Might not."

Krysty joined them. "Don't look around now," she said quietly. "No, don't. But in a minute, sort of casual, glance at Michael and that basking shark next to him."

"Why?" Ryan asked.

"They're both kind of huddled up, and she's got a servant to bring a cloak. But it slipped away and I'm sure she's pulled his dick out and is—"

The loud voice of Baron Mandeville interrupted her. Ryan looked quickly around, but the embroidered cloak was sedately in place over the laps of Marie and Michael and it was impossible to guess what might be going on under it. Though the face of the teenager was certainly flushed. He caught Ryan's gaze and stared pointedly away.

"Last contest of the day," the Baron shouted. "Sergeant Guiteau versus the woman doctor here. Six rounds at each distance. So quiet down, people."

Like a ghost appearing at midnight in a haunted chamber, Harry Guiteau was suddenly among them, holding a walnut gun case, inlaid with ebony filigree.

"Ready when you are, Miss Wyeth," he said.

"Mind showing me your blaster?" J.B. asked.

"Sure." Guiteau pressed the silver catches and flipped open the lid.

"Dark night!" J.B. took off his spectacles and polished them with a white kerchief, whistling softly between his teeth as he replaced the glasses, adjusting them on the bridge of his narrow nose. Then he peered into the custom-made case.

Ryan also looked in, seeing one of the most beautiful and unusual handblasters he'd ever encountered.

"What is it, J.B.?"

"Colt Whitetaler, Mark Two. It's triple-rare. Seen pix of them in the old specialist catalogs. Never dreamed I'd see one."

"More and better than that in my collection, Dix," Nathan Mandeville called. "Perhaps after breaking our fasts in the morning, we could take a look."

"I'd love that, Baron," the Armorer replied.

Guiteau took the weapon carefully out, handing it to J.B., who ran his fingers over it as though it were a genuine fragment of the true Cross.

"Eight-inch barrel, .357 Magnum. King Cobra. Combat grips, black rubber. Lovely balance. Stainless steel. The sight's brushed aluminum. One and a half to four times Burris scope. Millett satin nickel mounts. Made in about 1984 or so?"

"Eighty-six." The sec man smiled. "Only one thousand of the suckers were ever made. Baron reckons that this little beauty is probably the only one left in the whole world."

"Probably right," J.B. agreed. "Better be on form against this, Mildred."

"Not the size of what you got, it's how you use it that counts," she replied, walking calmly to take her place on the marked line.

The silvery scope set on the top of the Colt was markedly longer than the actual barrel, making the revolver look a little clumsy.

But Guiteau showed it wasn't clumsy by putting every one of his first six rounds into the small circle over the heart of the thirty-yard mutie.

Mildred took her time, lowering and raising her own revolver between each shot, standing sideways on, firing two-eyed, placing every one of the big .38s into the target.

She repeated the feat at the next distance, and a third time, producing a perfect performance at one hundred paces.

It was brilliant shooting with a handblaster.

But Guiteau managed to match her.

He squinted through the scope, firing a little faster than Mildred, but achieving a flawless score of three hundred and sixty from a possible three hundred and sixty.

He hadn't exchanged a word or a glance with Mildred, simply taking up his position and doing his job.

Now it was over, polite applause greeting each of the competitors. It didn't surprise Ryan to realize that Harry Guiteau didn't rank all that high in the popularity stakes at Sun Crest ville.

"Another draw," Mandeville called. "And I doubt that any man or woman in the whole of Deathlands, from the New York . . . Well, anywhere, could do better than these two marksmen."

"Why not find some way of splitting them, father?" Marie said. "I'm sure that the sergeant would want to defend the honor of his baron until the bitter end."

"I'll go on," Guiteau replied.

"Me, too," Mildred agreed.

"Let them fight a duel."

Michael snatched at Marie's arm when she made the suggestion, but she shrugged him off.

"No," Mildred said firmly.

"Scared?" Guiteau was sweating, though the sun was mostly gone and the afternoon was becoming much cooler. The eastern skyline was dappled with menacing purple clouds that warned of a building chem storm.

"I've killed people." She holstered her empty revolver. "When there was a reason. I won't kill you because some spoiled brat wants to get her kicks over it."

You could have taken the silence and sliced it thin with a straight razor.

Guiteau broke it, speaking directly to the baron. "I can't fight her if she won't face me."

Marie pushed Michael out of her way and leaned across her father, whispering intently in his ear. All the time she was talking, her brown, slanted eyes were fixed on Ryan, who stared back at her, wondering what was going on.

Mandeville nodded once, then shook his head, opening his mouth as though he were about to speak. He closed it again, then nodded twice more.

Marie straightened, smiling, and resumed her seat next to Michael, offering him her gloved hand to kiss, which he obediently did.

The crowd was restless, shifting and murmuring, unable to guess what was going on.

Finally Nathan Mandeville beckoned Guiteau to him, leaning forward and whispering, just as his daughter had.

The sec man showed no hint of emotion, his eyes looking vacantly over his master's shoulder toward the nearest towers of the ville.

He nodded and muttered something that seemed to be agreement.

With the exception of Michael, the rest of the friends were grouped tightly around Mildred. "Triple-red," Ryan mouthed. "Don't like this. The bitch had an idea, and it tied in with something been growing in the baron's mind all afternoon. You can bet your blaster it involves us in some way."

But the baron was back in Santa mode, all jolly smiles and good humor.

"A draw. These outlanders are fearful opponents, aren't they? They beat our best at wrestling and at shooting with the long blasters. Then a draw in knife-fighting, and here we have a woman who has taken our favored Sergeant, Harry Guiteau, all the way to the wire."

Far off to the east, Ryan's eye was caught by a ferocious slash of chem lightning, a brilliant pinkish silver that left its image on the retina long after it had disappeared. He waited for the thunder, but the heart of the storm was too far away.

Mandeville had also seen it. "We had best finish our afternoon's sport and relaxation before the weather sends us running to the ville."

Guiteau was back, standing at Ryan's elbow. "So, you had to all show off how good you were and what fine blasters you got." There was a strange note to his voice that hadn't been there before. Part of it was triumph for his own fine performance with the revolver. Part was an odd regret, as if something had happened that he deeply regretted but couldn't do anything to influence.

"So?" Dean said cockily. "We just showed that when you want an ace on the line, you send for us."

"Sure, son." He ruffled the boy's black curly hair. "But it would have been ... Shit, I'm losing it in my old age. Forget it, outlanders."

"What's this grudge fight coming now?" Krysty asked. "Servants from the ville want to settle an argument?"

"Sort of. From the lands around the ville. Opposite direction to where we found you all. Tribe call themselves the wildwooders. Ragged-assed bunch of poxed and rad-sick bastards. Steal game, birds and fish. Upsets the baron. Nobody likes a hunt as much as he does."

"So who is fighting?" J.B. asked.

"Wildwooders."

"It can hardly be a fair contest if these poor folk are set against your sec men." Doc shook his head sorrowfully. "I hope it will not be as unfairly one-sided as that poor devil who was butchered in the forest."

Guiteau sniffed, rubbing again at his scar. "Don't worry, Doc. Not them against us."

"Then who do they fight?" said Ryan.

"Each other, of course."

THERE WERE FIVE PRISONERS, all, it was thought, from the same family. A wizened old woman stood barely five feet tall, with white hair cropped so short that her scabby gray scalp showed through in several places. She was naked above the waist, her withered dugs hanging slack and barren.

A tall, gangling youth looked to be around fifteen, with the simperingly vacant smile of a triple-stupe. He didn't seem to have any idea of where he was or why he was there, and grinned amiably at everyone, in contrast to the vicious temperament of his grandmother, who spat ferociously at everybody who ventured within range of her spleen.

A middle-aged woman had a dreadful skin disease that had left her entire face and body a mass of running, suppurating sores. She had lost an eye and wore a filthy scarf tied over the empty, weeping socket.

The father looked fairly normal, standing with his hands chained behind him, head bowed, occasionally glancing around to see what was happening. His clothes were torn but clean, and there was an empty knife sheath at his belt.

Fifth was another son. Ryan's guess put him in his middle twenties, bearded, with long reddish hair. Like the rest of the family of wildwooders, his wrists were chained together. There was what looked like an untreated gunshot wound through his left shoulder.

The five were linked together with a long steel chain that was looped around each neck.

"How does this work, Guiteau?" Mildred asked. "They fight each other and then what?"

"One gets left alive."

"You mean they have to try to kill each other?" Ryan was disgusted. "While we all stand and applaud them? Son slaughters grandmother. Or mother chills husband? You're bastard sick, Harry. I'm leaving."

"No."

"I don't believe that you can compel us to remain here and watch this sick-brain spectacle," Doc said, his eyes narrowed with anger.

"You believe wrong, Doc," Guiteau replied. "Baron has plans for you all that he can tell you about some time. Not my place to do that."

"Obeying orders again." Mildred sneered.

"But he'd have you all gunned down without blinking if you went against his afternoon's sporting."

"Be a lot of blood spilled if that happened." J.B. made it obvious that this was a simple promise and not an idle threat to the sec man.

Guiteau smiled, genuinely amused. "Think that worries me or the baron, outlander? Main thing is that some of the spilled blood would be yours. All of you. Rest doesn't matter."

Nobody had noticed that Michael had walked from the raised dais and now stood by them, with Marie Mandeville holding his hand.

Krysty turned to the woman. "You truly don't have any sort of a conscience, do you?"

The mistress of Sun Crest smiled, showing perfect white teeth. "Conscience? Conscience, Krysty Wroth, is a dying moth fluttering in an empty attic."

"What happens to the one left alive?" Dean asked. "You let him go?"

"Sure," Guiteau replied. "But we kind of make certain he doesn't cause trouble for the baron again."

"How?"

"We call it the four by one," Marie replied. "They go free, minus one ear, one eye, one hand and one foot. We allow them to choose which. The left or the right. We are not barbarians."

"Generosity...that could be your big mistake," Mildred said, her voice thick with ironic anger.

The woman smiled and snapped her fingers, the dying sun glittering off the strange ring with the realistic human eye sealed into it.

"I'll still be generous long after the worms are shitting in your mouth, lady," she said. "Come on, Mickey. Come and watch the last of the sport."

Before any of them could say a word, she had led the teenager back to the dais, carefully draping her long cloak across both their laps.

"Someone better speak to that boy," Doc said, poking at the grass with the ferrule of the sword stick. "I am not one to talk ill of a lady, but that ferocious dragon whore is most certainly not a lady."

There was the rattling of steel as the chain was unshackled from the necks of the wildwood prisoners. Their cuffs were removed, and they were pushed by half a dozen sec men into a ragged line in front of the baron.

There was a distinct rumble of thunder, echoing around the sky, and more lightning from the east.

Ryan and the others finally sat down and waited for the day to reach its brutal ending.

Chapter Twenty-Seven

Oddly it wasn't the first time that Ryan had encountered this kind of punishment being meted out by a powerful baron.

There had been a ville in the bayous, with its center in an ancient tumbling church. The war wags had been passing by on a trading mission and arrived for the climax of the revolt. A number of sec men had plotted rebellion, but had been stupid or unlucky enough to get found out before they had a chance to put their plan into operation. Barons didn't usually appreciate treason, particularly from within their ranks.

The men were mostly burned alive.

But the leaders were a father and son.

And the baron saved his best for them.

There had been eight small glasses on the table in front of the two prisoners, each containing a measure of a colorless liquid. Seven of the eight held only water. The eighth was a deadly poison that would act with agonizing slowness. The survivor was promised he'd walk free, though banished from the lands of the baron.

The simple but malevolent idea was that father and son would take a drink from alternate glasses, until one of them stumbled upon the poisoned chalice.

But the baron was deprived of his sport.

Before either of them could begin the torturous process, the father turned and struck his son a ferocious punch to the stomach, knocking him gasping to the floor. Before the baron, his watching guests or any of the circle of sec men could act, the man snatched the glasses and drained them all.

Ryan remembered that the Trader had been disgusted when the baron had personally executed the surviving son as his father lay dying. But he hadn't felt that the broken promise was an issue worth drawing the blasters over.

There the setting had been the nave of the church, with the fragmentary remnants of a beautiful stained-glass window dominating the scene.

Now it was the grassy arena at the end of the shooting butts, with trees all around and the skies darkening, the chem storm moving toward them faster than a galloping horse. And the silent ring of onlookers.

The family of wildwooders stood in a ragged semicircle. The old woman had dropped to her knees and was plucking up dried leaves from the turf, touching them to her breasts, then crunching them between her gums.

The younger boy clapped his hands together when he was released, the crusted blood from the cuffs beginning to run crimson again.

Guiteau had taken charge of the proceedings, holding five identical horn-hilted daggers, with short six-inch blades. He stuck them into the ground, keeping a careful eye on the prisoners in case any of them went for him.

But they seemed to be completely passive and cowed.

"Listen up!" he shouted. "Baron Mandeville in his mercy has willed that one of you can go free from here, despite the crimes you committed by stealing a deer and several rabbits from the lands of this ville. There are five knives here. You are each to take one and then fight until there is only one survivor. Do you understand?" The prisoners remained silent. Guiteau spat on the ground. "Take the fucking knives and fight to the death."

The father of the wildwooders finally showed some response, ignoring the sec man, speaking directly to the baron. His voice was low and grating, so heavily accented that it was difficult to understand.

"Animals come from forest gods. Fed by sun and rain. Free for all men. You got not a right to say they's yourn. We don't fight son and grandam. Won't."

"Tell him, Guiteau," Marie Mandeville commanded. "Tell the ball-brained clod what happens if they don't fight."

"Yes, lady." He stepped in closer to the leader of the little group, poking him in the chest with the muzzle of the Armalite. "You don't get it, do you? You fight and one of you gets to walk free. Well, mebbe hop free. But you'll live. One of you. You refuse and you go to the cellars of the ville to the hot irons, the probes, the rack, the cold water and the screws and vices. You'll all pray to your heathen gods for death, and it won't come. Your eyes'll sizzle and you'll try to scream, but you won't have no tongue to scream with. Take the knives and get on with it. Now!"

He stepped away, not taking his gaze from them. There was a long rumble of thunder and the sky seemed to grow darker by the minute. A fresh wind had risen, soughing through the tops of the surrounding trees.

The father stooped and picked up the five knives, looking down at them as though he had no idea what they were.

"Yes." The syllable came from the red-bearded young man. "But not like they want."

"How?"

The son, father and mother all drew together, talking in urgent whispers, inaudible to any of the watchers.

"That storm'll be here if they don't get a move on," J.B. said.

Guiteau glanced back toward the raised platform, but Ryan realized that he was looking to Marie, rather than the baron, for orders.

The deaths came almost unnoticed.

The father spun on his heel with a grace that belied his clumsy, oafish appearance. He gripped the crouching old woman with surprising gentleness and cut her throat from ear to ear, driving the blade in, the soft crack of cartilage parting, and pulling it across from left to right.

The bearded son took out his brother. He put one arm around his neck, and, kissing him once on the cheek, thrust the knife in under his ribs so hard that he lifted the skinny boy clean off his feet. He held him as he died, then lowered him gently to the turf.

Ryan was aware that Krysty was silently crying.

"Don't let them—" Marie began, rising to her feet, her hair blowing in the wind like a funeral veil.

But her order was too late.

The mother waited for her doom, smiling as husband and son stabbed her simultaneously in the chest and back, the thud of the blows audible above the rumbling noise of the advancing chem storm.

The tall son dropped his bloodied knife and stood with arms spread, like Christ crucified, nodding to his weeping father to chill him.

The stubby blade sank home, the man giving the lethal twist to his wrist before withdrawing the dagger. His son fell to his knees, then slid forward on his face, like a wearied laborer taking to his welcome bed.

There was a moment of infinite stillness, the four bodies and the father frozen like flies trapped in amber.

Krysty touched Ryan urgently on the arm. "He's going to—" she began, but her "seeing" was too slow, overtaken by the event that she saw.

The wildwooder looked around him at the ring of staring faces, his eyes landing on Mandeville. "Dogs'll lick your blood," he said, and threw the crimson knife at the baron's throat.

If he hadn't seen it for himself, Ryan would never have believed it.

Michael stood up and leaned toward the rubicund figure at his side, reaching out with his left hand and grabbing the whirling dagger by its hilt, inches from the neck of the helpless Mandeville.

Simultaneously Guiteau squeezed off three rounds from his Armalite AR 190. Set for triple-burst, the bullets tore into the wildwooder's chest at almost point-blank range, knocking him off his feet, to lie still in the blood-slick grass beside the rest of his dead family.

One of the high-velocity rounds went clean through the man's body and ripped the right ear off a scullery girl on the far side of the butts.

There was a moment of chaotic confusion, with part of the crowd having no idea at all what had happened.

Several of the sec men spun to cover Michael, who was looming over their lord with a bloody knife in his hand. Others were staring wildly out into the woods, as if they were trying to locate the shooter who'd wounded the young woman.

Ryan had drawn his SIG-Sauer, ready to put a bullet into the first man who opened fire on the teenager.

"It's all done. Finished." Marie Mandeville's pure, cold voice rang out across the gathering, like a warning bell in a cathedral tower, holding the moment.

"Easy," Harry Guiteau said, lifting the blaster over his head, catching the eyes of the nervous sec men. "Outlander saved the life of the baron. Stray round caught the girl."

Krysty wiped her eyes, shaking her head. "Double-bad scene, lover," she whispered.

Ryan felt a few spots of light rain dash on his cheeks. He put his tongue out to lick the water, grimacing at its bitterness. "Acid," he said. "Sooner we all get back inside the ville the better."

The early years in Deathlands, after skydark, had been a time of neomythical horrors. The heavens were filled with all manner of rad-high nuke junk, circling around from the Star Wars conflict, dropping back to Earth with lethal and monotonous regularity. The whole globe and the skies around it had been hideously polluted by the holocaust, producing all manner of changes in the entire interdependent eco-structure.

One of the worst side effects had been acid rains—not like the bleeding-heart green liberals of the late nineties meant acid rain.

This was rain that could, so the stories went, flay the flesh off a man caught in the open. Burn him down to whitened bones within minutes.

From his journeyings with the Trader, Ryan knew that mutations of the atmosphere were rarely so powerful nowadays, though there were still places, particularly near the Gulf, where murderous acid storms could blow up.

The current chem storm was nothing like that, but the acidic taste was strong enough for Ryan to want to get out of it as quickly as possible.

It was obvious that everyone felt the same.

Rubberized capes appeared from nowhere to shelter the baron and Mistress Marie. They both headed toward the towers of Sun Crest, surrounded by a posse of sec guards. Ryan saw Michael at the woman's side.

The rest of them made their own way toward the fortified walls through the rising wind. The thunder was ceaseless, and one flash of purple lightning struck close enough in the forest for Ryan to be able to catch the bitter stench of ozone.

He glanced back once over his shoulder to see that the corpses had been left to lie where they'd fallen, the tumbling rain already washing away the thick blood.

"WISH WE COULD HAVE LUXURY like this after every chem storm, lover." Krysty was drying herself on a large white towel after enjoying a hot, scented bath. Their clothes had been taken away by the bevy of servants and were being dried.

Ryan had asked for some cream to ease the irritation of the acid rain penetrating behind the patch over his missing left eye, burning the tender flesh of the raw socket. The girl had brought him some light cream balm within a couple of minutes.

"Looking forward to a meal now," he said.

"I think the day went well..."

"You don't sound sure."

"I'm not." She had rubbed her hair dry, and it was now tumbled across her shoulders in a torrent of fire.

"Guiteau knows more than he lets on."

"Something bad?"

Ryan nodded. "Has to be. Baron says he'll show us his guns tomorrow. Real proud of them. What then?"

"We move on, I guess." Krysty helped herself to a nectarine from a ceramic bowl of fresh fruit. "Mmm, tender and juicy. Think he'll try to stop us?"

"Mandeville? Trader used to say that you never trust a man who smiles a lot."

"How about trusting a woman with the blackest hair in all of Deathlands?"

"Marie? Sort of woman that makes you want to count your fingers after you've shaken hands with her. Doc sometimes uses that old-time predark word 'evil' when he's talking about someone. Guess that applies to Marie."

"You best have a word with Michael, over the meal, Ryan. Set the boy straight."

"Guess so. Long as Marie hasn't got her claws into him too deep."

Krysty ran the tips of her fingers over his cheeks. "Could use a shave, lover. Then the clothes'll be back. Down to the meal. And a long talk to Michael."

Nearly everything happened like she said. Apart from Ryan having a quiet word of warning with the teenager.

That wasn't possible. Michael never came down to eat in the galleried dining hall.

Nor did Marie Mandeville.

Chapter Twenty-Eight

Michael Brother was two floors above the dining room in the exotic suite of chambers at the top of the tower that dominated the east wing.

"They belonged to my stepmother, Fuschia," Marie explained. "After her sad death, I took them over for myself. You like them?"

"Sure. When did your mother die?"

"Stepmother, Mickey. Fuschia wasn't my real mother. She died during the troubles when my father took power. Fuschia choked to death on a plate of strawberry jelly. Quite a mystery at the time, you know."

Michael was stretched out across the biggest bed he'd ever seen. Though he was stark naked, he wasn't feeling cold. A large fire of applewood crackled sweetly in the hearth.

A number of tall, slender vases of beaten silver stood around the rooms, all filled with wonderfully scented tapers. He remembered incense from his years at Nil-Vanity—Russian musk, summer lime, patchouli and sandalwood.

He felt wonderfully at ease. His limbs seemed slightly too heavy for his body, a thought that made him giggle to himself. He turned his head to admire the wondrous pattern on the coverlet, small squares of brightly colored satins and silks, sewn together into a pattern that seemed to draw the eye inward.

"More brandy?" Marie asked.

Michael blinked owlishly. The woman was sitting with her back to him, at the table where they'd just finished eating. She was wearing a loose robe, with a wildly complex embroidery of a fire-breathing dragon on it. Her long black hair shone with an unnatural luster. He wanted to go and brush it for her, with the ivory hairbrush with the handle carved like an erect male organ. Then he remembered that he already had brushed her hair for her. Before or after the meal.

"Before or after?" he whispered, puzzled that his voice was so quiet, as if his tongue had been removed and replaced with one that was slightly too large for his mouth.

From the back, Marie looked as though she were quite demurely dressed. But he could see her reflection in the long mahogany cheval mirror that stood against the far wall, to the left of the thick draperies.

The reflection wasn't demurely dressed.

Her breasts were uncovered, the nipples circled in a kind of soft red wax. Marie was sitting with her legs stretched out in front of her, slightly apart.

The teenager's slightly blurred eyes focused on the tops of her thighs. Her panties weren't like anything he'd ever seen before. They were a brilliant maroon color, with a silky sheen to them. But they were oddly split at the front, revealing bushy curls of jet-black hair.

He remembered that a novitiate at Nil-Vanity had once smuggled in a porno magazine, showing it around the dormitory after lights-out, by the dull gleam of a torch. It had naked or seminaked women, flaunting their bodies at the camera, touching themselves "down there" and actually using their own fingers to expose the pink inner lips. Most of the pix were such extreme close-ups that Michael had found it extremely difficult to work out what exactly he was peering at. He didn't want to have to face the mockery of his peers, so he pretended excitement. The real truth was he could have been looking at a plate of raw steak for all it meant to him.

But this was so different.

Marie Mandeville was also wearing long boots, loose above the knee and tight below. They were of immaculate white kid, with tapering heels of silvered steel, cast in the same shape as the handle of the ivory hairbrush.

She was singing quietly to herself, and caught him looking at her in the mirror, smiling at him. The woman stuck out the tip of her scarlet tongue and ran it slowly between her lips, opening her legs a little wider, allowing her hand to trail down over the maroon silk.

Michael knew that he was caught, helplessly trapped. Emotions raced through his body in a way that he'd never experienced before. Even in his wildest, midnight-moist dreams, he had never imagined such sexual power. Whatever this goddess required of him, he would have to do it.

"You like what you see, Mickey?" Her voice was low and breathy. "Tell me."

"Very much." The prominent state of his body's response would have made a lie quite grotesque.

"I have an idea, dear boy."

"What?"

"I'll come and join you on the bed and while we take some pleasure we can watch some vids."

"Vids? Old predarkies?"

"Goodness, no. Though goodness doesn't have much to do with these vids. Nathan has such wealth and power he can obtain everything. He bought one of the tiny number of working vid cams in Deathlands and some cassies to go with it. These are new and very exclusive vids that have only been seen by a special few close friends."

"Were those squawking parrots who were with you in the forest such friends?"

Marie stood, stretching her shoulders back, lifting her breasts. "Now and again, when I'm bored. But they are not 'special' like you are, Mickey. When the others are gone, you will remain here and save me from being bored."

Her words slithered through the cramped corridors of his mind, but didn't quite make sense.

"When the other are gone? Which others?"

"The one-eye and the red-hair and the others. They'll very soon be gone, but I can keep you safe."

She drained a goblet of pink crystal that had been a third filled with the fiery brandy. A small part of Michael's mind realized that he had become dangerously drunk. And so had Mistress Marie.

"Safe? Don't..."

She sat on the bed, crossing the legs in a whisper of leather. "Don't worry, child. Would you like something else to eat before we watch the vids?"

Part of Michael's mind wanted to pursue her odd, lateral comments. Ryan was going? And the others? But he would stay. Where would they go? The idea that he could stay forever in this languorous bedchamber with this amazing woman seemed like a glimpse of a profane paradise.

She reached out a long-nailed hand and gripped his erection, making him gasp. The sensation was so powerful that he was frightened for a moment that he would suddenly come all over her fingers and the silk coverlet.

"Do you need more food, I said."

"Oh, no. It was wonderful."

Though the truth was he hadn't much cared for some of the weird specialties she kept pressing on him. Oysters were slippery and cold, though he liked the way Marie threw back her head, mouth wide open, and gulped the oysters down, leaving a tantalizing thread of clear, sticky liquid dangling from her parted lips.

The fish eggs were bitter and salty, though she had boasted about their cost and rarity. But the steak, underdone, with creamed potatoes and garlic had been fine. So had the fluffy apricots, whipped up with cream and some kind of liqueur.

And the wines!

So many, some sweet and some dry. Some chilled and some at the temperature of the warm room. One of them had been delicious, fizzy and sharp. The heavy bottle had popped and foamed when Marie thumbed open the cork.

Her hand was still on him, squeezing hard, harder than Michael wanted, but he didn't protest.

"Go and turn off the lights, Mickey," she said. "Then press the white button on the table at the top of the bed."

"Sure."

"But first, a little kissing."

"Yeah." He leaned toward her smooth face, starting to close his eyes in anticipation.

"Not on the mouth, sweet one. Not yet. A kiss for the toe of each of my boots. Show you'll do what I tell you. Then a kiss on each knee. Then a long slow kiss just *here*. Her other hand slid between her thighs.

Michael nodded, though this wasn't turning out like he'd expected. He slid down off the bed, kneeling on the floor, taking her foot in his hand and kissing the soft leather, savoring the animal scent. He repeated the procedure on the other foot, then on the inside of each knee.

Her hands were on top of his head, locked in his hair, pulling him closer and higher, tugging his face into her body. His tongue, hesitant, flicked out, tasting her musky flavor, the mat of dark hair tickling his cheeks. Marie clamped her powerful thighs tight around his head, blotting out all sound, making it hard for the youth to breathe.

Seconds, or minutes, or hours later, the woman pushed him violently away from her, so that he sprawled on his back on the thick carpet. Her pale face was flushed, and her dark eyes narrowed as she looked down at him.

"That was exquisite, Mickey," she whispered. "So gentle and so pleasing. Later we can . . . But first the vids."

He rose clumsily and turned off the lights, so that only the glow of the fire illuminated the bedroom. He climbed back on the bed, finger poised over the button, hesitating.

"What is it?" A distinct touch of sharpness tinged her voice. "Do it."

"What did you mean about the others going, Marie?"

"Oh, nothing. Just my silly tongue running away. Just like your lovely tongue nearly ran away with me just now. All you need to think about is you being safe because I'll protect you."

Somehow, through the muddling effects of the mixture of alcoholic drinks, the teenager wondered how it could be, that if he was to be safe, then it seemed that it must logically follow that Ryan and the others might be in danger. It didn't make any sort of sense.

But now Marie Mandeville had wriggled her way up the enormous bed toward him. Her mouth was hot and deep and nothing else mattered. At one point Michael asked whether he'd be going back to his own room before the night was out. Marie smiled and said that he would go when she allowed him to go. He mentioned the worry of the patrolling sec guards. But she smiled again and patted his cheek, explaining patiently that her orders had cleared the corridors between her suite and the rooms of the visiting outlanders.

HE FOUND IT amazingly difficult to concentrate on the flickering vids projected onto a small white panel close to the fireplace.

The quality wasn't good, with the focus often blurring and the lighting inconsistent.

But it wasn't hard to see what the subject matter was of the films.

Michael wasn't able to watch all of them.

Some of the time he was being forced into repeating the performance from earlier in the evening, beginning with Marie's boots. With the added refinement of sucking the perverted shape of the heels.

Some of the time he was on the bed, flat on his back while the older woman straddled him, riding him as though he were a favored Thoroughbred stallion. She'd leaned forward to kiss him on the lips, biting at his neck so hard that she drew worms of blood, using her long, painted nails to scratch crimson weals over his chest and stomach.

And all of it was wonderful.

At one point she'd taken a tiny, beak-bladed knife and used it to cut up a fine white powder across an ornamental mirror shaped like a rose, forming it into narrow lines that she ordered him to sniff up through a tiny golden tube. Michael suspected that it must be what he'd heard Ryan and J.B. talk about as jolt, the common drug of choice in Deathlands.

But it was also wonderful. The jolt rushed through his brain and body, seeking out his extremities, making fingers and toes thrill and tingle. Though he'd already come three times into various secret places of Marie's voraciously lean body, the drug brought him again to a powerful erection, making the teenager feel that he could go on making love forever.

And ever.

After the fourth time, she finally seemed sated, lying back with her head on the pillow, the wondrous tempest of raven hair spread out around her.

And they watched the vids, endless combinations of men and women and boys and girls, some of them looking barely into their teens, a factor that made Michael begin to feel uneasy stirrings of concern about what was happening.

But the mixture of sex, drugs and drink still cloaked his conscience.

The couplings were limitless.

A masked woman, wrists and ankles tied to the corners of a bed, was being pleasured by five men at once, three of the men also being simultaneously penetrated by younger women with artificial strap-on penises.

"Isn't it the most wonderful thing to do?" Marie whispered. "To have power. Total power. To compel others to do *anything.*" The last word was drawn out forever.

She crawled down Michael's abused body, making him wince at the contact, as some of his scratches and bites were becoming painful. She touched him, giggling at his readiness. But the ornate silver human-eye ring that she wore scraped at his tender flesh, and he winced and cried out.

"Sorry, Mickey," she said, smiling at him, teeth white in the gloom. "But you mustn't pull away from me. Not ever, or I'll get angry and you wouldn't like that at all!" She squeezed his genitals so brutally that he nearly passed out. "Perhaps I should chain you up, dear little boy. We'll see about that later. But now I feel hungry again."

While she used her mouth on him, Michael stared blankly at the white rectangle on the far wall, hardly noticing what was going on.

Every possible perversion was there, including abuses of animals that disgusted him. For the first time he felt his penis beginning to lose its diamond strength. She felt it too, pushing her right hand between his spread thighs and using her index finger to keep him roused.

"Don't lose it now, or you might lose it forever," she whispered, looking up at him from between his legs, her eyes half-closed, lips swollen, looking, suddenly, much older.

He stared at the vid again, trying to concentrate on arousal, despite the growing nausea that he could feel seeding itself in the pit of his stomach. It was a dark room, with walls built from rough stone slabs. The only light came from a fire in the hearth, and the only furniture was a table with iron shackles at each corner. A youth was led into the room by two hooded sec men in the distinctive maroon livery of Baron Mandeville. A third person walked behind them, also hooded, slighter built. The youth's bright blue eyes were wide with terror. Unlike some of the earlier sections of the porno vids, this one had no sound.

The victim wore a long gown of white linen, fringed with yellowing lace. It was stripped off him and he was quickly placed on the table and tied there, his ribs strained with the effort of each frightened breath.

Michael felt the sickness rising.

There was a cut in the vid, jagged white lines, then the picture resumed. During the period of blackness, the youth had been brutally beaten. Bruises discolored his cheeks, and blood seeped from his mouth. He was crying.

The two sec men seemed to have vanished, but the third hooded and gloved figure was there, leaning over the stained table, hands pinching and slapping.

Michael tried to speak, but his throat was dry. Below, he was conscious of the woman making slurping noises that reminded him of a pig feeding in a trough. He knew he was going to be sick very soon, but he was afraid of Marie's anger.

Another cut, the vid camera repositioned so it concentrated on the youth's lower torso. One glove had been removed and the light from the fire sparkled on a ring on one finger, but it was too out of focus to see clearly. The hand was holding a knife, its blade less than three inches long, with a hilt of mother of pearl, inset with beads of lapis lazuli.

Gloved fingers touched the spot at the apex of the thighs and the knife moved nearer.

The hand. Ring. Human eye, set in silver.

Then blood splattered the lens.

Mouth, laughing in dreadful close-up.

Michael punched out, catching the woman across the cheek, vomiting his entire meal into her upturned face.

"Sick fucking bitch!" he screamed, his voice cracking in his horror, horror of what she was and horror of what he'd done with her.

Barely pausing to snatch his clothes, the weeping teenager raced from the bedroom, Marie's voice following him down the corridor outside.

"You're dead, prick! Dead with all the other outland fuckers. All dead!"

Chapter Twenty-Nine

At least the woman had kept her word about the guards. The long, labrynthine passages were deserted as the distraught Michael ran along them, losing his way twice before finally, on the ragged edge of insanity, finding the door that carried the golden numerals. A six and an eight.

There was a key in the lock, and he turned it, throwing himself into the darkened room.

Both Ryan and Krysty snatched at the handblasters tucked beneath their pillows as the door burst open and a dark figure came in, throwing itself on the bed, sobbing as though its heart had been broken.

"Michael?" Ryan said, easing off the trigger of the SIG-Sauer. "You nearly got your head blown off. What's wrong?"

"I'll close the door." Krysty moved quickly, glancing out into the corridor. "Nobody there. No sec men. But the key's here. I'll bring it and lock it from the inside."

By the time she'd made their room secure and turned on one of the wall lights, Ryan was hugging the teenager, arms locked tight around the trembling body.

Krysty sat by them, stroking Michael's head, laying one hand flat on his temples, trying to send healing signals, using the techniques that her mother Sonja had taught her back in Harmony ville.

"It'll be all right," she whispered. "Try and calm down. Steady your breathing and clear your mind."

"Tell us, Michael," Ryan urged, more aware of the realities and dangers of the situation. Something appalling had obviously happened to the young man. And whatever that was could spell disaster for all of them. It was vital they learned as quickly as possible what had gone down between Michael and the mistress of the ville. And then be able to judge what the repercussions might be.

"Give him time," Krysty said.

"Time we don't have, lover." He held the youth at arm's length. "Speak to me."

"Can't."

Michael was barely dressed, looking as though he'd just pulled on his clothes while running for his life. Krysty noticed scratches and bites around his neck and across his cheek, silently pointing them out to Ryan.

"You were with Marie Mandeville?" He shook him hard, trying to break through the wall of shock.

"Yeah."

"What happened?"

"Made love." Gobbets of tears coursed down his cheeks. "No! We didn't make love. We *fucked. She* fucked *me.* Kept fucking me."

"So? What was so bad about that?"

Krysty shook her head at him. "It was more than that, wasn't it, Michael?"

"Oh, yeah. More than that, Krysty. Jesus Lord, but I never saw such sick—" He almost choked on his anger and began to cry again.

"Was anyone else there?"

"No. Just her and me. She showed me some vids."

"Porno?" Ryan probed.

"Yeah. I mean..."

Gradually the story came out.

WITH THEIR OWN KEY, Ryan was able to enter the other rooms, waking everyone and bringing them silently back to his own chambers.

He and Krysty gave them the salient points of Michael's night. Before anyone else arrived, the teenager had gone into their bathroom, locking himself in, running a hot tub and sitting there, scrubbing at his skin as though he could somehow wash away the vile taint of Marie's body.

After the story was done, everyone sat in silence, trying to work out the implications for all of them. It was J.B. who spoke first, ticking off points on his fingers.

"One. He punched the daughter of one of the most powerful men in Deathlands. Two, he puked in her face."

Mildred laid a hand on his arm to interrupt him. "Main thing is that he rejected her. Bitch probably never had anyone turn her down before."

The Armorer nodded. He took off his glasses and peered through them, then put them back on. "Three is that it's now—" he glanced at his write chron "—quarter to four. Michael's been here for, how long?"

Ryan looked at Krysty. "I guess it must be close on a half hour."

"Yeah. Easily that."

"So, if Marie was so bastard pissed she wanted instant revenge, we'd already be dead meat. Dean, take a careful recce out in the corridor."

The boy turned the key in the ornate brass lock and eased the heavy door ajar. He stuck his head out and looked cautiously in both directions. Then he relocked it. "Nothing. Nobody out there at all."

J.B. nodded. "Good. Could be she won't want her father or anyone else to know what happened. Conclusion is that we aren't going to get chilled here and now."

"I find the most worrying aspect of this sordid affair is the threat that Michael detected. That we are all in serious danger of death." Doc looked around as the bathroom door opened and Michael walked slowly in, head down, not meeting anyone else's eyes.

"All right?" Mildred asked.

"Better. Cleaner. Ryan told..."

"Yeah, I did. We're just all talking it through. Main worry is that you reckon there's some triple-red danger for us coming up soon."

"Right." He sat on the bed beside Krysty, who squeezed his hand. "If I'd done what she wanted, been

what she wanted, she kept saying she'd keep me safe."
He laughed and shook his head. "She won't save me
now. I'll have to sink or swim with the rest of you."

"Swim," Mildred said.

THE TRADER ALWAYS SAID that the longer you thought
about escaping from danger, the less likely you were
to actually escape at all. He put it more simply.
"Faster you run, farther you get."

The one thing that none of them could understand
was why Baron Mandeville had treated them as his
honored guests if, all along, he was going to have them
murdered.

"When we were at the shooting and fighting," Dean
said, "one word and his sec goons could've taken us
all out."

"So, whatever it is, it'll be special." Ryan looked at
the others. "Let's try to get out of this place."

Mildred looked at Michael. "You up to this?"

"What I want is to be out of Sun Crest and breathe
clean air, then forget all about it. Back at Nil-Vanity
they thought they taught us about devils, Satan, de-
mons and original wicked sins. Evil." He sighed.
"They just didn't know squat about what real evil is."

THERE WASN'T ANYTHING that you could call a real
plan for the escape attempt from the ville.

It was such a massive, rambling building that there
hadn't been a chance to work out any potential weak-
ness. J.B. had sketched out a rough map, but it had an
awful lot of gray areas to it.

The wing that held their rooms overlooked stables, then a double wall, the outer lower than the inner. Both were topped with coils of razor-sharp antipersonnel wire. Beyond that was the river, then an open area of cleared brush that ended in the rolling deeps of the forest.

It had poured with rain for a good three hours after the afternoon's sport, and the river was visibly in turmoil, its foaming swollen surface shining in the moonlight.

The problem was that every single window was heavily barred and there was no time to try to cut them out. It came down to working their way along the passages, trying to keep moving downward and avoiding any of Baron Mandeville's sec patrols, finding an outer door and then...

Even that was so far ahead that Ryan hadn't bothered to discuss any plan beyond that point. He felt reasonably confident that they could get away if they could break out of the confines of Sun Crest. The trail back to the hidden redoubt wasn't difficult, and wouldn't offer too much advantage to horsemen. Though they would then have to face the ghoulies again.

FROM THE BRIEF acquaintanceship with the tight regime of the ville, Ryan knew that it was only a matter of time before they encountered sec men. Marie might have cleared the upper floor to enable her young lover to return to his own room unseen, but the rest of the place would still be crawling with the maroon uniforms and their Armalites.

Ryan led the way, moving in their usual skirmish line.

Krysty was second, then Dean and Michael. Mildred and Doc preceded J.B., who guarded their rear. Everyone had a blaster drawn and ready.

Mildred had been the only one of the group to oppose their escape attempt. "Could be Michael misunderstood. There's been no threat against us. Once we try to break out and start chilling Mandeville's men, there's no turning back."

But she'd been overruled.

Ryan paused at the forking of the corridors. A narrow staircase spiraled to the left. He remembered that they'd come that way on their first night, following Mercy Weyman. She'd said something about it leading to a suite of tower rooms that held the baron's collection of Bright Carvings.

Ryan took the right-hand passage, which he knew would eventually bring them into the gallery above the dining room, then a short set of broad stairs into the large hall. A few yards more and there was a door that opened to the inner courtyard.

And once there—

Doc stepped on a creaking board, freezing with a pained expression on his face. "I must say that I'm most awfully sorry," he whispered.

The ville was silent.

Stained-glass windows at a half landing showed the martyrdom of some early Christian saint, standing against a large wheel, pierced with dozens of golden arrows, his smooth face showing only a beatific and vaguely puzzled smile.

The moon filtered through the window, casting colored shadows across the band of friends.

The place was so still that Ryan could hear the faint distant pounding of the powerful water generator. Most of the wall and ceiling lamps had been switched off for the hours of darkness with only one in ten of them leaving small islands of light in the ocean of blackness.

The vast space of the banquet hall was almost impenetrable. Ryan moved into it from the bottom step of the flight of stairs, his left hand reaching out ahead of him to avoid bumping into one of the chairs or the long table itself.

Once they were safely across, they'd be within spitting distance of one of the outside doors.

The lights all came on at once, like a thunderbolt from a summer sky.

"One stupe move and all of you get to be dead, here and now." The voice belonged to Sec Sergeant Harry Guiteau, leaning on the rail of the gallery, with twenty or thirty of his guards ranged around him, their Armalites covering the hall below.

Ryan noticed that there was someone standing close behind the man, in the shadows. All he could see was the sheen of her long black hair.

Chapter Thirty

The atmosphere at the breakfast table had been distinctly strained.

The moment the lights snapped on, Ryan had realized that they were hopelessly trapped. Though they had some serious weapon power, it would have been simple suicide to open fire on the armed men above them.

Moving at Guiteau's command, they'd slowly, one by one, laid down their blasters. It had been no surprise that the leader of the sec force had carried out his orders with efficiency and simplicity. Each of the seven companions had been led away, back to their rooms, under heavy escort.

Ryan had been kept to last.

Marie had disappeared, probably to her own chambers, to relish her triumph.

Guiteau slowly walked down to the hall, unable to restrain a smile. "Really triple-fucked now, outlander, aren't we? Haven't got the Trader to come rolling in to rescue you with his war wags rumbling and trumpets blowing."

"Clever of you to notice, Guiteau. So, what happens now? Or are you waiting for orders from that sick-brain bitch?"

"Words, words, words. If it's any consolation, Cawdor, the kid throwing up over the mistress doesn't make a lot of difference. What's going to happen on the morrow was going to happen the moment we saw you out in the woods. Just a matter of when, not if. The boy might have lived a few weeks longer if he'd played the game with the mistress. But it would all be the same." He drew his finger across his throat. "You saw the butterflies in their pretty clothes? She lets them live awhile, while they don't bore her. Within six months they'll be all food for ravens."

"Nice lady."

"Sure. But talk doesn't do a thing. You know that, Cawdor. There's roads we've both been down."

"Is there..."

Guiteau shook his head. "Not a thing. You can't threaten me, and you sure as shit don't have anything to bribe me with. No. It'll be done tomorrow."

"How?"

The sec man grinned. "Me to know and you to find out, Cawdor."

"Why feed us and entertain us first?"

"Part of the way the baron likes it. Part of his pleasure. Part of the sport."

THEY WERE ESCORTED separately down to the hall for their breakfast. Maroon-uniformed men watched cautiously from the minstrels' gallery above. Neither the baron nor his daughter had appeared by the time Ryan and the others were halfway through their meal, though Harry Guiteau had joined them, sitting and sipping a large mug of black coffee and nibbling silently at a sweet cinnamon roll.

The food was, surprisingly, just as good as it had been before, but it was served by armed men rather than by the aproned young women.

Krysty called out to the sergeant. "If you're going to chill us, isn't this a waste of a decent meal?"

"Not me going to chill you, lady. Not directly. And the chilling'll be helped if you all eat well."

It was the clue that Ryan had been looking for. The clue that gave the answer to the puzzling jigsaw.

"A hunt," he said.

Guiteau looked sharply over his shoulder, to make sure neither of the Mandevilles was there, then glanced back at the prisoners, trying to school his face to indifference. "How's that?" he said nervously.

"Of course. Skydark, Ryan!" J.B. punched his right fist hard into his left hand. "A hunt. Like that poor bastard we saw getting his belly ripped open. We run and they chase. That's it, isn't it, Guiteau?"

"No."

"Lying bastard!"

"It's not." But his unease was obvious.

The woman's voice came from above, drawing every head. "Oh, yes, Ryan Cawdor. You've guessed well."

"Thanks."

"Later this morning you and your friends will be taken out into the forest surrounding the ville and given a sporting chance of escape."

"With our blasters?"

Marie shook her head, unsmiling. "You know better than that, outlander. But you may all keep your knives. See how kind we are?"

"You murderous, foul, evil bitch!" Michael was up on his feet, holding his index fingers crossed toward the woman. "Sooner you die, the sooner the earth's a better, cleaner place.'

"When this day is over, I shall make sure that you are mine, boy." To Guiteau she said, "Any man harms this fast-tongued lad in the hunt will swim the moat with thumbs and toes tied. Tell that to your people, Sergeant."

"Aye, Mistress."

She disappeared again, but they could all hear her heels clicking along the stone corridor. Michael sat down again at the long table, slowly, his hands trembling with the red-mist violence of his rage.

Harry Guiteau caught his eye and laughed. "Say what you like, lad," he said. "Nothing'll make a difference now. Cawdor, a word with you."

Ryan sipped at his fresh chilled apple juice, then put the glass down, rising to move and stand by the burly sec man. "What is it?"

The answer was so quietly spoken that Ryan had to lean close to hear it. "If you care anything for that boy, then you'll do well—when the end of the hunt's near—to take him and cut his throat, quick and mer-

ciful. She—'' he jerked his thumb to the gallery
''—won't be either quick or merciful to him. Take my
meaning, do you?''

''Yeah. Thanks for that.''

''*Da nada, amigo.*''

AFTER BREAKFAST, they were again escorted to their
rooms and locked in.

The last words from Guiteau were that they would
be brought downstairs once more, probably around
noon. They should make sure that all of their possessions were together, as they wouldn't be returning.

That was all he said, then refused to answer any of
their questions.

Ryan stretched out on the big canopied bed, trying
to relax, readying himself for what he knew might well
be a terminal ordeal for all of them.

Krysty went into the bathroom. When she came
back she lay down by him. ''This going to be it,
lover?''

He shrugged. ''Been plenty of times we thought we
might be catching the last boat downriver. I guess that
one day it might be true. Might be now.''

''We have much of a chance?''

''Not much. Best sec men I've ever seen. Plenty of
them. Armalites are in good condition. Horses. Likely
they'll give us a start of around ten or fifteen minutes. Not long enough to get far. Then they come after us and ride us down.''

''We split up?''

He nodded. "Haven't thought it through, Krysty. Might be a chance of one or two of us getting away."

"Or we can go down together?"

"Yeah."

"How many are going to be hunting us?"

He rubbed his chin thoughtfully. "Probably the baron, his beautiful daughter and pretty well all of the sec men. In fact . . ." He stopped.

"What?"

"Nothing, love. Just the tiny green shoots of a possible chance. Just a chance."

WHILE THEY WERE RELEASED and herded together in the corridor just before noon, Ryan maneuvered himself next to the Armorer, heads close together, talking intently to him. Krysty watched, knowing that this was something that she could never share. She and Ryan were as close to each other as it was possible for any two human beings to be, but when it came to details of the arcane and intricate crafts of combat and death, Ryan would go to John Dix above all people.

At least it showed a glimmer of hope in what she felt was an utterly bleak situation.

As they were marched down, J.B. called out to Guiteau. "Sorry we don't get to see the baron's gun collection. Must be something special. Where's he keep it?"

"North tower. You can get some satisfaction from the thought that all of your blasters are already up there, labeled and on show. But I guess you know that you won't ever be getting to see them yourselves."

Each of them had submitted to a cursory body check to make sure they weren't carrying concealed guns. Most of them had knives, but they were ignored.

Baron Mandeville was waiting for them in the great hall, standing on a platform close to the main door, hands behind his back. He looked as though he'd just come from a bath, with his white hair still damp, and the scent of perfumed oils surrounding him. He was dressed in a heightened version of antique fox-hunting clothes—crimson jacket, fawn jodhpurs tucked into highly polished riding boots, with short, blunt spurs. He had an unidentifiable revolver in a deep holster at his hip and carried a silver-handled riding crop.

"Stands there like he's waiting for his sled and reindeer to go and deliver the Christmas presents," Michael whispered, making Doc, next to him, splutter with laughter.

"Time has come, outlanders," Mandeville announced, tapping the whip against the side of his boot.

Before he said anything else, he was aware that everyone was looking past him to a small staircase, where Marie stood looking at the assembly.

She wore a simple white blouse, with a ruffle of lace at her throat, black leather riding breeches so tight that they looked like they'd been sprayed onto her, and the same soft maroon boots she had on when they first saw her, with the same savage Mexican rowel spurs. Her gloves were scarlet leather, and she carried a vicious quirt. Her astounding hair was pulled back and tied with a ribbon of azure silk.

Her slit eyes burned toward Michael, but he, to his great credit, held his nerve and smiled at her, then turned away and spat on the stone floor.

"I hope you keep that courage after the hunt when you and I are alone again," she said.

"Fuck you, lady." It was Mildred speaking, and she gave Marie the finger. "Let's get on with this sad and sorry charade, shall we?"

THE BARON HAD GESTURED for his sec boss to tell Ryan and his friends what the rules of the game were. Outside the ville, they could all hear occasional rumbles of thunder, promising a return of yet another of the vicious chem storms that were whirling around Kansas. Through the tall windows it was possible to see that the day had become darker.

"You have a fifteen-minute start by my chron," Guiteau told them. "You get to the main gate and go from there. Stay together or split up. Doesn't matter. After the rain, there's no way you can hide your tracks from us. We come after you. Run or hide. Up to you. We catch you and you all get chilled." He hesitated and glanced at Marie. "One way or another, fast or slow. Remember what I said to you, Cawdor."

Ryan nodded, saying nothing.

"No questions, outlanders?" the baron asked, beaming at them as though he'd just wondered if anyone wanted more chestnut stuffing with their Thanksgiving turkey.

Nobody spoke. In the silence Marie gave a small, uncontrollable giggle of anticipation that was one of the most chilling and obscene sounds that Ryan had ever heard.

"I NEVER SAW so many sec men," J.B. said, observing the proceedings for the hunt with a dispassionate fascination. "Going to leave the ville short."

"Yeah," Ryan agreed.

Mildred was at their elbow. "No point in at least asking if they'll spare Dean, is there?"

"No." Ryan looked around him, seeing that the chem storm was not that far away, with lightning lacing the sky. The wind flurried, and he felt a brief spatter of small rain in his face. Tasting it, he found that it didn't have the bitter acid tang of the previous storm.

Both the baron of Sun Crest and his daughter had disappeared into the ville, no doubt to take some last-minute refreshment before hunting seven human beings to a brutish death.

But dozens of sec men circled the courtyard, watching the prisoners. Harry Guiteau stood among them, peering down at his chron in the gathering gloom. "Looks like you'll die wet, Cawdor," he shouted, getting a burst of laughter from his men.

"I can live with that." Ryan's retort also brought the reward of broad grins.

"I reckon time's about up, outlanders. Fifteen minutes from . . . Now!"

Chapter Thirty-One

The gaudy was on the eastern edge of the old town of Everett, thirty miles from Seattle, overlooked by the magnificence of the Cascades. But nobody was that interested in the view of the snow-topped mountains.

Everyone was much too busy watching the developing situation at a quiet table in one corner, near the stairs, watching the skinny little guy with the droopy mustache and the older, grizzled man who sat with him.

They'd been in the area for several days. All that was known was that they'd been making a point of approaching any travelers or packmen, giving them a generous handful of jack and a message to carry. Local curiosity had immediately revealed the nature of the message.

It was for the traders to give to a one-eyed man named Ryan Cawdor, if they should encounter him on their travels. Or a small, quiet man with glasses named John Dix. The message had been short and simple.

Success. Will stay around Seattle for three months. Come quick. Abe.

He was the one with the mustache. And a stainless-steel Colt Python on his hip. The older man, who didn't seem to have any name at all, carried a beat-up Armalite that looked like it had seen better days.

The older man also looked like he'd seen better days. He had an occasional racking cough that doubled him over, and he seemed to live mainly on a diet of milk and eggs.

What was obvious to the locals of Everett was that these two outlanders weren't short of jack, which made them extremely interesting.

Now, with the late-afternoon sun slipping away across the ocean a few miles west, that interest had finally reached its head in the gaudy. Its name, on a shingle that hung crookedly outside, was the Passion Pool.

On the landing of the crowded building, the sluts—those who weren't in the tiny bedrooms actively earning their keep—leaned on the scarred balustrade and watched the drama below them. Some were virtually naked, with only a stained wrap over their shoulders. Others wore skimpy underwear designed to reveal far more than it concealed.

Everett, like many frontier villes, didn't have anything that you could call a baron. Just a loose assortment of men and women, holding various powers. Powers that waxed and waned—waxed as they flourished, often briefly, and waned as they died, often unexpectedly.

Currently the leading force in the township was a family called the Byrnes—the Bloody Byrnes. The family had six sons, aged thirty down to eighteen. Their father had been hanged in Tupelo four years earlier for barn-burning, and their mother helped out in the Passion Pool, boasting openly that she could pick and choose which of her sons she could sleep with any night.

Now she watched proudly as her boys prepared to rob the two insignificant strangers.

All six of them stood around the table, which bore the greasy remnants of a recent meal—strips of limp bacon rind, a hunk of stale bread crust and two mugs containing the cold dregs of coffee sub.

A faded blond girl was with the brothers, showing the characteristic septic spots and rash around her mouth of the habitual jolt addict.

"I said that you insulted my sister," said the oldest brother, Brandon, leaning and pushing his face between Abe and the Trader. "We don't like fuckin' outlanders who don't show respect to our women. Understand?"

Trader nodded, his face quite without emotion. "I understand what you say. You can move away."

"Why?"

"Your breath stinks worse than a pig's shithole."

"How's that?" Brandon Byrne was genuinely bewildered, wondering whether he'd somehow misheard what the old man had said to him. "Say again."

"Lousy fuckbag said you smelled like pig shit," repeated Dermot, second youngest of the family, winking at Brandon.

"You don't hear me, mister," Brandon said, pressing manfully on, though his Neanderthal mind was trying to tell him something wasn't right here. The little guy and the old-timer should have been messing their breeches by now.

"They said they wanted me to suck both their dicks at the same time and wouldn't pay me nothing after I done it for them," the whore squeaked.

"There." Brandon nodded solemnly. "That's why you got to hand us over all your jack for our sweet little sister and the wrong you done her."

Abe was watching Trader carefully, hoping that there might be some sort of clue before the action began. Six triple-stupes against the two of them, in what might prove to be a hostile killing ground, weren't good odds. But he knew, without a trace of a doubt, that Trader wasn't going to give any of their jack to these peckerwood brain-dead bastards.

"You hear me, stranger?"

"I hear you," Trader replied.

"So. Me and my brothers want to know what you intend to do for us?"

"Hurry it up, boys!" their mother shouted from the top of the stairs.

"Shut it, Ma. Speak to me, mister."

Trader cleared his throat. "Your sister isn't your sister. She's a nickel-and-dime little slut from Norleans." He glanced for a moment at Abe, giving him the clue he'd been waiting for. "And all I got to say is this."

The word "this" was said with no particular emphasis, so the outburst of violence was totally unexpected.

Except by Abe.

His reflexes had been honed to a singing needle point since the six Byrne brothers had arrived at their table to harass them for jack.

Despite his age and his illness, Trader wasn't a man to mess with.

During the brief conversation, he'd been weighing up the opposition, judging them as small-ville bullies, thugs who were good at picking on a storekeeper and hassling him for some protection jack.

But not up to serious combat.

Trader's left hand cut back like the edge of a two-by-four, into the groin of the youngest brother, who was standing close to that side of the table, crushing his genitals up against the sharp leading point of the pubic bone. The boy didn't even get time to scream before his lights went out and he dropped unconscious to the barroom floor.

Long before he hit the planking, two of his brothers were done for. Trader always used to say that the most important thing to do was take out the leader of the pack.

While his left hand was pulping the manhood of the littlest Byrne, his right hand was bringing up the Armalite. He used it as a club, swinging the butt around and into Brandon's face, splitting his lips, splintering seven of his jagged front teeth and filling his throat with his own blood.

Almost simultaneously Trader kicked the table out of the way, into two more brothers, slowing their reactions to his sudden attack.

Abe was a shard of a second behind his old leader, relying on his Colt, able to take advantage of the fact that none of the Byrnes was bothering much with him, taking his silence and stillness for passivity and fear.

The four-inch barrel cleared the greased holster and the first of the six .357 rounds struck Dermot Byrne smack through the center of his muscular chest.

Abe's second round hit the brother on his immediate left, who was staggering off balance from the tumbling table. It was aimed just above belt height.

"Close action and you don't fuck with clever tricks. A hit'll put anyone down. While they're down you can think about what you'll do next."

He could almost hear the Trader's voice at one of their old regular war wag crew meetings, distilling the advice that had made him among the most powerful, feared and hated men in all of Deathlands.

Less than three seconds had clicked by and four of the six men were out of the action, though Brandon was still upright, spitting out fragments of teeth in a spray of watery blood.

Now the Trader was on his feet, and the Armalite was braced against his right hip. Two triple bursts and two men went down, chests torn apart, blood spraying over everybody within fifteen paces.

Abe looked at the man he'd shot in the belly, who was down on his knees, both hands trying to hold his looped intestines from spilling in the dirt, looked at him and then carefully put a round between his eyes.

Three of the six were clinically dead.

The man that Abe had shot in the chest had staggered as far as the bar, where he was leaning hopelessly, blood trickling steadily down his legs. Trader turned on his heel and brought the blaster to his shoulder, switching to single fire, blowing half the brother's face over the flyspecked mirror behind the bottles and smeared glasses.

Abe was standing now as well, both of them watching the reactions of the rest of the room, the muzzles of their blasters raking across the line of men and whores, most of whom raised their hands or shrugged as a sign that they weren't going to get involved in the slaughter.

"Who the fuck are you?" Brandon mumbled through his broken teeth.

"You don't need to know that," Trader replied, shooting him once through the heart at point-blank range.

As the sixth body went sprawling in the lake of blood, Trader and Abe became aware for the first time of a strange, monotonous sound in the gaudy, keening above the gasps of the onlookers and the weeping of one of the sluts, the one who had played the part of the aggrieved sister of the Byrnes.

It was an astounding drawn-out scream, high and rasping, sustained on a single endless note, coming from the plump woman on the stairs. Tears coursed through the mascara around her staring eyes.

When it finally faded away into relative stillness, with only a man near the door shuffling his boots as if he were thinking of running for safety, Trader nodded to her. "You'd be the mother of these men."

It was a statement and not a question.

"You chilled them all, you rotten, murdering bastard! All of them."

"Not quite. This one—" he nudged the youngest of the family with the toe of his combat boot "—survives, though if he lives to be a hundred I doubt he could father any more of your vicious spawn."

"Danny? Danny's still living, is he? Oh, then spare him to be a comfort to me in me old age."

Trader stared wordlessly at her, and not even Abe, who had known him for so long, could guess what was going through the older man's brain.

"Come here," he said finally, watching while she walked unsteadily down the stairs and across the frozen room, the soles of her tawdry high-heeled shoes making sticky, sucking noises as she stepped through the blood of her five sons.

The boy that Trader had struck in the groin was still deeply unconscious, eyes shut tight, a dark, wet patch spreading across the front of his cotton pants.

"This is your Danny, is it?" Trader asked.

"You killed them all but him. I wouldn't want to live on if anything happened to him. My youngest and dearest."

Trader shot her once through the center of the face, a neat dark hole appearing in her left cheek to the side of her fleshy nose. Most of her brains sprayed out of the large hole that the tumbled bullet smashed in the back of her skull.

"You didn't have to..." began the half-breed bar-keep, his voice trembling.

"You heard her," Trader replied. "Didn't want to live if this boy was chilled. So, I obliged her."

"But the boy isn't dead, mister." The voice came from a tiny man with a large boil throbbing on his neck, just above the line of his collar.

Trader smiled at him, as cold as meltwater. "You're right, friend. Hadn't noticed that. What a stupe I am." He lowered the Armalite and blew away the side of the boy's head, firing casually, one-handed. "He is now."

The only sound was Abe reloading the spent rounds in his Colt Python and the young gaudy slut crying in the arms of an older whore.

"We moving?" Abe queried.

"One more thing," Trader replied. "Never leave a job until it's all done."

He walked over to the girl, gently moved her away and looked at her.

"Didn't mean to," she stammered. "They made... made me say what you done. Sorry for..."

"Sorry never pays the bill, girlie," he said, and shot her once, in the left side of the chest, watching her fall at his feet, blood clotting in her hair.

He turned to Abe. "Now it's done."

Chapter Thirty-Two

The chem storm was closing in around them as they ran away from the gates of the ville, grouped together, following on the heels of Ryan Cawdor.

Off to the north the sky was darkened by great bursts of rain sweeping down from high altitude. It looked like it would be on top of them within less than the fifteen minutes start that they'd been given.

The first target was to reach the fringe of the trees across the stone bridge, where the river was close to bursting its banks, taking them out of sight of any watchers within the shadowy windows of the ville.

Ryan held up his hand as soon as they were safe, checking his chron. "One minute and twenty-two secs," he said.

"Why don't we try to get back to the redoubt?" Michael asked.

"Wouldn't make it. The point about this hunt is that there isn't any way we can win it. Whatever we do they'll still ride us down and chill us. They got the time, the men and the blasters." Ryan looked back. "Can't see us from here. Come on."

He turned sharply to the right and began to dodge between the pines, making sure there was always a fringe of the forest between them and the nearer walls of the ville.

"We're going to try and get back in!" Dean exclaimed. "Hot pipe, Dad."

Doc was always the one who found it difficult to travel fast over rough terrain.

"Sneak into the lair of the great white worm itself," he panted. "Your schemes are always a source of wonderment and delight to me, my dear Cawdor."

THE IDEA HAD BEEN triggered by the realization that Sun Crest would be left distinctly short of sec men once all of the hunters had left in the pursuit.

But it was a plan hedged about with potential problems and opportunities for total, terminal disaster. They had to find a way into the fortified building, then get to the arms collection. If they could get that far, then the balance of power would tilt a little in their direction.

After that...

Ryan stopped again, checking his chron. "Six minutes and forty seconds."

They were close to the main generator, where the river foamed and tumbled over the huge lichen-covered wheel. It was possible to make out the massive stone building through the trees, less than a hundred paces away.

Lightning crackled a few miles off, and a curtain of rain came sweeping down, veiling the walls of the ville itself, close beyond the generator. Under the spreading branches of the dense wood, the seven companions remained dry.

For the plan to have any chance of success, its timing was crucial.

If they made their move too soon, then the hunt wouldn't have set off and they might as well slit their own throats. If they left it too late, then they might well be tracked down before they could try to break into Sun Crest.

"Rain'll make tracking harder," J.B. said, his face a white blur in the Stygian gloom.

"Going to be around a hundred riders all bursting out of the main gate in about six minutes from now." Ryan brushed away a spot of cold water that had already filtered through the dense foliage above him. "Bound to have the dogs with them. But the scent won't be that strong, and they could easily get jammed up together on that main trail."

"Should we have tried to cross the river?" Mildred asked. "Heard that hounds can't follow over flowing water."

J.B. answered her. "River's flooded. Try to cross it and you get drowned. Better this way."

More lightning flashed, turning everyone into wide-eyed, pallid ghosts. This time it was followed by a deafening crash of thunder that rolled on and on, the volume reaching close to the pain barrier.

"Won't help the dogs any," Krysty commented.

Nobody answered.

J.B. looked at his chron. "Five minutes before they start after us."

"What if they cheat and come early?"

Ryan smiled at his son. "No need for that. What I've seen of Harry Guiteau, he'll give the word when exactly fourteen minutes and sixty seconds are up."

The only window in the mill that looked over the woods was high up. The black sky reflected off it, turning it into a blank mirror, making it impossible to see if anyone was on watch behind the dusty glass.

The rain had become torrential, and all of the friends were starting to get wet. For a brief moment it crossed Ryan's mind to wonder whether the Mandevilles might abort the hunt, but he instantly dismissed the idea.

He led the way closer to the pounding wheel. There was now so much noise from the raging water and from the storm around them that it was pointless to try to move with any stealth. He'd noticed a couple of tin wires running from the mill to the nearest point of Sun Crests's walls, which he guessed was some kind of comm device. Ryan held up his hand, gathering everyone around him.

"They get a chance to warn the sec men left in the ville, then we're done. We have to be triple-fast."

"Two minutes," J.B. warned.

Now they were out of the cover of the pines, all of them soaked to the skin, pressed flat against the streaming granite walls. Here was the first step of the long, perilous road to safety.

RYAN AND THE ARMORER counted down the last seconds in unison. They both had knives drawn, as did the others, except Doc who had unsheathed his sword stick.

"Fifteen, fourteen..."

A rumble of thunder seemed to shake the mill to its foundations.

"Eight, seven, six..."

The lightning was purplish, streaked with a jagged pattern of neon pink, accompanied by the characteristic chem storm smell of sulfur and ozone.

"Two and one and go!"

Ryan was first up the stairs, careful not to slip on the wet, slick slabs of gray stone. There was a huge oak door, studded with iron bolts, and a whorled brass ring the only way of trying to open it. He grabbed at the handle, feeling it squirm away from his damp fingers. Then he had it, turning it to the left, aware of the latch lifting.

The place was throbbing with the ceaseless vibration of the great wheel turning, powering the generators that provided the ville with its electricity. The hall of the mill was deserted, with a staircase winding toward a higher floor.

Ryan's fighting nerves told him that the clock was now running against them, ticking off their lives as the hunt began its remorseless pursuit.

The noise was so all pervading that it seemed to numb the other senses. Ryan sprinted up the angled stairs, rounded a corner and found himself almost on top of a pair of men in maroon overalls. They had their backs to him and were sitting at a long bank of dials and gauges.

It wasn't a time for hesitation.

He had the panga out in a flash and hacked the head off the shoulders of the servant on the left, while J.B., with one of his pair of thin stilettos, stabbed the other in the heart.

Neither victim could have known what hit them, death plucking them from light to darkness in the beat of the heart.

The blood still fountained from the gashed neck of the one man as Ryan raced halfway up the next flight of stairs, the Armorer right behind him.

Reaching the very top of the mill, the men checked every side room and dusty landing.

"Empty," J.B. pronounced, looking around the attic, under the eaves of the echoing building.

"Right. Let's go wreck the power controls, then head for the ville."

Back down to the second floor.

"Break everything you can," Ryan said. "Everything. Is there a master control that'll jam the wheel?"

"Do that and the mill could come apart. Most frightfully dangerous, my dear fellow."

"Here," Michael called.

Despite the tension and danger, Krysty laughed. "Never have guessed it was this lever."

It was set in the outer wall, a great steel bar six feet long, painted a brilliant red. It was dusty, showing that it had hardly ever been used. The piece of card above it was also faded by the passage of time: Warning! This Brakes Main Wheel Axle. Only Use In Emergency On Direct Order of Chief Miller. Do Not Engage While Power Is Being Generated.

Peeling off the gray stones to the right of the big lever was another, larger notice, which simply blared, in large crimson capital letters, the single word: DANGER.

J.B. looked at it carefully, then turned and gave Ryan one of his rare smiles. "Best get everyone else outside, except you and me," he said. "Could be sort of exciting."

"Why?" Dean asked.

"Like going flat out on a war wag and then throwing her straight into reverse," the Armourer replied.

"No arguments," Ryan shouted above the bone-shaking rumble. "Wait around the corner, out of sight of the ville." Another thought occurred to him. "Krysty, get the overalls off that dead man and give them to me."

"The one without... No, course. Too much blood."

Mildred helped her as they stripped the stabbed man, tossing the maroon garment to Ryan.

"Great. Now wait out there."

He struggled into the overalls, finding them a tight fit over his coat, but it would only be for a moment's extra time, a moment that might be vital.

"Right. Let's do it, J.B., and see what happens."

They both gripped the lever, feeling it vibrate at their touch, as though it were connected to the heart of some monstrous beast, dwelling in subterranean caverns.

It was very stiff, and it took all of their considerable joint strength to shift it.

"More," the Armourer gasped.

They felt a hideous grinding sensation, and the steel bar jerked, almost pulling itself from their hands. But they clung on, forcing it farther.

"Fireblast!"

The lights in the mill flickered. Came on again with a desperate brightness, then dimmed once more.

"Bit more," Ryan panted.

They threw everything at it, finally wrenching the control all the way down. The noise was unimaginable.

And stopped.

The lever flopped out of their hands like a broken-backed snake and clattered to the floor.

All of the lights went out.

The only sound now was the racing river outside the open door and the rumbling of the chem storm, with its hissing torrents of rain.

Ryan was first out to join the others, feeling clumsy in the borrowed clothes, blinking in the downpour. He glanced once more at his chron.

"Hunt's been on for nearly two minutes," he said. "But they won't be organized yet. Time for us to try the ville. So far, so good, friends."

Chapter Thirty-Three

Sun Crest was in pitch darkness, but none of the hunting party had the least idea that there was anything wrong.

They had surged from the main gates of the ville into the teeth of the chem storm. As Ryan Cawdor had predicted, the weather had produced chaos for the dozens of riders and their baying pack of dogs.

Two of the leading sec men's mounts went down on the cobbles of the inner yard as soon as the signal was given, bringing down another ten in flailing, cursing confusion.

By the time some sort of order had been restored, helped by the savage whip of Mistress Marie, and they were out near the edge of the forest in reasonable discipline, nearly two whole minutes had been wasted.

Despite the raging chem storm, they all knew that time was still massively on their side, and not one of the huge gang of sweating, soaked hunters was worried.

Which isn't quite true.

Sec Sergeant Harry Guiteau had a strange, nagging doubt at the back of his mind, a doubt that made him push his men on into the forest. He allowed the hounds to run free as they tried to pick up a scent from the sodden mud underfoot.

Marie Mandeville was riding like a fury, her long black hair already streaming water, the flanks of her stallion specked with crimson droplets where the Mexican spurs were doing their vicious work.

Her father was jogging comfortably along, beaming at all of his men, whistling to himself.

There was utter confusion for at least two more minutes, where the trails parted, until the belling of a group of the hounds showed they'd finally caught a scent.

"For the river!" shouted one of the pretty boys who rode as close to Marie as they dared.

His cry turned the moment and everyone set off toward the stone bridge at a flailing gallop, whooping and cheering at the thought that the hunt might turn out to be blessedly short, so they could all make haste back to the ville for hot baths, drink and food.

"Didn't figure the old Trader's man for a double-stupe," Guiteau said to himself, spitting out a mouthful of cold rainwater. "No way."

SUN CREST WAS in total darkness, and even from outside the rain-drenched walls, it was possible to hear shouts of concern.

The door stood at the base of the north tower, with its ornate Gothic pinnacles and mullioned windows. An electric sec alarm was at its center, as well as a large iron knocker in the shape of a bear's paw.

Ryan lifted the knocker and let it fall, hearing the deep sound echo away.

Nothing happened.

The storm was still raging, with almost constant thunder and lightning, though Ryan had thought, a few moments ago, that he might have caught the sound of baying dogs through a second or two of silence.

He hammered again with the knocker. The maroon overalls were soaked through, their color almost black. Ryan gripped his panga in his right hand, concealed behind his back. J.B. was flattened against the wall to his left, the others lined up behind him, ready for the move if someone opened the door.

If nobody let them in, then survival could be measured in short minutes.

"Mebbe we better run for it, Dad."

Ryan ignored Dean's worried voice, using the knocker as if he were beating the heat out of the ville.

There was a small, barred ob window in the side of the door, and it slid back. All Ryan could see was a white oval of a face peering at him.

"Mill's broke," he said urgently. "Power's down. Got to check inside before Baron Nathan comes back. Quick, open up."

He spoke quickly, as if he were on the wrong side of panic, keeping his head turned away, relying on the uniform as his pass.

There was a deafening crash of thunder, smothering whatever the person inside the door replied. Ryan shouted again at the top of his voice.

"Open the fuckin' door or you can be the one tells Baron and Mistress why the ville's blacked out!"

He heard bolts grating and a key turning.

The moment the door began to move he hurled his shoulder against it, pushing in, so that the invisible person inside was knocked off balance. Ryan stabbed with the panga, using the broad point, feeling it jar against solid flesh. Hearing a gasp of pain and shock, he twisted his wrist, giving the blade a savage jerk as he withdrew it.

Blood gushed hot over his wrist, and he felt the life drain away at his feet.

Everyone was jostling around Ryan, and he was aware of J.B. pushing past him, across the narrow hallway, and cautiously easing open the stout door beyond that led into the rest of the ville. There was nobody on the bottom floor of the north tower, and they climbed quickly to the next level, past priceless tapestries showing medieval hunting scenes.

The Armorer was in the lead, keeping flat against the wall, trying to avoid the oak treads of the broad stairs, not that anyone was likely to hear creaking over the noise of the chem storm.

On the second floor there weren't any lamps lighted, nor were there any sec men or servants.

"Where are the damned blasters?" J.B. hissed, staring back into the pit of blackness.

Ryan had automatically taken up the dangerous position of rearguard and he stopped a moment. "Just said they were in this tower, didn't they?"

Krysty spoke. "Next floor."

She was right.

The precious gun collection of Baron Nathan Mandeville was on the third floor, where several emergency lamps had been lighted.

And where three sec men were waiting.

SOME OF THE DOGS picked up the trail of the fugitives, leading toward the water mill. But most of them had missed the cutoff and were still racing excitedly on through the downpour, vanishing from sight, barking and snapping at one another.

Two horses went down in the confusion, the rest of the riders bottled up and screaming.

Harry Guiteau had suddenly realized what Ryan Cawdor's plan might be, and he was trying to spur through the chaos, yelling out for order.

THE THREE SEC MEN were all standing on the landing, carrying several unlighted oil lamps, two of them with glowing tapers. J.B. spotted them and retreated without being seen, beckoning to Ryan to join him near the top of the stairs.

"That overall could get you the few steps you need," he whispered.

"Start coming before those bastards even work out who I am," Ryan replied. "Not going to be much time for this. Let Doc follow on third. His sword stick could be just what we need here."

There was no point in waiting for a better time or a better chance.

Ryan gathered himself, slipping the panga out of sight behind his back and powering himself up the last few steps and onto the landing at a dead run.

The guards were less than twenty feet away from him, slowed by their burden. One turned, spotting the maroon clothes and started to smile.

"Been outside in the rain and—" he began.

And died.

Ryan slashed the sec man's throat open, then lunged at the chest of the second uniformed man, who went to meet his Maker, puzzling over whether he should try to drop the valuable predark lamps before unslinging the Armalite from his shoulder.

J.B. tried to stab the third guard, who parried the blow with one of the brass lamps, the steel ringing off the bowl. His mouth was opening to shout for help when Doc killed him with one savage thrust of the rapier, piercing his heart.

"Stamp on those lights," Ryan hissed to his son, watching as the boy quickly trod out the naked flames before they had time to ignite the pool of spilled oil that reeked among the broken glass of the lamps.

There was a neat sign, in ornate lettering, nailed to the wall at the entrance to a room that resembled the picture gallery: The Nathan Mandeville Armory.

A couple more oil lamps stood on a wooden table a little way into the long room, both lighted. Ryan picked up one, J.B. taking the other.

"Let's get our blasters back," he said.

CURSING AT THE TOP of his voice, Sec Sergeant Harry Guiteau eventually managed to heel his horse nearer to the mounts of the baron and his daughter. During the time it took him, he'd also checked his chron.

Close to ten minutes had elapsed since he'd given the outlanders the signal to run for their lives, ten minutes that had been nothing but a bedlam of noise, rain and uncontrollable animals, canine and equine.

"Baron!"

"What is it!?" Mandeville's white beard had lost its spring and curl and now looked like some desperate Arctic animal clinging to his chin for protection. The merry little blue eyes were like chips of ice.

"I can't see lights in the ville."

"So what?"

Guiteau realized that his lord was way beyond any sort of sense or reason, locked into a blind rage.

"So, I think Cawdor's fucked the power mill."

"Bastard liar." Mandeville swung at his face with the crop, the barbed steel tip missing Guiteau by less than an inch as he swayed back out of range.

"Imbecile!" The cold, vicious fury in Marie Mandeville's voice penetrated through the crimson mist of her father's insensate anger, rising above the neighing of the horses and the baying of the dogs.

"Don't talk to me like . . ." he began, quailing as he met his daughter's eyes.

"Guiteau."

"Lady?"

"I believe you're right."

"I can take a few good men and go to the mill."

"We'll come with you." A thought occurred to her. "Take twenty. No more. And send the rest of the blundering stupes back to the main gate of the ville. Tell them what might have happened. I think they're going for their blasters. We might still be in time to cut them off at the mill."

THERE WAS NO OTHER SIGN of life within the ville as the seven companions moved slowly into the entrance of the gallery, the two lamps casting pools of yellow light for a few yards ahead and behind them.

Ryan told Michael, as their best hand-to-hand fighter and fastest mover, to remain behind on the dark landing with the spilled oil and the three corpses to listen for any sign of danger.

"I'll get your Texas Longhorn Border Special for you," he said to the teenager.

"I'll stay with him, Dad."

"No."

"Why not?"

Ryan's fingers clenched and his knuckles whitened, but Krysty felt his surge of anger and spoke quickly to the boy.

"Do like you're told, Dean."

"Sorry."

GUITEAU EMERGED from the darkness of the mill, his face tense, voice tight. Lightning flickered around the ville, making his cheeks glow with a ghostly pallor. The horsemen and Marie Mandeville waited.

"Yeah," he reported. "Broken the main drive gearing. Takes days to repair. And chilled the two men."

"So where are they now?" Mandeville spat.

All eyes turned toward the looming bulk of Sun Crest.

Guiteau pointed, blinking away the rain. "There. Lights moving in the north tower," he shouted.

Chapter Thirty-Four

John Dix was showing more emotion than Ryan had ever seen from the sallow-faced Armorer. Twice he stopped, putting down the smoky lamp to wipe his spectacles again.

"We got to move, J.B., you know."

"Of course, of course."

The room that seemed to be at least forty paces in length was simply filled with armaments. There were all manner of bows, spears, swords and daggers, dating from every period of history, all jumbled together in the same way that the collection of paintings had been.

And blasters of every shape, size and age.

At any other time Ryan would have happily spent a full day in savoring the weapons. But now there was only a snatched moment to glance at anything that particularly caught his eye. Some had neat labels pasted beneath them in their display cases, but many more had little or no information: an 1860 Henry; a unique Genhart repeating rifle with its revolving cylinder placed horizontally on its top; a trim breech-loading derringer made by David Williamson over two hundred years earlier; a Gerngross breechloader. J.B.

threw over his shoulder the information that it was simply a modification of an earlier needle gun.

J.B. had paused to shake his head at a wonderful example of a Kentucky musket that dated from way back before the Revolutionary War.

"Can't we take some new blasters, Dad?" Dean asked, admiring a magnificent Sharps buffalo rifle.

"No. They said that our own weapons are up here. We take those and then get out."

"My God, what are these?"

J.B. skidded to a halt and brought the lamp back to see what Mildred had been admiring.

The case contained a number of tiny little guns, smaller than a man's palm, with a hole through their engraved butts.

"Knuckle-dusters. Single shot. Fire one bullet, anything from a .22 right up to a big .44. Accurate up to about eighteen inches."

Krysty kept looking over her shoulder to where Michael was keeping watch. "I think they're coming," she said. "Not inside the ville yet, but it won't be long."

J.B. was so worked-up that his normal placid nature had vanished. "Skydark! The best blasters in the whole of Deathlands and I can't even look at them."

Now, conscious of the increasing pressure, Ryan began to walk faster. His good eye caught familiar and unfamiliar names as he passed the rows of oiled and gleaming metal: Colt, Astra, Browning, Detonics, Cimarron, Steyr, Iver Johnson, Heckler & Koch, Hammerli, Smith & Wesson, Beretta. The list went on and on, a litany of all that was wonderful about the world of predark blasters.

There were revolvers, shotguns, rifles, automatics, machine pistols and even an LMG, tripod-mounted. A couple of gren launchers made J.B. hesitate.

"No ammo," he said, moving to the far end, raising his voice. "Here's our blasters."

Everyone ran to join him, Doc bringing up the rear. Ryan whistled, beckoning for Michael to leave the landing and retrieve his own centerfire .38.

The storm had eased for a couple of minutes, but now it came surging back with renewed violence. The north tower of the ville shook with the sustained rumble of thunder and a flash of lightning that seemed to hang endlessly suspended, filling the gallery with a shimmering silver-purple light.

It had been so brilliant that, when it faded, it left all of them temporarily blinded.

Doc's deep voice broke out of the darkness behind them. "By the Three Kennedys! But this is a miracle. Come join me and look."

Everyone was too busy gathering up their guns and buckling them on.

Ryan felt fully dressed at last with his SIG-Sauer in his right hand, the bloodstained panga sheathed once more. The Steyr was slung over his shoulder, he was ready to go.

J.B. worked the action of the Uzi, head to one side, listening critically. "Needs fieldstripping and oiling," he muttered, placing the Smith & Wesson M-4000, fléchette-firing scattergun across his back.

"I say, you people," Doc called plaintively. "Do come and look here."

Dean flourished his massive 9 mm Browning Hi-Power, the metal shining in the warm, golden glow of the two oil lamps.

Krysty and Mildred both gripped their blasters, grinning at each other.

The odds were just what they'd been a few minutes ago, and the danger was even more intense. But now they could give a good account of themselves.

They heard smashing glass from the gloom, halfway along the gallery.

"Doc?" Ryan picked up one of the lamps and started off toward the old man, when he heard a loud booming sound from somewhere below them in the tower.

"They're here," he said.

HARRY GUITEAU WASN'T a man much given to disabling attacks of panic, but he had bitten his lip so hard that blood flowed over his chin, unnoticed in the teeming storm.

His heart was pounding with the certainty that the outlander had managed to outthink and outflank them. His men were good, well trained, and their Armalites were kept in tiptop condition. But he'd seen the blasters that Baron Nathan had taken into his collection and knew what they could be capable of, particularly in the wrong hands.

He corrected himself. "Right hands," he said, unheard by anyone above the thunder and the pounding at the door at the foot of the north tower.

Marie Mandeville was possessed by a terrifying cold rage. She sat her stallion quietly, watching as the mud-soaked sec men attempted to break into their own ville, knowing that it wasn't possible to communicate with the main force who'd been sent around to the front courtyard entrance. The strong likelihood was that they would have no idea that something had gone grievously wrong at the north flank of Sun Crest.

Rain trickled down her smooth cheeks, dribbling off her chin and onto her gloved hands.

Despite her calm exterior, she was twisted with anger, desperate to have the outlanders taken prisoner so that she could have her way with them. Pay them back for this, for having to sit like a triple-stupe outside her own home in the middle of the worst chem storm in years.

Her fingers tightened on the riding crop, wanting to spur her horse in among the servants and lash them into greater activity. But enough fragments of sanity remained for the woman to know that this wouldn't be productive. She caught Harry Guiteau's eye and gestured to him.

"Shoot the fucking door apart!"

Guiteau had also lost patience, ignoring the questioning look from the baron.

"Take out the hinges with the Armalites. Rest keep out of the way."

It was vital that they didn't delay any longer. It was difficult, with all the lightning reflecting off the barred windows, but the sec sergeant was certain that he'd seen lamps moving along the weapons gallery.

The rifles opened up, shredding the door to white splinters of torn oak.

RYAN WAS ALMOST at Doc's side when he heard the pounding stop. An indistinct voice shouted an order, then, moments later, came the crackle of gunfire.

"Shooting off the bolt or the hinges. What did you find, Doc?" he asked, seeing the shards of shattered glass on the floor. "Got to be real quick now."

"But look at this, my dear fellow. Who would have ever thought it possible? I glimpsed it during that eternal flash of chem lightning."

Now they were all gathered around the delighted old man, who was holding a blaster in his hands, with as much reverence as if it were the original Holy Grail.

"Gaia!" Krysty exclaimed. "It's a Le Mat, isn't it? Just like the one you lost."

"Not like the one he lost," J.B. said. "This one is... What's the card say?"

Mildred picked it out carefully, avoiding the jagged edges of the display cases, angling it to the lamp so that she could read the cribbed script.

"Says that this is the General Stuart Le Mat. Commemorative limited edition model, made in 1987. Numbered from one to five hundred. With twenty-four karat gold on many of its surfaces. To remember the indomitable spirit of the 'last cavalier,' J. E. B.

Stuart. Then there's some technical bit about the two barrels and firing one round of 18-gauge and nine rounds of .44 caliber.''

"One you lost fired .36s, Doc.," the Armorer said. "So you got even more punch."

"There was a box of ammo for both barrels," the old man told them. "I filled my pockets with them."

Ryan admired the blaster. Along the scattergun barrel, the lower one, was the golden name of "Gen. J. E. B. Stuart" and the capital letters CS on the cylinder, along with various dates from the life of the famous Civil War commander. Also in gold were crossed swords and some delicate acanthus bordering.

"Loaded?"

"Indeed, John Barrymore, it is," Doc said proudly. "I made certain of that."

"Then keep a good hold on it. Sounds like you're going to be using it real soon."

RYAN HAD LOCKED and bolted both the outer and inner doors, expecting the hunters to track them down quickly. In fact, it had taken several invaluable minutes longer than he'd figured. Now they all had their blasters, and it sounded like the sec men still weren't inside the ville.

Outside, the rain had eased from a blinding torrent to a normal downpour.

The ville had been built with a view to defense. It took nearly two hundred rounds from the Armalites to shoot away the hinges of the stout door in the wall. But once through that they faced another door, almost as strong, and in such a confined space that it was difficult for Guiteau's men to attack it.

He had glanced sideways at his mistress, surprised that she seemed to be showing no emotion. He realized, with a shudder, that her eyes weren't looking at him, weren't looking at anything. They were staring inward, a half smile showing she was already savoring the orgy of torture and sexual murder that she saw awaiting her that evening.

Guiteau wasn't quite that confident.

THE SEVEN FRIENDS were grouped at the landing by the three dead men, looking down into the black stairwell. Ryan held one lamp, J.B. the other, but their mellow glow only reached a few steps into the darkness.

"They get in, then they'll likely come straight here," Ryan said. "Guiteau'll know we're after the blasters. What we need now is to get outside again before they realize we're gone."

"They'll know this place like a rabbit knows its own warren," Krysty said. "They can hunt us down and take us by sheer numbers. Listen."

The gunfire was louder and clearer than before.

"Through the first door." J.B. looked behind them. "Can't be long before the rest of the garrison starts wondering what all the noise is and comes running. Then we get caught between the hammer and anvil."

Ryan nodded, his mind racing through the options, selecting and rejecting: to go deeper into the core of the ville and then buy some time, or try to get out as quickly as possible.

There was only one realistic chance.

"We're moving," he announced.

"Where, Dad?"

Ryan jerked a thumb down the stairs, toward the shattering noise of the sec force trying to break into their own fortress. "There."

Chapter Thirty-Five

Marie Mandeville's horse was alongside Guiteau's, and she was leaning from the saddle to speak to him. Despite the pouring rain, he could almost taste the feral scent of excitement that oozed from her body through the soaking clothes.

"I will have blood if they aren't all taken quickly," she promised.

"I know that, Mistress. They can't get out. The rest of the ville's secure. And we're out here. There isn't any way they can escape us, eventually."

"Eventually?"

Like most of the men in the ville, Harry Guiteau had spent a little while as bedmate of the woman. The look in her eyes made him shudder with memory. And he had escaped more or less whole from their couplings.

He had been one of the lucky ones.

"Eventually, Mistress. But if they split up and try to hide within Sun Crest, it could take some time to snare all of them." For a fraction of a moment Guiteau thought he was going to feel her silver-hilted whip across his face, and he flinched instinctively. But

Marie controlled herself. "Yet we will take them all," he added hastily.

To his relief, he heard a great cheer from behind him and turned to see his men beckoning and calling out that they had finally managed to break down the second sec doors to the north tower.

He dismounted and ran forward, Marie at his heels, leaving their horses to be taken care of.

"Keep away and let me go first!" he bellowed, forcing his way through, aware of the instant relief of being out of the teeth of the chem storm.

The vestibule was as black as pitch, and Guiteau almost immediately stumbled over something.

Someone.

"Woman," he said, raising his voice to order the chattering group of sec men to keep quiet. "They chilled a woman. Must be up the stairs, getting their blasters back."

"Let's go get the outland bastards," someone shouted. In the echoing vault the sec sergeant couldn't recognize the voice, but it drew an enthusiastic yell from the others.

Guiteau pulled a face in the darkness, whistling softly to himself. If Ryan Cawdor and the others had really gotten their blasters back, then there was some blood going to be spilled in the next few hours.

They must have used some trick to get the serving girl to open the outer door for them. With most of the garrison out on the hunt and the destruction of the mill stopping all power, it would have been deeply confusing. Even so, it crossed Harry's mind that the woman was lucky to be dead. That way she was spared punishment from Mistress Marie.

After pushing their way in, they'd dragged her body out of the way through the unlocked second door, bolted both, then headed upward.

He stood still, elbowing back at someone who was trying to push past him. "Wait, damn you!"

It was difficult to visualize precisely where he was standing. The main stairs were ahead of him and to the right, circling up, with one of the dusty old tapestries covering the small alcove beneath them. There was no other corridor available to the outlanders to escape.

They had to be higher, on the second or the third floors, where the guns were. They had to be.

Guiteau was trying to decide how many of his shrunken party he should leave behind as a last line, in case Ryan or any of them managed to get past and escape through the two broken doors. Three would be enough.

Then he heard the hiss of a lash and the unmistakable sound of the quirt striking flesh, a gasp of pain and shock, only just behind him.

"Out of the way, or I'll bury you facedown in cold pig shit. Why have we stopped?"

"Thinking about putting a rearguard to—" Guiteau began.

"Don't think. You get good jack to do what you're told. Up the fuck-damned steps right now. All of you. And I want them taken alive, if possible. Particularly I want Michael Brother and the one-eyed man unharmed."

"But if any of them—" Even in the total blackness, he realized he could actually *see* her anger, knew he was wasting breath and laying himself open to bleak disaster. "Fine. Sure. Let's all go kick some outland ass."

Harry Guiteau had hardly noticed that there had been a sudden and total shift of power in the last five minutes. Somehow Baron Nathan had become a peripheral figure. Seeming shocked by the odd turn that events had taken, he had given up the lead to his voracious daughter and was now standing disconsolately among his armed servants.

"Anyone got a lamp?"

Several of the men had self-lights, but the rain had affected most of them. Eventually three or four managed to get theirs working, giving a weak and fluttery yellow light around the cramped space at the bottom of the stairs.

Above them, the top four floors of the tower were totally dark and silent.

"Go first, Guiteau," Marie ordered.

"Sure." Carrying the Armalite in his right hand, the disfigured left hand moving cautiously up the damp banister. A brace of sec men followed him, with Marie coming fourth. Plodding doggedly along at her heels was the baron, water still glittering in the fronds of his snowy beard. The rest of the group pressed close behind.

Outside the tower, one of the tethered horses snickered softly in the easing rain.

The noise of the thunder was moving southward, and there was only a lingering, occasional flash of the pink-purple chem lightning.

The rasping of their wet boots on the stone stairs carried clearly to Ryan and the others.

IT WAS DESPERATELY crowded in the tiny alcove under the stairs, with only the dusty wall hanging between them and the posse of sec men.

Everyone had their blasters drawn and ready, nerves strung taut, waiting for someone to rip the tapestry back and reveal them in the darkness.

But the minds of Guiteau and the sec force were directed upward to the baron's priceless gun collection and the threat it represented to the ville.

Ryan put his eye to a ragged tear in the flimsy material, seeing that the lobby was now empty, except for the ruin of the two doors and the motionless body of the woman. The occasional flashes of lightning gave enough illumination for him to be sure that there was nobody left downstairs, though a flickering glow from above and the noise of the feet told him they weren't far away.

"How long, J.B.?" he whispered.

"About three minutes. But those old clockwork detonators aren't that reliable. Might not even ignite the stuff."

Outside on the wet, trampled turf, Ryan could hear the horses, moving nervously, and could see half a dozen or so of the pack of hounds, left behind when the main body of the hunt had gone around to the main gate. They whimpered unhappily, too frightened to enter the tower.

"Can't we go now, Dad?"

"Soon. Real soon."

"WHAT'S THAT SMELL?"

Guiteau turned to the man behind him who'd broken the silence. "Lamp oil, you stupe. So you all better be fucking careful with those self-lights. Start a fire here and the whole of Sun Crest could go up."

He'd divided the force on the first landing, sending ten of his men to explore that level and also to try to make contact with the rest of the garrison.

With the baron, Marie and the remainder, he was halfway toward the part of the Tower where the blasters and the rest of Mandeville's weaponry were kept in their showcases.

His keen hearing caught a sound from the blackness below, and he stopped. It was a whimpering dog. Then came a sound that could almost have been a thudding blow or a punch. And the whimpering stopped.

Fifty feet blow, Michael rubbed the edge of his hand and pushed the corpse of the hound out of the alcove.

"What's wrong, Guiteau?" Marie hissed.

"Heard... Down below, by the door." The fear that had been simmering at the back of his mind when he'd been thinking about posting a rearguard came flooding back to him. And he remembered the curtained space below the stairs.

But he still wasn't sure enough to risk annoying the woman by making a mistake.

"Well?" she snapped.

The sec sergeant made a decision. "I'm going to go back down." He glanced around on the winding stairs, checking the faces in the uncertain shadows.

He spat the command once more, sending six of the sec men toward the next floor, while he and four others readied themselves to descend again.

Baron Mandeville seemed to have slipped away into his own thoughts. He suddenly spoke up, loudly. "What the damnation fuck is going on there?"

"Guiteau suspects a trick," Marie replied. "Some of the servants are going on to the top of the tower and we are going back down again."

"We?"

"Keep your voice quieter, Father. Yes. Guiteau, four men and me."

"And me," the baron replied less loudly.

At ground level, Ryan and the others had heard the briefly raised voices, but it hadn't been possible to catch what was being said.

"Less than a minute," the Armorer whispered. "Best move out into the open before any more of the dogs get brave enough to come in here after us."

Ryan led the way, picking a careful path over the dead hound, the splintered wood and the body of the woman servant that he'd chilled only short minutes before.

The half dozen sec men emerged on the top landing, feet splashing through the puddled oil and the broken glass from the lamps. They held their lights high above their heads to minimize the risk of igniting the volatile liquid, spotting the corpses of their colleagues. Only one of them saw the device.

The clockwork detonator was two and a quarter inches in diameter, code-marked in trim white paint: FMGE 5577, overstamped Special Forces Vietnam.

J.B. had packed it into a nest of black powder, placing a handful of low-caliber ammo in among it. He added a couple of dubious Second World War hand grenades, making sure that the edges of the lake of spilled oil was soaking into the bomb.

And, of course, there was the plastic container, holding a lethal mixture of napthenic and palmitic acids, marked with the single word Napalm.

"What the fuck is—" the sec ban began, pointing with the barrel of his rifle.

The dial clicked its way around to zero.

The spark came, detonating the small amount of hi-ex, setting the whole mess off with a thunderous roar of noise and red-orange light.

It converted the six sec men into staggering, fiery dolls, waving their arms and screaming in little voices as the jellied flames consumed them.

Whatever the napalm touched caught fire.

Guiteau and his group stopped, all hanging on to the handrail for support.

Not far below them, Ryan and the others were halfway out the door when the bomb went off.

And the invincible ville of Sun Crest, in the old state of Kansas, began to die.

Chapter Thirty-Six

While hastily preparing his makeshift booby trap, J.B. had broken open several of the cases that held samples of explosives or grens, hoping that the explosion would scatter the flames and set fire to the whole gallery.

It succeeded beyond his wildest expectations.

Within a dozen heartbeats the dry wood and the elegant draperies were ablaze. Even with the power on to work the pumps, it was doubtful that much could have been done to save the ville. The damage might possibly have been limited to the north tower if there had been light for the defenders to work out what was happening. And work together to fight the inferno.

But the place was in almost total darkness, most of the servants massed in and around the main courtyard and hallway inside the front entrance.

Within seconds there were more muffled explosions, one of them blowing out a row of windows on the topmost floor, splinters of glass showering around Ryan and his companions. Slavering tongues of fire protruded from the shattered casements, licking hungrily at the damp air.

The chem storm seemed to have sucked all the light from the sky, leaving the land midnight black.

"To the trees, quick!" Ryan shouted.

The one-eyed man led the way, the others tumbling out of the narrow doorway onto the muddy grass, among the frightened horses and panicked hounds.

"Take mounts?" J.B. yelled.

"Too spooked. We got the blasters and they're in chaos. Once we get in the trees we head to the redoubt and watch our backs. I don't think they'll follow us too close."

Both men had paused on the side of the cleared land nearest to the ruined mill, having to raise their voices above the roaring of the swollen river.

"That blood-eye bitch and her father might want to hunt us down, whatever the cost," the Armorer shouted.

At that moment there was another cataclysmic flash of lightning and a demonic peal of thunder that made the earth shake with its violence.

Simultaneously Harry Guiteau raged from the doorway, followed by four sec men. A second later Marie Mandeville was out, with her father a few steps behind her.

Ryan was closest to the forest, J.B. at his shoulder. Because of the size of the entrance and the broken wood that blocked it, the others were strung out, Doc and Dean only a few yards ahead of the sec sergeant.

On the heels of the thunder and lightning, the downpour of torrential rain began anew, cutting visibility to less than fifty paces, blurring the action.

"Take them!" Marie screamed, her hands raised as if she were about to claw her own eyes out of their sockets.

But now the scales had tipped radically in favor of the outlanders.

The sec men were both outnumbered and outgunned. They skidded to a halt, Armalites only half-raised.

The baron had drawn his revolver and was steadying it, aiming toward Ryan, who was about to gun him down with the SIG-Sauer. Only Doc was quicker.

His ornate, gold-plated Le Mat boomed, its lower barrel firing the single 18-gauge round at the baron at almost point-blank range.

The scattershot ripped through the man's curling white beard and opened up his throat, slicing the arteries apart and flooding his lungs with his own blood.

He staggered a few steps backward, tripping over his spurs, crashing down, hands reaching out helplessly toward the doorway of his ville.

The shot was the signal for everyone to open fire.

Ryan put down one of the sec men, while a burst from the Uzi destroyed two more.

Krysty chilled the last of them with a couple of well-aimed rounds from her snub-nosed, double-action Smith & Wesson 640.

But not everything went the way of the outlanders.

Marie dodged to the right, stooping and picking up her father's fallen blaster, snapping off two rounds toward Michael's crouching figure.

Harry Guiteau lived up to everything that Ryan feared about him. He saw the reality of the danger in a single glance and moved toward the only possible cover—the tethered horses, dodging toward them, firing a dozen rounds from the hip as he ran. He didn't expect to hit any of them, but knew it would be enough to make them all duck down.

Dean tried to run away from the sec sergeant, but his boots slipped in the wet earth and he fell over, dropping his big Browning.

Guiteau never hesitated, diving like an eagle on a lamb, scooping the boy under his arm before vanishing among the skittish horses.

Dean yelled out, the cry muffled by the sec man's iron fist. The two of them, along with Marie, were hidden among the dozen or so animals.

"Chill the horses?" J.B. shouted.

"No. He'll take out the boy." Ryan had dropped to his knees, holding the Steyr rifle, using the Starlite night scope to try to get a clear shot at either Marie or Guiteau. But all he could see were the kicking legs of the horses, making it impossibly risky.

The flames were now shooting twenty feet from the broken windows of the tower, and they could all hear explosions from the ammo.

Krysty was at Ryan's side, looking back at the burning building and the sprawled body of the white-bearded baron, his red-clad arms and legs spread wide.

"Looks like Santa fell out of his sled," she shouted.

Guiteau's voice rose above the noise of the fire and the storm. "Any moment now and you get a hundred armed men on top of you, Cawdor. Give up and I'll guarantee the boy lives. Best offer you'll get all day.''

He appeared, crouched and almost totally hidden behind Dean, the muzzle of the Armalite digging into the boy's chest, his finger on the trigger. A silhouetted figure in the gloom, lit by the baroque glare of the flames.

"Tell him to go fuck his dead mother, Dad!" Dean screamed. "Run, Dad."

"Let him go, or I'll put you down." The voice, surprisingly, was Mildred's.

"Even if you could hit me in this light, nothing'll stop my finger squeezing and blowing the kid away."

Ryan was aware that time was racing by at twenty times its usual speed, and that what Guiteau said was true. The rest of the ville's garrison could arrive at any moment, and the standoff would quickly be over.

Out of the corner of his eye he saw Mildred standing like a statue carved from jet, her right arm extended, the ZKR 551 pointed at the sec sergeant.

"No, don't," he said.

"Be all right," she promised, hardly moving her lips.

"Boy dies," Guiteau called, crouching even lower, so that she could see very little of his head or body.

But that didn't matter.

The Czech revolver snapped once, the flat sound totally insignificant against the bedlam of noise that surged all around them.

Ryan was watching carefully, ready to blast the grizzled sec man the moment after he shot his son. He didn't know how Mildred could possibly take him out while simultaneously preventing him from firing the Armalite. He couldn't believe what he saw.

At forty paces, uphill, in dreadful light, Mildred had put the Smith & Wesson .38-caliber round precisely where she'd aimed it.

Both Guiteau's index finger and the trigger of the automatic rifle were blown off.

There was a cry of shocked pain. The Armalite fell to the wet grass, and Dean scampered toward the rest of the group, dodging sideways like a little crab.

Harry Guiteau stood still, blood gushing from the severed joint, shaking his head in amazement.

"Best shot I ever saw," he said wonderingly. "Best I ever—"

Mildred put a second round through the bridge of his nose, silencing his voice forever.

"Dark night!" J.B. breathed reverentially.

"Thanks," Dean panted, arriving to a skidding halt in their midst.

Ryan looked at the burning ville, the dead bodies sprawled in front of the broken door, the horses, flanks glistening in the rain, the flames making them look like fiery creatures from the spirit world.

"Let's go," he said.

"No."

"No, Michael? Why not?"

"The woman."

"Leave her be."

The teenager shook his head, staring, stone-eyed, at the horses, with Marie Mandeville lurking somewhere among them, still holding her father's revolver.

"Got to finish it, Ryan."

"No time."

"Time for this." He started to walk back toward the burning north tower, holstering his own Texas Longhorn Border Special .38.

"Chill her if she appears, Mildred," Ryan said. "Don't wait. Just do it."

There was a crack of thunder and a brilliant magnesium flare of vivid chem lightning, almost blinding everyone.

"Shit?" Mildred cursed. "Done my sight for—"

They all heard the vicious crack of the baron's revolver, held in the hands of his vengeful daughter.

The ribbon of azure silk had fallen out, and her hair tumbled unchecked, soaking wet, reaching below her waist. The white blouse was transparent in the rain and she stood spread-legged, the spurs on her maroon boots gleaming in the firelight.

"You bastard little fuck-brain!" she screeched, her face contorted with a blind rage, eyes narrowed to razored slits.

The gun flashed twice, bucking in her hand. Michael never deviated from his path, walking slowly and steadily toward the woman.

Ryan had the Steyr to his shoulder again but, against all his impulses, he didn't shoot, instead waiting and watching.

Another shot. This time the bullet visibly kicked up a clod of mud a yard to Michael's right.

"It's an Iver Johnson Cattleman model," J.B. said. "Sounds like it's firing a .44. Five rounds gone. Just one more to go."

Now the gap between them was less than ten yards, and still the bare-handed teenager didn't hesitate.

The revolver was steady in her gloved fist, centered on his chest.

"No," Krysty breathed. "She's going to miss."

Marie Mandeville fired the blaster a sixth time. Michael seemed to sway to one side, like a cobra dodging the charge of a mongoose. Ryan felt the wind of the bullet passing him by, like the warm breath of the hooded man with the scythe.

The somber sky lowered over the last act of the drama.

Marie stared at her nemesis, pulling the trigger on the empty blaster, again and again, the dry clicks barely audible to the six watchers. With a sob of frustrated anger she threw the revolver at Michael, now less than five paces from her. His hand plucked the gun from the air, throwing it over his left shoulder without a single glance.

"Should we not do something to deter the young lad from this act of murder?" Doc asked, answering his own question. "No, I suppose in conscience that there is no valid moral reason for the woman to carry on defiling the earth."

It was more melodrama than drama: the backdrop of the burning building, the rearing, frightened horses, the skulking, terrified hounds, the bodies on the grass that streamed with rainwater, the thunder and lightning seaming the sky around them, the beautiful woman, in her tight, elegant leather pants, falling to her knees in front of the inexorable figure of vengeance, face turned up to him.

The young man, his black hair pasted flat to his skull by the storm, reached out to her with his pale, strong fingers.

Only the two of them heard that last brief exchange of words. Only one of them could possibly have told it to anyone else. But he never did.

The passing of Marie Mandeville, mistress of the mighty ville of Sun Crest, was blessedly brief, far more brief than her corruptly evil and perverted life merited.

They heard the small noise of a brittle bone snapping, then the lifeless head lolled to one side, the eyes staring blankly.

Michael laid the woman on the grass.

"May the Lord have mercy upon the richly deserved ending of the life of milady," Doc said.

"Amen," Mildred breathed.

"Now let's go," Ryan repeated. "Once we get safe into the woods I don't believe that the sec men'll have any stomach for following us. Not with their home burning down about their ears and their leaders stiffening in the dirt."

J.B. touched his arm. "Look. We got company."

A number of ragged and filthy men and women stood in the shrubs at the fringe of the forest, watching them in motionless silence.

"Wildwooders," Dean said, hefting his recovered Browning.

"Easy." Ryan laid a hand on his son's shoulder, gesturing to the scene behind him. "It's over," he called.

Krysty murmured in surprise. "Remember that curse."

One or two of the hunting dogs, bolder than the rest, had sneaked, belly-down, to where the corpse of their master lay, his head almost severed by Doc's Le Mat, and started to lick the blood from the body.

THE WILDWOODERS HAD FADED back into the shadows beneath the dripping trees as mysteriously as they'd appeared, without a word or a sign.

It was time to be moving on.

The glow from the fire lighted the sky behind the seven friends as they crossed the stone bridge over the south fork of the Antelope, heading back toward the distant redoubt.

Ryan had been right.

Disheartened by the reversal in their fortunes, all in the space of an hour, the inhabitants of the ville made no effort to pursue the destroyers of their lives.

Chapter Thirty-Seven

It was evening when they got to the bluff at the edge of the plains that concealed the entrance to the redoubt.

"Anyone want to break for the night and rest up? Move on at dawn?"

Ryan's suggestion was greeted by universal disapproval, Doc voicing it for everyone else.

"The past few days have been most exceedingly trying, have they not? Well, my dearly beloved brothers and sisters, let us bravely go toward the new world and get the jump completed. Then we can, perhaps, rest awhile."

"Long as the bastard cannies don't try for us again," Dean said.

Michael spoke for the first time since executing Marie Mandeville. "We can handle them," he said. "Fact is, we can handle just about anything."

But none of them was ready for the unspeakably vile smell that oozed from the entrance to the redoubt. It seeped out at them before they'd even taken a step inside the military complex.

"Least we know what it is," J.B. said, clamping a hand across his nose and mouth.

"Doesn't make it any sweeter." Ryan had knotted his white silk scarf around his face.

"Reckon most of the muties will have left." Krysty looked around, staring out over the plain behind them when a gentle breeze whispered in the tops of the trees. She glimpsed the faint orange light that was the burning ville. "Difficult to feel anything about the place. But I can't 'see' much life. Just the most death I ever felt, anywhere, anytime."

THE SCENE INSIDE WAS barely describable.

Despite their ability to devour most kinds of carrion, it was obvious that the digestive system of the cannibal muties hadn't been able to cope with the thousands of rad-poisoned, rotting corpses that had filled the redoubt.

Many of them lay dead, showing every sign of having died in hideous agony, knees drawn up to their chests, hands clutching their swollen abdomens, lips tugged back off yellowed teeth in a rictus of terrible pain.

A few were still alive, and their low cries echoed along the stinking passages and chambers of the vast fortress. But none of them tried to attack the seven invaders. Ryan picked a path around the dead and the dying, the SIG-Sauer cocked and ready in his hand.

"Think I'm going to be sick, Dad."

Before anyone could say a thing, the boy was as good as his word. He bent over, hand against the lichen-smeared wall, puking copiously.

Doc instantly emulated Dean, bringing up the remnants of his last meal at Sun Crest, then wiping his mouth with the swallow's-eye kerchief.

"By the Three Kennedys! I once walked though Hell's Kitchen in the bowels of New York, during a summer heatwave. Many a poor soul went to pay their respects at the court of good King Cholera that year. But the miasma, vile though it was, could not hold a candle to this damned place."

"Not far to the elevator, Doc," Mildred said. "Once we get down into the basement level, close to the gateway, the smell shouldn't be as foul."

Ryan laughed. "One of the few times I'm really looking forward to making a jump."

THE ELEVATOR STOOD SECURE, its doors closed.

In the open space at the junction of several corridors, a small group of the muties stood together, watching in silence as the seven outlanders advanced.

"Cover them," Ryan said.

He looked at the coded panel beside the doors, checking his memory for the combination of letters and numbers that would give them access.

"Green with envy, Claude Monet painted nineteen pictures in his blue period. Five of Edward Edgar's compositions made him red with anger."

Everyone stared at Doc for a few moments in total incomprehension. Mildred tumbled to what he was saying first. "Nice one," she said admiringly. "Excellent mnemonic for the code on the doors."

Then Ryan realized what was going on, working slowly through Doc's memory aid. "Green, C, M, nineteen, blue, five, E, E. Red. Yeah, that's what I make it."

He punched in the code, waiting for several fraught seconds before the mechanism responded. Once before, they'd had terrifying trouble with a broken elevator, and it wasn't an experience that he wanted to repeat.

Finally there was a pneumatic hiss, and the dull metal doors slid apart.

"Inside."

Ryan stood and kept an eye on the cannies, four male and two female, but they were so apathetic that they seemed to be merely waiting for death.

J.B. went in first, turning with the Uzi at the ready. Mildred was second, then Doc and Dean. Michael came next, with Krysty last.

Ryan holstered his blaster and joined the others, reaching out to press the button that would take the elevator speeding to the lower level.

"Look out!" Michael shouted.

The doors were already sliding shut, but one of the muties had decided to attack them.

It ran in curious slow motion, holding a jagged-edged dagger that looked like it had once been part of a pruning saw. The cannie's mouth hung open and a thread of green saliva dangled from its thick lips.

But it was too late, and the gap had narrowed to a few inches as the creature finally arrived. The knife jabbed out, but the warning had given everyone time enough to back away out of reach. The doors clamped shut, just above the mutie's elbow, gripping it for a moment.

Ryan reacted fastest, drawing the eighteen-inch panga and hacking at the trapped arm. He put all of his strength into the blow, feeling the sharpened steel cut through skin, flesh, muscle and bone, the blade severing the limb just above the wrist.

There was a muffled groan and the hand dropped inside the cage, the stump of the arm being instantly withdrawn. The doors had begun to open, reacting to the obstruction, but now they hissed smoothly shut.

"Come on," Dean whispered. "Yeah..." He smiled and punched the air, as the elevator finally began to drop.

They all stared in fascinated horror at the bloody severed hand. It had released the knife, but the stubby fingers were still opening and closing, the crooked, broken nails scraping on the dusty metal floor.

"I fear that I may be about to lose the remainder of the contents of my stomach," Doc muttered.

But he held on until the doors opened once more, revealing the corridor that stretched toward the mattrans unit.

THE SMELL OF DEATH and corruption was less overpowering down in the cooler passages that wound toward the gateway, but it was still there, lingering at the back of the mind like a constant reminder of mortality.

The cherry-red armaglass walls of the chamber stood cold and empty.

"Everyone ready?" Ryan asked, waiting while J.B. joined them, having made sure that the sec doors were safely locked, keeping that part of the complex secure.

"Mebbe we should all hold hands," Michael suggested. "After what happened last time, next jump we might all go someplace else and then not be lucky enough to get back together again."

"Not a bad idea." Krysty looked around. "Let's do it this time, okay?"

Doc stepped in first, the heels of his cracked knee boots tapping on the metal disk in the floor. He was holding his prized new golden Le Mat in his left hand, the sword stick in the right. As he sat down, leaning against the wall, he laid both weapons across his lap.

Mildred sat next to him, the beads in her hair clicking softly against the armaglass. J.B. joined her, carefully putting his weapons by his side.

Michael and Dean pushed each other in the doorway, kidding as they jostled, finally sitting down crosslegged, leaving a gap for Krysty and Ryan.

She went in and took her place, sighing. "Still hate a jump."

Ryan took a last look at the Kansas redoubt, then firmly closed the heavy red door.

The lock activated the mat-trans process and as he sat beside Krysty, the first tendrils of white mist were appearing near the ceiling of the chamber.

"Ready or not, here we go," Mildred said, holding hands with J.B. and with Doc, who gripped Ryan's left hand in his right, the rest of the friends completing the circle.

"For what we are about to receive." Michael grinned at the others.

"Hope it don't stink."

"You mean 'doesn't' stink, Dean," Krysty corrected.

"Yeah. Just so we go where the sun shines bright and we can have a real hot pipe of a time."

"I'll settle for the sun." Ryan looked at J.B., feeling the feathery fingers of the jump beginning to slide across his cortex. "What're you thinking?"

The Armorer had finished folding his glasses and putting them safely in a pocket, taking the hands of Mildred and Michael again. "Thinking about the most beautiful blasters in Deathlands and how I destroyed them."

"Trader used to say that some you won and some you drew."

"Wonder where Abe is?" J.B. closed his eyes, falling silent.

Ryan felt his hand being squeezed by Krysty and suddenly thought that it would be nice to tell her how glad he was they'd survived another close one. How much he loved her.

But the disks in floor and ceiling were glowing brightly, and time was running out. The jump was on.

It took an enormous effort of will, but he managed it. "Love you," he said, the words sounding infinitely far off.

He thought she responded with pressure on his fingers, but he couldn't be sure.

Ryan closed his eye.

Join Mack Bolan's latest mission in

THE TERROR TRILOGY

Beginning in June 1994, Gold Eagle brings you another action-packed three-book in-line continuity, the Terror Trilogy. Featured are THE EXECUTIONER, ABLE TEAM and PHOENIX FORCE as they battle neo-Nazis and Arab terrorists to prevent war in the Middle East.

Be sure to catch all the action of this gripping trilogy, starting in June and continuing through to August.

Book I:	JUNE	FIRE BURST
		(THE EXECUTIONER #186)
Book II:	JULY	CLEANSING FLAME
		(THE EXECUTIONER #187)
Book III:	AUGUST	INFERNO
		(352-page MACK BOLAN)

Available at your favorite retail outlets in June through to August.

Don't miss out on the action this summer—and soar with Gold Eagle!

TT94-1

Take
4 explosive books
plus a
mystery bonus
FREE

Mail to: Gold Eagle Reader Service
3010 Walden Ave.
P.O. Box 1394
Buffalo, NY 14240-1394

YEAH! Rush me 4 FREE Gold Eagle novels and my FREE mystery gift.
Then send me 4 brand-new novels every other month as they come off
the presses. Bill me at the low price of just $14.80* for each shipment—
a saving of 12% off the cover prices for all four books! There is NO extra
charge for postage and handling! There is no minimum number of books I
must buy. I can always cancel at any time simply by returning a shipment
at your cost or by returning any shipping statement marked "cancel." Even
if I never buy another book from Gold Eagle, the 4 free books and surprise
gift are mine to keep forever.

164 BPM ANQY

Name	(PLEASE PRINT)	
Address		Apt. No.
City	State	Zip

Signature (if under 18, parent or guardian must sign)

* Terms and prices subject to change without notice. Sales tax applicable in
NY. This offer is limited to one order per household and not valid to
present subscribers. Offer not available in Canada.

AC-94

**A biochemical weapons conspiracy puts
America in the hot seat. Don't miss**

STONY MAN™

SECRET ARSENAL

With a desperate situation brewing in Europe, top-secret
STONY MAN defense teams target an unseen enemy.
America unleashes her warriors in an all-out counterstrike
against overwhelming odds!

Bolan delivers a death warrant to a
conspiracy of blood and hatred in

DON PENDLETON'S

MACK BOLAN®

DEATH'S HEAD

While in Berlin on a Mafia search-and-destroy, Bolan
uncovers a covert cadre of Soviets working with German
neo-Nazis and other right-wing nationalists. With the clock
ticking, Bolan hunts rogue Spetsnaz shock troops and
skinheads out for blood…uncertain that his own people
won't shoot him in the back.

Are you looking for more

DEATHLANDS®

by JAMES AXLER

Don't miss these stories by one of
Gold Eagle's most popular authors:

TOTAL AMOUNT	$	
POSTAGE & HANDLING	$	
($1.00 for one book, 50¢ for each additional)		
APPLICABLE TAXES*	$ _____	
TOTAL PAYABLE	$ _____	
(Send check or money order—please do not send cash)		

To order, complete this form and send it, along with a check or money order for the
total above, payable to Gold Eagle Books, to: **In the U.S.:** 3010 Walden Avenue,
P.O. Box 9077, Buffalo, NY 14269-9077; **In Canada:** P.O. Box 636, Fort Erie, Ontario,
L2A 5X3.

Name: _____

Address: _____ City: _____

State/Prov.: _____ Zip/Postal Code: _____

*New York residents remit applicable sales taxes
Canadian residents remit applicable GST and provincial taxes.

DLBA

A new warrior breed blazes a trail
to an uncertain future in

JAMES AXLER

DEATH LANDS ®

Twilight Children

Ryan Cawdor and his band of warrior-survivalists are transported
from one Valley of the Shadow of Death to another, where they
find out that the quest for Paradise carries a steep price.

In the Deathlands, the future looks terminally brief.